Dear Reader,

Home, family, community and love. These are the values we cherish most in our lives—the ideals that ground us, comfort us, move us. They certainly provide the perfect inspiration around which to build a romance collection that will touch the heart.

And so we are thrilled to have the opportunity to introduce you to the Harlequin Heartwarming collection. Each of these special stories is a wholesome, heartfelt romance imbued with the traditional values so important to you. They are books you can share proudly with friends and family. And the authors featured in this collection are some of the most talented storytellers writing today, including favorites such as Brenda Novak, Janice Kay Johnson, Jillian Hart and Patricia Davids. We've selected these stories especially for you based on their overriding qualities of emotion and tenderness, and they center around your favorite themes—children, weddings, second chances, the reunion of families, the quest to find a true home and, of course, sweet romance.

So curl up in your favorite chair, relax and prepare for a heartwarming reading experience!

Sincerely,

The Editors

Although **Susan Floyd** has been writing all her life, she didn't start finishing books and submitting them until 1997. Since her first book was published, she's found herself on a wonderful journey in the company of fellow romance writers and the editors at Harlequin Superromance.

As her writing career continues to blossom, her teaching career is settling down. Susan has taught Developmental English at the Westside satellite campus of Merced College and before that she taught research and academic writing skills at the University of California, Santa Cruz.

She also is a (sometimes) avid gardener and cross-stitcher.

HARLEQUIN HEARTWARMING

Susan Floyd

Phoebe's Gift

TORONTO NEW YORK LONDON
AMSTERDAM PARIS SYDNEY HAMBURG
STOCKHOLM ATHENS TOKYO MILAN MADRID
PRAGUE WARSAW BUDAPEST AUCKLAND

Recycling programs
for this product may
not exist in your area.

ISBN-13: 978-0-373-36454-1

PHOEBE'S GIFT

Copyright © 2011 by Susan Kimoto

Originally published as ONE OF THE FAMILY
Copyright © 2000 by Susan Kimoto

This edition published by arrangement with Harlequin Books S.A.

For questions and comments about the quality of this book
please contact us at Customer_eCare@Harlequin.ca

® and TM are trademarks of the publisher. Trademarks indicated with
® are registered in the United States Patent and Trademark Office, the
Canadian Trade Marks Office and in other countries.

www.Harlequin.com

Printed in U.S.A.

Phoebe's Gift

For Michael Floyd,
the man who heals the cracks in my cosmic egg.

CHAPTER ONE

UNDERWEAR. AND LOTS OF IT. Tumbling out of an overpacked suitcase and scattering freely in all directions, the colorful fugitives raced down the dirt road across the perimeter of a cornfield, their destinations in the hands of a tiny renegade windstorm common to the California Central Valley in mid-September. Leaning against an iron corral fifty yards from the front of their mother's house, their bodies angled in much the same way, Mitchell Hawkins and his fifteen year old sister, Katie, a slight replica of her older brother, paused from their work to watch the spectacle unfolding before them.

About one hundred and fifty Holstein cows moved restlessly behind them, oblivious to the stranger who broke into an undignified run to pursue her undergarments. Her cool demeanor cracked as she snagged the fleeing articles, stuffing them—for lack of a better place—into her T-shirt. A trio of heeler pups, free roamers until old enough to work with their parents, pounced on the intruders and wrestled them to the ground.

Mitch watched with veiled interest.

"Here, doggie, doggie. Nice puppy. You don't really want those." The dairy's newest tenant tried to coax a paisley unmentionable from the tenacious jaws of one puppy, while not losing sight of another scampering away with something red.

In her initial interview, Phoebe Douglas had been well spoken, polite, impeccably dressed, clearly on her best interview behavior. She smiled profusely, nodding with perky enthusiasm, letting slip that she had spent much of her childhood on a farm, nonproductive though it was. Mitch was impressed, even drawn to her effusive grin. Her handshake was business firm, her nails neatly manicured but not overly long.

He liked that.

It had been a while since Mitch had been in the company of such a woman and even though he didn't have much time to devote to personal interests beyond the farm, a pretty face would provide a nice distraction from the day to day work on the dairy. Maybe, she'd be a good influence on his rather rebellious teenage sister.

Then, he'd given Phoebe a tour of the dairy.

He couldn't keep the pride out of his voice as he walked her through the enterprise that his father had built from nothing. But when he noted midsentence that what he was saying took less precedence over where she was stepping, any camaraderie he felt for her faded. With new eyes, Mitch observed the wrinkle of her finely sculpted nose as they passed the cows and her panic as she frantically waved away a proliferation of small black flies drawn to her expensive perfume. If Phoebe Douglas had indeed been raised on a farm, she retained no love for the life.

He watched her use her ankle to surreptitiously nudge away the boldest of the heeler pups, just eight weeks old, who trod with muddy paws on the fine leather of her toes.

Phoebe gave him a game smile, "So, I'll be sharing the main house with your mother, Bess, and your sister…uh…?"

"Katie," he supplied. He watched her shoo the pup away more forcefully.

"And she's fourteen?"

"Fifteen." When the other pups, encouraged by the success of their brother, clustered around her finely tapered ankles, Mitch couldn't hide his amusement. But then, he took pity on her and scattered the pups in the direction of the four winds with an authoritative command that even caused her to jump.

"Thank you," she said gratefully, her very pretty gray, green, gold eyes meeting his directly. Two dark fringes of long eyelashes lifted up.

He studied her for several moments, noting how terribly out of place her pale linen suit looked in relationship to her surroundings.

"I'm not sure why you want to live on the dairy," Mitch finally said.

She turned bright red and just for a split second, he saw in a hurried flutter of those long lashes, a desperate child. Then, she shuttered that part of herself, lifting her chin a notch as if to remind herself, more than him, who she was.

"It's not that I want to live on a dairy. But have you priced the rents in San Jose lately?" she asked bluntly, her hazel eyes shifting away from his. She leaned down, completely absorbed in brushing the mud from her shoe. However, she only succeeded in smearing it, then gazed helplessly at the dark, wet mud on her hand.

"Can't say that I have," he admitted, then added with a directive nod of his head. "There's a sink over there, some soap."

She looked around the barn until she spotted the sink in the corner. "Thanks. Rents are now over $900 for a *studio*. One-bedrooms are running over twelve hundred," she informed him, her voice terse.

Mitch shook his head, speculating. "So the computer industry drives the rents up even in a recession. When the salaries are inflated, everything becomes inflated."

She glanced at him in surprise. "From housing to cappuccinos to egos," she said heavily, as she searched for soap. Finding the well-used bar, she thoroughly washed her hands. Twice. "Some people have resorted to renting floors for about as much as you're asking for a room."

"Floors?"

"Living room floors." Her voice was tinged with forced humor. "You supply your own sleeping bag." She found a small clean rag and with considerable effort, dabbed at her shoes. She looked up. "Well, at least, I'm not there yet. Even if I have to drive four hours a day."

Silenced by her honesty, Mitch found himself liking her again. Obviously, she needed a place to stay as much as he needed a tenant.

She straightened and asked point blank, "So, can I have the room?"

With no better offers or, more accurately, no *other* offers, Mitch shrugged and said, "Sure."

Phoebe immediately dug into her purse and produced a cashier's check for first and last months' rent plus a generous deposit that he hadn't even requested.

"What's the possibility of me getting the room that has the bay window?" she inquired, her voice purely business now. Back in character, she flashed a winning smile.

"Bay window?" Mitch frowned, then looked at her in shock. "Katie's room?"

"It's bigger, with more light," she explained.

"I don't think—"

"I'll pay more." She produced yet another cashier's check.

Even with the checks in his hand, enough to get new tires on the truck and furnish Katie with some practical school shoes, a winter coat and maybe a new outfit, Mitch harbored serious misgivings about what he had just done. It was nuts to uproot his sister, his very moody—to put it nicely—sister, for a stranger who would probably go crazy in the isolation of Los Banos. Although the small town boasted a state-of-the-art skate park for the youngsters, it lacked many of the amenities urban dwellers might expect—not one indoor mall. It just got its first multiplex movie theater. Life on one of the three hundred and fifty odd family-owned dairies scattered across the sprawling county was even more isolated. He doubted Phoebe Douglas would last even a month. But his truck needed new tires and Katie needed shoes. The next day, he cashed the checks.

Now, Mitch watched Phoebe strategically study the towering corn silage mound covered by neat rows of old tires. She stared at a pair of boy shorts that had blown up like a parachute and dangled just out of reach. He shot a glance at Katie, whose narrowed blue eyes and tight lips told him all he needed to know about his young sister's feelings.

"I hope it falls on her," Katie muttered bitterly, her voice filled with hormonal angst. "Then I can get my room back."

Mitch turned his gaze back to Phoebe, who was still trying to snag her undergarment. Finally, after a quick look around her, she jumped and took an inefficient swipe at it. Twice. The pups barked at the entertainment. Even Blue, their father, came to investigate, sniffing inquisitively around her feet. Triumphant on her third try, she stuffed the shorts down her shirt and continued her hunt, curious pups at her heels.

At the edge of the drainage ditch, Phoebe

crouched down, her position precarious as she plucked three items out of the murky water, shaking them out, scattering her canine audience with the spray. Then, she scrambled across the trench into the cornfield, the stalks towering over her, their golden tops shimmering with the breeze and the sun. She hopped over another ditch and disappeared from view.

"Well, you're out of luck, kid," Mitch said evenly, alert as Phoebe shot out of the cornfield, shaking her head violently, her honey colored hair wisping out from the elegant French braid. She flailed at her shoulder blades in a vigorous attempt to fend off some flying creature.

Mitch laughed out loud.

When she whirled to identify the laughter, he quickly knelt, pretending to examine a section of laminated wire he and Katie had just restrung. He glanced up again as their renter walked wearily back to her car, a late model Lexus complete with gold accents. He pushed his cap up and used his sleeve to wipe the sweat off his forehead and then settled the cap down again.

"It won't be so bad," he reassured Katie, squinting against the September sun right into his sister's dour expression.

"It's going to be awful," Katie snorted.

"She's got a ton of clothes." Jealousy tinged her voice as the nearest cow nudged at her. Distractedly, she patted the Holstein between its eyes as she stared at the woman, now laying the suitcase across her trunk.

Mitch sighed and tightened a bolt with a grunt, shifting his gaze away from his sister, her tone pricking at him as she scuffed the toes of her worn tennis shoes. They watched as Phoebe pulled out the bottom of her T-shirt and dumped the bras and panties back into the suitcase. Then she quickly shut the lid and hurried into the house, glancing over her shoulder at them with an embarrassed smile.

"Why does someone even need all that underwear anyway?" Katie muttered, her eyes fixed on a fragile piece of rose silk fluttering their way. She kicked dust at it.

Mitch leaned over to retrieve the little scrap of material and shoved it in his shirt pocket. It hadn't helped that their renter had taken so long to move in. She had taken the keys a month ago when he had accepted her checks. He grimaced as he remembered how they had only given Katie a day to vacate the room she'd grown up in.

Bess wanted to give the room a good cleaning, the walls a fresh coat of paint, and the worn rug a thorough shampoo. She had him retrieve his old single hardwood bed from the attic and made Katie clean and polish it until it gleamed. Insult to injury for Katie, Mitch knew. He had even taken an afternoon off to purchase a new mattress, extra firm. After all their hurry, the room had sat empty, until their renter arrived midmorning last Saturday, leaving a trail of clothes and shoes piled around the room before she gave Bess the vague assurance that she would be back the following weekend.

After Phoebe had left, Mitch spotted Katie in her old room, fingering the material of a fine suit, slipping her foot into a polished high heel a size too small, holding an expensive beaded evening dress up to herself. His throat closed as he looked at her now. Although slight, Katie was taller than Bess, making Mitch acutely aware that she was no longer the six-year-old girl who had dogged him relentlessly when he first returned to the farm after college.

Then life had been so easy. His father, Pete, had been in his prime. The dairy ran at peak production. In fact, they had just finished expanding the milking stations to take on more cows when— Mitch shook his head, keeping at bay the painful memories, forcing his thoughts to return to Katie. He'd never said anything about catching her in the renter's room, but he hoped that once Phoebe moved in to stay, there would be no repeats of such behavior.

He stood up and stretched a kink out of his back. Then he draped his arm across his sister's thin shoulders. "I know it's an adjustment, Katiekins. But, remember, we all agreed—"

"No!" she shrieked suddenly, the pitch shrill enough to make the cows moan. She wrenched herself away from him, eyeing the edge of panty that poked out of his pocket. "You and Mom agreed. I didn't. You and Mom didn't have to move out of your rooms. I did. Nobody asked me if I wanted this. I don't want to share a bathroom with some stuck-up woman from San Jose who thinks she's better than us!"

"I don't think she thinks—"

"I don't care!" Katie's voice grew tighter, more thin, her eyes tearing with her distress.

Mitch stared at his sister, keeping his face neutral to mask the sudden acceleration of his own heartbeat. The volume of Katie's fits always unsettled him. "We did agree," Mitch reminded her and waited.

The pause was long, but then Katie's shoulders relaxed.

"I know, I know. It will help with household expenses." Mercurially, Katie was rational again.

Mitch breathed a sigh of relief.

"So why the rotten attitude, squirt?" Mitch asked, his voice mild, trying to gauge his sister's state of mind.

"When we talked about it, I thought we were going to rent a room to someone young. A college student or something. Not, not—that!" Katie gestured at the woman who returned to her car, her T-shirt smoothed and tucked back into her slender, tailored jeans, her hair neatly ordered once more. "And you didn't say anything about me switching rooms," she accused. "It's not fair! Dad built my room!"

Mitch stared down at his sister. No. It wasn't fair. Nothing in the past two years had been fair. It wasn't fair that she had to work every afternoon feeding calves instead of participating in school activities with her friends. It wasn't fair that she had lost a father who adored her. It wasn't fair that Bess was so consumed in her grief she couldn't— Mitch looked away, swallowing hard, his own guilt stabbing his already churning stomach. No. None of this was fair.

Katie got a gleam in her eye and a sly smile. "I know what…"

Mitch looked at Katie warily. "What, squirt-let?"

"I'll move in with you—"

"Not a chance. You'll stay right where you are."

"Please, Mitch, please," Katie begged, her blue eyes appealing, the sweet girl again. She wrapped both her hands around his wrist and tugged. "You can have the bedroom. I'll sleep on the couch," she added generously.

"No. The trailer's too small. I can barely move without bumping into myself. Besides, I'm always up late. You'd be in the way."

"That's because you're always working. But if I lived with you, you could relax more."

"No," Mitch said shortly.

Katie got another glint in her eye. "Then why don't we switch? You share a bathroom with her and I'll live in the trailer."

"Nope."

"What if I move in with Carlo? He's got that milker's house."

"No. The last thing Carlo needs is you hanging on him."

"Carlo likes me."

Thank God for that. Carlo, their milker and general around-the-farm handyman, was the only family member not affected by Katie's turbulence. But Carlo had been like that for as long as Mitch could remember. Carlo, as old as the mountain range that surrounded them, was as much a part of the dairy as the cows, his presence hardly ever felt as he quietly went about his business.

As a kid, Mitch would sit at the dinner table and listen to his father and Carlo talk business, notwithstanding the occasional off-color joke along with bursts of laughter. Mitch always laughed, too, though he wasn't quite sure what he was laughing at. Bess would shoot them a warning glare, and his father would just chuckle and give her a pat, telling her the boy had to hear these things sometime.

In retrospect, the jokes weren't even that bad.

During the days that followed the senior Hawkins' death, Carlo asserted himself with uncharacteristic force, so that the bank wouldn't call in their loans, allaying the fear that Mitch was too inexperienced to handle the dairy alone. Carlo had been talking retirement, then, of returning to Portugal, but never mentioned it again, the vigor and energy in his stride uncommon for his years as he worked side by side with Mitch, hauling loads that would cripple a much younger man. Thank God for Carlo.

"Carlo has to like you. That's what we pay him for," Mitch retorted, sending her a quick wink and then held his breath. When she made a face at him, Mitch grinned and said, his voice serious, "It's just for a little bit. Until we get over the hump."

"I thought we were doing good," Katie said quickly, her blue eyes riveted to his face for signs they weren't.

He reassured her. "We're doing fine, but we don't have money for the extras. You know—" he gave her a meaningful nudge "—like those new shoes you just got."

"But the cows are fine, right?" Katie confirmed, sending a worried glance over the sedate herd.

Mitch nodded but shook off the chill that settled between his shoulder blades. "Yes, sweetheart. The cows are fine." He paused and then said practically, "If the cows weren't fine, we'd need more than one renter to make up for it. Your bathroom time would be seriously compromised."

Katie didn't laugh.

Mitch put his hand on the top of her head and gently squeezed the way he used to when she was younger. "This is temporary," he whispered. "We need the money just for a little bit. Can you help us out?"

After a long, tense moment, Katie finally nodded.

"Good girl," he said approvingly, ruffling her hair before letting go. He looked up and saw Phoebe standing on the front porch with his mother, staring at them. He draped his arm around Katie's shoulders. "Once you get used to her, you'll be okay. Let's go and formally welcome the lady. C'mon. Chin up. You've lived through worse."

Katie's bottom lip quivered as she allowed herself to be led to the porch, her voice tight. "I wish Daddy hadn't died."

Mitch gave her a reassuring squeeze. This time she didn't pull away but leaned into him, her body stiff with her efforts not to tremble. "I know, munchkin," Mitch said, his voice gruff as he planted a soft kiss on the top of her head. "Me, too."

PHOEBE DOUGLAS SHIFTED uncomfortably as Mitch and Katie walked slowly towards her, their heads bent in conversation, Mitch coaxing a reluctant laugh from his sister. Phoebe closed her eyes to shut off the images of Audrey flooding back to her. Phoebe had left Michigan ten years earlier to escape such loud, unexpected volatility, desperately seeking ways to soothe her fragile self-esteem, finally finding comfort in the sterile surroundings of the hospital where she worked, and in middle-class values, shopping malls and fine clothes.

Phoebe painfully remembered her mother's comments only two days ago.

"I knew it couldn't last," Audrey Douglas had groused into the phone. "It didn't take long for a good man like William Holworth III to know what kind of woman you—"

"Momma, I can't talk now," Phoebe had invented suddenly. "I'll call you." Even after all these years, her mother could reduce her to a trembling preteen, making her forget that she, by her own hard work, had landed an excellent administrative position at the hospital, which, along with a generous salary and benefit package, had elevated her into a whole different socioeconomic bracket. That's how she'd met Will, urbane, handsome, seemingly wealthy Will, who—the day after their first date—pulled strings with a bank so she could finance a condo during a record run of skyrocketing housing prices in the Silicon Valley.

It was her own fault. She had been so infatuated with Will, one of three sons whose father owned a Fortune 500 packaging plant, so delighted by his strong family ties and his "ordinariness," despite his supposed millions, that she chose to turn a blind eye to the simple truth that the fortune Will believed to be his was, in fact, his father's. For a brief stint, as brief as the two years of their relationship, Phoebe had been catapulted into another world laden with conspicuous consumption, dinners out at exorbitant prices and weekend trips to luxurious spas.

She was living an upper, upper-class lifestyle—which she financed with her credit cards—on a middle-income salary. Always a willing participant, but absent when it came time to pay for the luxuries they'd just indulged in, Will would shake his head with a disarming grin and remind her about his cash flow problems. At first, she didn't care. His attention was worth the price, Phoebe told herself, until she couldn't even pay the minimum balances. When she pointed this out to Will, he'd console her out of her panic, confident that she'd find a solution. But then the creditors started calling, and Will returned his key to her, telling her that he didn't think their relationship would work in the long run, that his father wouldn't be pleased if he married a woman who would be such a financial liability. By that time, Phoebe was glad to see him

go, furious with him but mostly with herself
for not just believing in but also paying for
Prince Charming.

Surrounded by the bills she couldn't pay,
Phoebe did what she could to stay afloat, but
after six months, it had become evident that
drastic times called for drastic measures. She
had to get the mortgage monkey off her back
and thank goodness she wasn't underwater.
With shaking determination, she rented out
her condo while she put it on the market and
started the search for a cheaper place to live—
that took care of the mortgage. She chose to
deal with her debt with old-fashioned denial.

Her fiscal health wasn't the only thing to
suffer damage during her association with
Will Holworth. Will had a way of prying into
the deepest corners of her soul, opening up the
wounds and calling it healing. From the start,
he seemed inordinately interested in hearing stories of her childhood, something that
at first, Phoebe preferred not to discuss. Her
childhood had been pretty grim and not nec-
essarily dinner table conversation. But Will
probed, developing an almost voyeuristic ob-
session with it. Finally, late at night, looking
intently at the shadows of Will's handsome
face, his dark hair tousled by their recent intimacy, feeling his hand soothingly caress her

forearm, Phoebe revealed bits and pieces. She told him about Tucker, the youngest of her siblings, the little boy she raised until she left home. He would be a young man, now.

Heal the childhood wounds, Will gently urged. Because she had felt so insulated by the promise of a new life with Will, she'd believed he and his notions of a happy family could shield her from her mother. Floating on a cloud of pre-engagement bliss, full of hope, Phoebe initiated contact with Audrey Douglas, dismantling nearly a decade of careful, deliberate separation.

But even if Phoebe had changed, Audrey hadn't. Apparently, it was Phoebe's fault that her sister, Stella, had married a chronic gambler and brother Todd needed a lawyer, who specialized in aggravated assaults. Thanks to the technology of caller I.D., Audrey now had Phoebe's phone number and she used it liberally, usually when she needed money. The only reason Phoebe didn't change her phone number and tell Audrey to get lost, was because Phoebe knew she'd only make sense out of the whole mess with her family when she was finally able to talk to Tucker. There were things that she needed to explain, that he wouldn't have understood then, but if he had grown into the man she'd hoped he would become, he would understand now.

So she sent Audrey money, sometimes taking out cash advances on her credit cards, just to keep her at bay. Larger amounts of cash seemed to buy Phoebe more time and every so often Audrey would throw her a bone and pass along a phone number that she promised would connect Phoebe with Tucker. But the phone numbers were always wrong or permanently disconnected. More and more, Phoebe was convinced Audrey had no idea where her youngest child was.

After two years of William Holworth III, along with her reluctance to cut Audrey off for fear she would lose her brother forever, Phoebe's tenuous financial hold had swirled into an ever growing vortex of debt that threatened to swallow everything she had worked for. Her panties blowing across the plains of this Los Banian dairy farm was merely a symbol of how quickly her carefully constructed world had unraveled.

So here she was now, standing on the front porch of the Hawkins' dairy. Bess Hawkins, the matriarch, had been courteous, but her voice held a brittleness, an emotional distance that discouraged friendly small talk. The duo approaching seemed no more inviting. Katie, the walking hormone, was downright surly. And Mitch, her official landlord, had seen better days. Although the dairy appeared prosperous, with a new barn and milking station, their herd of Holsteins seemed smaller in comparison to the other dairies she had passed on the way. The dairy's circumstances must have consumed the entire family, because they all acted, talked and walked like each shouldered a heavy burden.

Phoebe glanced quickly at Mitch and Katie, her eyes skittering away from the intense dislike in the teenager's directly into the reserved brown eyes of her brother. Gorgeous brown eyes, despite the dark circles under them. She remembered those eyes, a pure almond-brown, framed with thick dark lashes that were surprisingly feminine for a man who looked every inch the farmer—from the short cut of his light brown hair to the lean drape of his plaid shirt, cuffs rolled, revealing powerful, tanned forearms, ending with huge, rough hands.

"You remember Mitch and Katie," Bess introduced her, and gestured to the young woman to come and stand next to her. "You'll be sharing a bathroom with Katie."

"That'll be fine." Phoebe's smile died when it collided with a stony stare and returning scowl. Even so, Phoebe said carefully, "Thank you for giving up your room. I know how hard that must have been. I certainly appreciate it."

"I guess you need the closet space more than I do," Katie said, resentment emanating from her very stance, her thin arms crossed defensively across her chest.

"Glad you made it," Mitch intervened with a brief, friendly grin, and gave Katie an admonishing bump when he extended his hand.

Phoebe grasped his hand, calloused and tanned from years of work on a dairy farm. His grip was gentle, almost intimate, as his thumb grazed the back of her hand. She looked down in astonishment at the hard ball of silk that he pressed into her palm. Her face grew hot when she realized what it was.

She hesitated just a fraction of a moment, before she released his firm grip, primly putting her hands behind her in order to stuff the errant panty into her back pocket. She tentatively sought eye contact, surprised to find pure levity dancing behind his very sober expression. Bess and Katie were none the wiser.

"Thank you," she said, her reserve lowering as a grin involuntarily burst forth.

"Don't mention it," Mitch said, his voice deep, tone conversational. "Still working in San Jose?" As he spoke, Mitch draped both of his arms around his mother and younger sister, both silent, both stiff as boards.

"Yes," Phoebe replied.

"What is it that you do again?" His voice was politely curious, as if he was used to filling space for his conversationally impaired family.

Phoebe forced herself to relax, to meet him halfway. "I'm a hospital administrator."

"A hospital administrator." Mitch nodded. "And what do you administrate?"

"Human resources. You know, hirings, firings, evaluations. Pretty boring stuff."

"Do you like it?" His curiosity was a little more genuine, as if he couldn't imagine liking such a job.

"Actually, I do," Phoebe said wryly. "I'm kind of an eight-to-five gal. Partial to fluorescent light."

He shuddered as if the prospect of spending the day indoors was akin to a jail sentence. Then he looked at her speculatively. "That must be a rough commute."

"About two hours," she admitted, feeling a bit foolish and then gestured toward her car, the Lexus. "I don't mind driving."

Mitch gave a dry whistle of male admiration. "I wouldn't either if I had that car."

"I like your truck better," Katie blurted suddenly.

"It's not quite in the same class," Mitch observed, appearing slightly embarrassed by his sister's loyalty.

Phoebe smiled in understanding. "I'm sure that for what you do, your truck is indispensable."

"It's got over 200,000 miles on it," Katie said, her voice filled with pride. "Mitch changes the oil every two thousand miles. And he just got new tires—"

"You know, Katie," Mitch interrupted with a loud cough. "I need your help in the barn. If you'll excuse us, Ms. Douglas."

"It's Phoebe, please," she said anxiously.

"You have a nice afternoon, and make yourself at home, er, Phoebe." Mitch gave her a friendly nod and walked away, tugging at his younger sister's ponytail. "Squirt, you coming?"

Katie heaved the sigh of one greatly beleaguered, but obediently followed him without a goodbye or a backward glance.

Bess went back into the house and said shortly, "Your rent covers meals, too. We eat breakfast at 6:00 a.m., lunch at noon, and dinner at 6:00 p.m. Only two meals at Thanksgiving and Christmas."

Following her, Phoebe nodded but hoped to be long gone before the holidays even approached. "During the week, I'll need to leave by five-thirty in the morning and probably won't be home until after dark," Phoebe offered politely.

"We eat breakfast at 6:00 a.m., lunch at noon, and dinner at 6:00 p.m. Only two meals at Thanksgiving and Christmas," Bess repeated with emphasis.

"I usually pick up something at work—"

"If you use the kitchen, Katie does the dishes. Don't make more of a mess for her or she'll let you know."

"I'm sure she will," Phoebe said with a teasing grin.

Bess just looked at her.

Phoebe stopped smiling and then added quietly, "I'm used to washing up after myself."

It wasn't so bad, Phoebe tried to reassure herself. After all, they *were* strangers forced to live with each other. Bess had to open up a private family home, while she had to vacate her beautiful two bedroom condo, just walking distance from the hospital where she worked.

She stared at Bess's grim features and wondered what circumstances demanded so much emotional control.

"I hope you'll like it here," Bess said stiffly. "You'll be sharing a bathroom with Katie."

"Yes, I realize that." They waited for a minute and then, Phoebe said awkwardly while moving toward the bedroom. "Okay, then. I guess I'll sort myself."

"Dinner's at six," Bess reminded her and disappeared into the silence of the house.

Phoebe went to her room. She glanced at her watch. Four hours until dinner. Goodness knew she had enough to occupy herself until then. She surveyed the boxes that crowded into the room. She grimaced as she reluctantly opened one.

Even though she had paid extra for the bigger room, pristinely cleaned, newly painted, there was no way that even half the clothes she'd brought would fit in the standard-sized closet. She took a deep breath trying to fight the feelings of claustrophobia, of being trapped, of being a teenager desperate to leave behind her home life. She closed her eyes to compose herself. She wasn't fifteen and this wasn't Michigan. This was merely a place to stay, a transition into a new phase of life.

When she opened her eyes, she looked around with new appreciation. This room was lovingly designed with a picture window as the room's focal point. Feminine moldings graced the ceiling and hand carved borders framed the built-in bookshelves. The masculine, mission-style bed was distinctly out of place. A canopy bed, like the one she had spotted in Katie's room, was much more appropriate. Phoebe absorbed a stab of guilt. No wonder Katie was so resentful. To Phoebe, this was simply a larger living area. To Katie, this was probably the only room she had known.

Phoebe put the boxes on the floor and cleared off the bed. She sat down and tested it. Very firm. How long had it been since she slept in a single bed? When she first came to California. Then, it was a novelty to sleep alone and not have to endure Stella's flailing elbows. But now, this youth bed was a far cry from her queen-sized feather bed, quickly liquidated so she could bolster her checking account for the next wave of bills.

The picture window began to rumble, the whole house rattling fiercely, causing her to leap up to steady her Tiffany lamp. A famous California earthquake? She peered out the window. Nope. Only Mitch on a gigantic tractor attacking the tire covered silage mound.

Rrrrr. He moved forward, the arms of the big scooper cutting into the mound. Rrrrrrr. He backed up and swiveled the arms to dump the silage into a large feed wagon about the size and shape of a classic dump truck. She craned her neck, and realized that her corner of the house was just to the right of a pole barn, a gigantic carport for the huge machines. Mitch attacked the mound again and again, and she watched fascinated until he finished, the edge of her loneliness pleasantly dulled.

MITCH CLIMBED OFF THE tractor, with the peculiar feeling that he was being watched. He looked in the direction of the house, very surprised to see Phoebe in the bay window staring at him. She seemed as out of place there as she had the first day she'd visited in her linen suit. He pushed down a feeling of guilt. He should have warned her about Katie, about Bess. But then he shrugged it off. She wasn't going to be around much anyway. Just on the weekends. He raised his hand in greeting as he pulled himself into the cab of the feed wagon, grinning when she ducked out of the window.

With an embarrassed laugh, listening for the roar and hum of the engine starting up, Phoebe lay down on the bed, pulling herself out of Mitch's view, her cheeks hot. She studied the graceful arc of the headboard, naturally distressed from years of wear. She ran her hand up and down the cool slats and felt a nick in the smooth wood. She peered closer for a better look. Initials were painstakingly carved on one thin edge, the periods heavily pronounced.

M. R. H.

Phoebe smiled at the discovery of a family secret. She peered cautiously out the window, only seeing Mitch's baseball cap in the cab of the wagon, trying to imagine him as the small boy who had made his mark on his possession. The vision that leapt before her was startling. It was Tucker.

CHAPTER TWO

PHOEBE SAT STRAIGHT in her high-back executive chair and stared at the late afternoon office memo. The administration always saved bad news for the four-o'clock mail drop-off on Fridays. This was a doozie. Phoebe blinked rapidly to control the tears that threatened to overwhelm her.

After a week of living in Los Banos, Phoebe wanted good news. The atmosphere at the dairy was simply bleak. Although Bess proved to be an excellent cook, mealtimes were silent gatherings. It wasn't strained, per se, just devoid of conversation, laughter. Over the weekend, dairy emergencies had kept Mitch and Carlo absent from most meals so Phoebe had been forced to eat alone with Bess and Katie. The fifteen minute meals felt like hours. On Monday morning, Phoebe had been anxious to steal away at the crack of dawn to start her commute.

Phoebe rose abruptly, closed the door to her office and sat back down, swiveling to gaze out of her fourth floor window, studying the traffic patterns of the busy parking lot. She read the memo again, denial almost choking her. She was being downsized, as the administration liked to call it. Phoebe laughed a little weakly at the irony. She was administration. But even administration had administration. And hers had decided her job could be consolidated and given to an assistant. Angrily, she crumbled the memo in her hand and hurled it across the room. First the condo, now the job.

She put her head down on her desk and banged her forehead softly on her blotter pad. How did her life get this way? How could it get worse after she'd worked so hard to make it better? She took a deep breath, collecting herself. This wasn't worse.

Worse was hitchhiking at the age of fifteen in the dead of one of Michigan's sub-zero winters to California. Worse was lying about her age so she could find a job that kept a roof over her head, clothes on her back, and food in her stomach. Worse was going to night school after pulling a ten-hour double shift in the restaurant where she waited tables, then studying until three in the morning, only to wake up at six to do another double shift so she could make her tuition for the next semester.

Now, she wasn't fifteen. She wasn't running away to be safe, to find some peace. She was in Los Banos to start over. She looked on the bright side. At least she didn't have the Hawkins' schedule. After her week in their residence, she understood the root of their stress. Dairy work wasn't simply hard, it never ended.

The washing machine hummed constantly. When Bess wasn't cooking or cleaning, she was on the phone placing orders for grain, calling the vet late at night, when the big lights went up and nobody slept. While Phoebe realized that the whole Hawkins' family was clearly overworked, she had yet to ascertain whether work made them distant or whether work gave them the excuse for that distance. She shook her head. The Hawkinses' interpersonal relationships were not her problem.

Katie, however, was.

Katie, if possible, was even less friendly, shooting her nasty looks when they passed in the hall, deliberately slipping into the bathroom when Phoebe tried to use it. Katie also seemed to have no compunction about liberally sampling someone else's shampoo and conditioner. When Phoebe tried to initiate some ground rules, such as cleaning wads of hair out of the shower drain and putting towels back on the rack rather than leaving them in soggy pools on the floor, Katie gave every indication of only tenuous control over adolescent rage. Phoebe guessed that the teenager might actually be looking for a fight, so refused to be baited—for now.

However, soon she and young Katie would need to have a rational discussion, because in her own state of mind, she just might give Katie the fight she was looking for. Phoebe sighed. Even extensive training in conflict management didn't make dealing with her own conflicts any easier. She fingered her Realtor's business card with budding hope. Perhaps Diane was selling her condo at this very minute.

The phone rang sharply. "Phoebe Douglas," she said quickly.

"Phoebe, pumpkin!"

Phoebe's heart sank. "Momma, I told you not to call me at work."

"That's because you haven't given me your new phone number."

"It's because I don't have one yet," Phoebe said smoothly. "When I get it, I'll—"

"Phoebe, your sister's in trouble." Audrey got straight to the point.

Phoebe winced but didn't say anything. This phone call was going to cost money.

"What?" Audrey Douglas's voice turned

hateful and raspy. "Not saying anything? Don't you care?"

"Yes. I care." Phoebe closed her eyes against the tone. "What's wrong with Stella?"

"That husband of hers lost their rent money. If she doesn't have four hundred dollars by this evening, they're going to be evicted. Her and those three babies."

"And what do you want me to do about it, Momma?" Phoebe felt very, very tired.

"Why, we need you to wire the money," Audrey replied as if it were a natural conclusion. As an afterthought, she added, "If you send a hundred dollars more then they can have some food to eat."

Phoebe wanted to scream, but asked patiently, "Doesn't Stella get food stamps?"

"She used them. I don't think you know how expensive it is to live with three small children."

"Momma. I can't afford—"

"Don't tell me what you can't afford. Sitting up in that big office with a secretary."

"Momma! Listen to me. There's no more money. I'm sorry about Stella. But I can't help her out—"

"I have a new number for Tucker..."

Phoebe closed her eyes tight so the tears wouldn't leak past. She'd done that when she was a little girl, when her father was yelling at her and didn't want her to cry. After a full minute of silence, Phoebe said, her voice weary, "Okay, Momma. I'll wire Stella the money tonight."

"Five hundred dollars?"

"Five hundred dollars. Now where did you get the new number for Tucker?"

"You're a good daughter, Phoebe." Her mother's voice was sweet and gentle as she rattled off the new phone number, vouching for its validity. "I ran into a friend of his who gave it to me."

Phoebe hung up feeling as if she'd been trampled on. She hated her mother and felt guilty that she hated her mother. But she fingered the envelope that she had scrawled the new number on. She knew it wasn't real but she had to try. Later.

It was after five, and Phoebe peeked out of her office. The administrative staff had already gone home. With no chance of interruption, she rummaged through her purse and took out a three-inch wad of credit cards held together by a rubber band. She lay them out on her desk and started to sort through them, relying on her mental tallies to estimate her credit limits for each.

During her days with Will, she had collected them like trading cards yet had somehow managed to keep current on everything. But now, even in her terrible situation, Phoebe found herself inextricably tied to the plastic just to make ends meet. How ironic that even though she was in too deep a year ago, the credit card offers still kept coming. And she kept filling them out and getting new cards, with additional credit limits. For a time, those offers were gold to Phoebe. Each new card she got in the mail gave her a reprieve from her increasing financial pressures and allowed her to indulge in the costly game of denial.

Phoebe selected two cards, flipping over the back to call the 1-800 number. Using automated information, she felt a rush of relief to find that she had guessed right. She had seven hundred dollars left on one and three hundred on the other. She memorized the logo on the card with the seven hundred dollars. She'd use that to send money to Stella. She'd keep the other one for an emergency.

A sharp knock on the door startled her. She quickly pushed her credit cards together wondering who could be knocking on her door after hours. She hastily bound together the cards and dumped them back into her purse, pulling a folder in front of her so it looked as if she was working.

"Come in," she called, striking the pose of a calm executive.

A young man, probably barely out of his teens, dressed in a baggy sweatshirt and jeans entered solemnly and stood across from her.

"Yes?" she inquired professionally, "How may I help you?"

"Are you Phoebe Douglas?"

"Yes."

He handed her a legal sized envelope. "You've just been served. Have a nice day, ma'am," he said politely and turned to go.

Phoebe stared at him stunned, dropping the envelope on her desk. She waited for him to close the door behind him before she allowed the moan to escape from her mouth. What in the world was she being served for?

With trembling fingers she opened the envelope. *Notice to appear before the court clerk for nonpayment—* She couldn't read any further, overwhelmed by the image of a large stereo box, doubling as her nightstand, filled with unopened notices. She'd even cut a slit out of the side of the box so she would never have to actually open it. She merely lifted the decorative slipcover, pushed the unopened envelopes into the hole and pretended this debt wasn't happening to her.

Phoebe shoved the document, envelope and

all into the back of her leather planner and grabbed her keys as she headed out the door. Forcing herself to smile at the hospital staff, Phoebe made her way to the parking lot. First she would wire Stella her money and then she would go have some dinner.

IT WAS AFTER MIDNIGHT when Phoebe quietly unlocked the door to the Hawkinses' house, grateful that Bess kept the front porch light on for her. The cows were silent, waiting patiently for their 3:00 a.m. milking. As Phoebe entered, she tried to dim the noise of the shopping bags, and clicked off the front light.

Once she'd wired Stella her money, Phoebe had headed for the comforting refuge of her favorite shopping mall, losing herself in the anonymity of the crowd. She wandered up and down the tile floors, finally treating herself to dinner. She was starving and had no cash so she used her emergency card, telling herself that it *was* an emergency.

After dinner, she continued to walk through the shops, reluctant to go home, and stayed until the mall closed. She knew that she shouldn't have bought anything, but the handcut crystal bowl was perfect for a wedding gift for her secretary who had pulled her out of more than one jam.

When she found that her favorite lingerie shop was having an autumn blowout clearance sale, Phoebe fingered the luscious silks and settled for three pairs of panties to replace the ones destroyed by the dairy pups. On a whim, as a treat, she also fatalistically purchased a bottle of English rose lotion. At the rate that Katie was going through hers, goodness only knew when she could afford another bottle. As Phoebe presented her preferred status card, she pushed away her feelings of guilt.

However on the way home, when Phoebe negotiated the nearly deserted highway that took her farther and farther away from civilization, she could not squelch the general anxiety that grew the closer she came to the dark, isolated dairy. With her bags rustling conspicuously, Phoebe tried to walk quietly past the living room.

"Out late, aren't you?" a masculine voice inquired softly.

"Oh!" Phoebe jumped and looked over her shoulder. Mitch sat in a well-worn armchair. "Do you always sit in the dark?" she inquired testily.

A broad smile gleamed at her from the shadows and he obligingly leaned over and put the lamp on.

"Better?" He studied her, and then confessed, "Sorry. I think I was asleep."

Phoebe immediately regretted her tone. "I'm sorry," she apologized and lowered her voice with her index finger over her pursed lips. "Go back to sleep," she whispered. "I'll be out of here in a quick second. Sorry for waking you up." Phoebe turned to retreat down the hall.

MITCH WATCHED HER SLIM form begin to slip away and called out, "Buy anything good?" He forced his voice to be awake, alert even.

Phoebe stopped and turned in surprise. Mitch was certain that he saw guilt pass across her face. In the past week, he really hadn't seen much of her. When he got up in the morning, he could see the light in her room from the kitchen window of his trailer. By the time he was getting onto the tractor to feed the cows, she was getting into her car. If he saw her, he always raised an arm to greet her. About half the time, she waved back. However, that was the extent of their interaction. He sat up and looked at her expectantly, as she stood poised in the shadows of the foyer, clutching her bags as if she harbored some dirty secret. She looked at him doubtfully. When his eyes met hers, she visibly relaxed as if realizing that there was no guile in his question, just curiosity and perhaps his own need for conversation.

"Just some presents," she said lamely.

"Can I see?"

Phoebe looked at him again. He kept his features blank.

She shrugged, said, "Okay," and moved to sit on a pea-green ottoman in front of him. She sat with her knees tucked together, her feet apart to balance her new purchases on her lap. Mitch tried not to stare. His heart beat a little harder as she shifted on the ottoman to move closer. He could see the transparency of her skin, an almost flawless complexion. Made a man want to run a finger down a slightly plump cheek to verify that it was truly as soft as it looked.

"My assistant is getting married next summer." Her voice, low so as not to wake Bess or Katie, interrupted his thoughts, pulling him back from staring at her skin to her the person. "So I thought she might like this." Phoebe pulled out the decorative bowl, pushing aside the bag it came in, carefully unwrapping the bubble wrap that protected it.

"You shop early," Mitch observed and then hefted the bowl, turning it around as he studied the cut lines. She had expensive taste.

Phoebe seemed absorbed in watching the glass sparkle as he examined it from all angles. "Crystal," he concluded, and then added, "Very nice crystal."

"Thank you."

"Usually given for weddings then put away for special occasions," he said with an amused glint.

"True," Phoebe admitted with a quick smile that caused his throat to close just the slightest bit. Her long eyelashes fluttered. "But it's sure pretty, don't you think?"

"Beautiful," he agreed. He leaned forward and handed back the bowl, feeling the slight brush of her hand as she took it. He indicated to her other bag. "What else did you buy?"

"Underwear and lotion."

"Underwear?" He looked at her, unable to suppress his grin. "Still haven't found them all?"

Her wry laugh almost knocked the breath out of him. "I had a few casualties. And I couldn't resist. These were on sale."

"Do you need more underwear?" he asked seriously, disconcerted by gold flecks in her eyes. She smelled like fresh roses. "Seems even if you lost half of what you had, you'd have more than enough."

"Obviously, it's not about need," Phoebe

said with a slight flush to her clear skin. She withdrew from him, suddenly absorbed in gathering up her belongings.

"Really?" He regarded her thoughtfully. "What is it about?"

"I don't know," she said, as much to herself as to him. Then she flashed him a bright smile. She was back in character. "I wish I knew. It makes me feel good."

"Ah," he said with a nod. "Like cows."

"What?" Phoebe laughed again, obviously not expecting the turn in conversation. Her professional persona disappeared and she stared at him, interested in what he had to say.

"Cows," Mitch repeated, feeling less able to communicate when she gazed at him so intently. He added lamely, "Cows make me feel good."

Phoebe nodded, her expression serious. "I'd guess they'd have to. You spend all your time with them."

"They're not complicated. They just do their thing." A silence fell between them. Finally, he cleared his throat and asked, "So, you hungry?"

Phoebe glanced at the clock and Mitch followed her gaze. It was nearly one in the morning.

"It's kind of late to eat, isn't it?" she asked uncertainly.

"It's never too late for meat loaf. I can throw together a couple of sandwiches."

"I haven't had a meat loaf sandwich in—"

"Probably too long," he interrupted, getting up, moving away from her, partly because he was hungry, and partly because if he didn't, he would act on that impulse to run his finger down her cheek.

Halfway to the kitchen, he stopped and turned to look at her. She was still seated. "Coming?" he asked quietly. He really wanted her to come.

"Yes, I am." She hesitated for just one second more, then stood up, kicked off her high heels and padded across the living room in her stocking feet to join him. Mitch smiled when he realized she had just lost two inches.

FEELING BETTER THAN SHE had all day, Phoebe leaned up against the counter and watched Mitch slice two thick pieces off the slab of meat loaf that he'd pulled from the refrigerator. Man and meat. Phoebe chuckled, surprised at how masculine he looked rummaging through a drawer to find a knife.

"Katie's fifteen?" she asked casually.

Mitch nodded as he arranged the pieces of meat loaf on the bread.

"It's a hard time to be a girl," Phoebe observed with a reminiscent shudder.

"For Katie it seems to be," Mitch agreed with a wink and then commented more sympathetically, "It's too young to be counted as an adult, too old to be a kid."

"I guess Katie's just—uh—normal."

"You mean those violent mood swings are normal?" Mitch grinned as he placed each sandwich on a separate plate. "Do you want it cut long ways or kitty-corner?"

"Kitty-corner, please." She was surprised at the hunger that rumbled through her stomach. The sandwich looked delicious.

"Katie hasn't always been like she is now," Mitch said quietly, his voice serious. He paused to put the bread and meat loaf back into the refrigerator. "She's got a lot on her plate, right now."

"She seems to like working on the farm," Phoebe offered.

Mitch grimaced. "That's a small favor, because she's doing more work than I'd like her to." He spoke matter-of-factly, then added, "She knows that we're doing the best we can." He gave her a small grin that made him look like a mischievous boy. "At least I don't have to worry about any dating issues that she might have."

Phoebe smiled, the good feelings that emanated from him spreading across her back like a welcome blanket. She could almost forget about that memo and the subpoena and Audrey. Mitchell Hawkins could be very charming when he wanted to be. Would Tucker be like him? "Eventually, though," Phoebe ventured, "she'll need more of a life."

There was now an amused look on Mitch's face. "More of a life than what?"

Phoebe bit her lip, embarrassed. "I'm sorry. That wasn't very complimentary, was it?"

"No, it wasn't. But you're forgiven. I understand where you're coming from."

"I just meant—"

"Be careful, now."

She acknowledged his point and tried again. "I just imagine that most farmers are born into the work, rather than choose it."

He considered what she said and then nodded thoughtfully. "You're probably right. I was."

"Did you ever think about doing something else?"

He laughed outright. "Not until very recently." He pushed a plate toward her. "Eat your sandwich. I need sleep. The days come early around here."

Phoebe obediently bit into her sandwich, surprised when he took his plate and headed for the back door.

"Sleep well," he said with a departing grin.

"You, too," Phoebe echoed, the house falling quiet.

She took her time finishing the sandwich, savoring the taste and the texture of the meat loaf. She slowly washed up her plate, dried it and put it away, peering out the kitchen window into the darkness. Too late to try the number Audrey had given her earlier. She'd try sometime this weekend. She then gathered up her bags and headed toward her room where she switched on the light and blinked.

That morning, she had left in a hurry after trying on several coordinates, leaving them scattered across the room. But, now, they lay neatly arranged, blouses matched with skirts and jackets, with the shoes' toes pointed forward in perfect order underneath each suit. She paused and studied what had been done with the outfits and smiled. Someone showed a, well, creative sense of color.

Was it Bess? She shook her head and put her packages on the floor next to the closet. Katie? The sullen teenager just didn't seem the type

to be interested in such things. Carlo? Hardly.
Mitch? Phoebe laughed, feeling lighter than
she had all day, the warmth of his conversation still in her mind. Bemused, she hung up
her clothes, carefully keeping the outfits in-
tact, admiring the skill of her phantom coor-
dinator.

SATURDAY, PHOEBE AWOKE from a fitful sleep,
as the tractor rumbled by. The clock blinked
5:30 a.m., and she rolled over and nearly fell
off the mattress, sorely missing her queen-
size bed. She felt a wave of self-pity as she
stared into the dark. She didn't just miss her
bed, but her bed in her room in her condo in
her neighborhood. She squinted into the darkness, the headlights on the tractor illuminat-
ing the silage mound. She could barely make
out Mitch's form. And then she curled back
under the covers, falling back asleep with the
fuzzy realization that there were no Saturdays
for dairy farmers.

It was nearly ten when she woke again. The
sun streamed through the picture window, evidence of a clear September morning. If this
were one of her normal Saturdays, she'd get
dressed and leisurely amble three blocks down
to the bakery and get a cinnamon latte and a
bear claw. There she'd read the morning paper

and amble back. Then, she'd do a quick clean of her condo and plan her weekend, talk to her friends, maybe go grocery shopping.

Outside her window, there was nothing but the silage mound, cornfields, Mitch's trailer and a whole Saturday to spend doing what? After a quick shower, Phoebe slipped past the living room where Bess and Katie both sat on the floor surrounded by a kaleidoscope of color and shape.

In the kitchen, Phoebe fished the number Audrey had given her out of her back pocket as well as her cell. After punching in the numbers, she waited, her heart pounding in her ears. One ring, two rings, then the tinny voice of the operator informing her the number had been disconnected. She blinked back tears, trying not to be disappointed—again. She swallowed hard, unwilling to face the fact that she was out five hundred dollars and no closer to contacting her brother, thanks to Audrey.

Phoebe closed her eyes and took two calming breaths before joining Bess and Katie. They both looked up simultaneously when she entered, almost as if they had forgotten she lived there, and Phoebe felt the tension rise in the room. Finally, Phoebe said, "Hi."

Katie ignored her and became absorbed in

finding exactly the right piece of calico. Bess said abruptly, "You missed breakfast."

Katie snickered.

Phoebe smiled uneasily. "I'm sorry. Some Saturdays, I like to sleep in."

"You should let me know, so I don't cook for so many," Bess informed her, her hands moving automatically as she arranged the fabric shapes.

"I'm sorry," Phoebe repeated and squatted to look at the pattern that Bess and Katie were creating. "This is beautiful. What's it going to be?"

"Quilt," Katie spoke for her mother.

"For any special occasion?" The awe in her voice was clear as she admired the gradation of color, from soft blues and yellows in one corner to dark purples and reds in the other.

Bess gave her a quick glance, but then looked away, almost as if she didn't want to participate in any kind of conversation that would build an understanding or, God forbid, friendship. Phoebe understood. She'd been there herself. Katie replied in a voice full of pride, "Mom makes the best quilts in the county. This is probably for a raffle, right, Mom?"

Bess ignored her daughter and turned a square, studying the pattern on the material.

Apparently, that fear of friendship also extended to her daughter. Phoebe glanced at the young girl. But Katie seemed used to her mother and continued to sort unperturbed. The silence grew thicker.

Phoebe stood up and announced. "Well, I thought I'd go explore the town this morning. Is there anything I can get from the grocery store?"

"We shop on Mondays," Bess said and glanced up at Phoebe. Her faded blue gaze just lasted a split second.

"Okay." Phoebe nodded and then deliberately addressed Katie. "Do you want to go with me, Katie, to show me around?"

"No," Katie replied.

"Well, then. I'll be back in a little bit."

"Lunch is at twelve," Bess reminded her without looking up again.

"Okay. I'll be here," Phoebe promised and made a mental note not to be late.

When Phoebe was outside, she shook her head to clear away the conversation, appreciating the September morning that was cool despite the vestiges of summer lingering in the air. She had missed the heat wave a week or two earlier, but the day still promised to be in the mid-eighties. She took a deep breath.

The dairy smelled sweet today. The pups were nowhere in sight.

"And where are you going?" a deep voice asked behind her as she inserted her key into the car door.

Phoebe jumped and then laughed nervously. "Do you always do that?"

"Do what?" Mitch's eyes squinted in the brightness of the sun. He adjusted the brim of a plain blue baseball cap to shade his eyes.

"Surprise me."

"You walked right past me," he told her lightly. "So, where are you off to?"

"Town. I thought I'd explore it."

"And that will take you twenty minutes. Then what are you going to do?" he asked deadpan.

Phoebe felt a pleasant shiver run up her back. How nice to be teased. "I don't know. I asked Katie if she wanted to come—"

His eyes narrowed with interest. "Really? What did she say?"

"No." Phoebe laughed ruefully at the girl's frank rejection. "I guess I'm not much company for her."

PHOEBE WAS AS BEAUTIFUL in the morning as she was at night, Mitch realized with dismay. Dressed casually, in a pair of khaki shorts and a white sleeveless blouse, she still looked out of place. Maybe because it was a fancy sleeveless blouse, with little flowers on the collar. Her hair was loose, but carefully groomed to fall around her face, the sun glinting gold off several silky strands. She looked like a model, down to the fashionable sandals and her pale pink toenail polish.

"Ask me," popped out of his mouth before he could stop it.

"What?" She stared at him with surprise.

"Ask me whether I want to come," he repeated, shuffling through his mind what he could put off until this afternoon. How long had it been since he had taken a morning off? He couldn't remember.

"Don't you have to work?" Her voice was uncertain, as she glanced around the farm.

"I always have to work," Mitch admitted, suppressing the image of five somewhat urgent chores that should be done this morning. "But we're in between calves. The cows are fed. The milking area's scrubbed down. I can get away for a little while."

"Oh." Phoebe looked around.

Mitch waited.

The fall day was spectacular, bright, with just enough chill to remind him that the seasons were changing. He watched Phoebe inhale deeply, lost in some sort of memory. Then she physically shook herself and smiled brightly at him, asking in her most perky professional voice, "Would you like to give me the official tour of the city?"

"Sure," Mitch accepted immediately, then added, "if you don't mind making a stop or two."

"Lunch is at twelve," Phoebe reminded him dryly.

Mitch chuckled, feeling a lightness under his feet. "Mom's a little rigid with her time schedules. Don't worry, this won't take nearly as long as you think."

PHOEBE LEARNED THAT Mitchell Hawkins was not prone to exaggeration. It took them longer to get to town than it did to explore it. He directed her past the newer strip malls to the older downtown, a main street consisting of the town essentials—a family run grocery store, post office, several banks, along with a shoe store, two jewelry stores, a sewing machine repair shop, cobbler, a flower shop or two and a corner drug store complete with a lunch counter. They parked under a big shady tree, just beginning to change colors, and as Phoebe browsed through the small antique and gift shops, Mitch strolled along next to her.

But shopping in Los Banos wasn't a solitary affair. Mitch knew several people, introducing her as his new tenant. Everyone smiled at her and welcomed her to the town, asked how she was liking the area. She found she wasn't lying when she declared that she liked it just fine. She glanced up at Mitch and decided that she liked her landlord just fine, too. When she was finished with the downtown, Mitch directed her to the autoparts store.

"We have an account," he said briefly. "Benefits of a small town."

Phoebe stayed in the car and admired the ready smile he had for the owner, who walked him out of the store, talking animatedly, giving her a friendly nod.

Mitchell Hawkins was really a very attractive man, Phoebe realized with a small flutter in her stomach. If one looked past the farmer to see the man, the chiseled planes of his face, the creased dimples in his cheeks and the way his eyes crinkled at the sides when he smiled. She squinted, imagining him in an Armani suit, cut to accentuate the breadth of his shoulders and his tall, straight posture. She nodded approvingly. Get rid of that cap, grow his hair a little longer; he'd be stunning. She started when he tapped on her hood, gesturing toward her trunk. She looked around and then obediently popped the trunk of her car for a case of tractor oil.

"Thanks for the ride," Mitch said with a grin as he got back into the car.

"Don't mention it." Phoebe studied his face more closely. He had very nice features, made nicer by that incredibly endearing smile of his. "Say—would you like to drive home?"

Mitch shook his head in automatic denial. "No. I don't think so."

"Don't be polite. What guy doesn't want to drive a different car, just to fiddle with all the doodads and see how it runs?" Phoebe unfastened her safety belt and opened the car door. "Come on."

Mitch grinned and obligingly switched seats with her. After a brief orientation, he settled back and pulled out of the parking lot. Phoebe relaxed in the passenger seat, impressed by Mitch's ease with the vehicle.

As they drove home, he asked casually, "So how fast can this go?"

Phoebe laughed. "I have no idea. I think I've gotten it up to eighty with no problem."

"You want to see?" Mitch gave her a speculative look.

Phoebe met his brown gaze to see if he was

serious. The wicked twinkle in his eyes challenged her. Her heart pounded. That mischievous boy was almost irresistible.

"Sure," she agreed, her voice nonchalant, hoping that he couldn't hear the pounding of her heart.

He turned onto a deserted stretch of country road. "It's just a little detour," he assured her.

Phoebe watched the needle on the speedometer climb, past eighty, past ninety. By a hundred, she had a tiny sense of thrill, by a hundred and ten, she was clutching the side of her leather bucket seat. Mitch immediately stepped off the gas.

"I think we could've gotten to one fifteen, one twenty easy," he said, his voice fully appreciating the fine motor craft. "But I stop when the ladies start hanging on."

"You know, it's different if you're doing the driving," she admitted, with unabashed relief as Mitch slowed down to make a quick, tight U-turn. "If you're a passenger, the topography just blurs."

Mitch grinned in agreement and said, "It's all about who's in control."

He headed in the direction of the dairy and they fell silent until Phoebe cleared her throat and asked, making her tone light, "You haven't been trying on my clothes, have you?"

"What?" Mitch asked, his tone immediately guarded.

"I just noticed last night—" Phoebe ventured as he slowed for a large tractor ambling down the side of the road. The driver waved at them. Mitch waved back.

Phoebe carefully modulated her voice to the most neutral tone she possessed and started again. "I just noticed last night that my clothes had been, uh, rearranged."

There was a long silence and Phoebe darted a quick glance at Mitch. The change in him was lightening quick. Gone was the playfulness. He stared straight forward, his mouth tight, his body angled away from her, all the easiness of their small trip to town drained away. She hastily added, forcing herself to sound cheerful, "Not that I really care. Nothing was damaged or anything. I just thought it was weird, that's all."

Mitch heaved a sigh and said quietly, his voice low and embarrassed, "I'll have a talk with Katie."

"No, no. Don't do that," Phoebe protested, feeling terrible for having brought it up. "I just wondered, that's all."

"No. I should have talked to her sooner."

"Sooner?"

"I caught her in your room while you were still moving in, but thought it was just curiosity, so I didn't call her on it. Anything missing?" Mitch asked frankly.

"No. Nothing's missing at all. And if it were," she said and tried to poke fun at herself, "I probably wouldn't notice."

He didn't laugh.

"I'll take care of it," he assured her, his tone clipped, his hands tightening and loosening on the steering wheel.

Phoebe didn't like the sound of that and fell silent. Mitch drove the rest of the way home, his features grim and set. Finally, as he turned down the dirt road, the family house looming up before them, Phoebe suggested, "Why don't I talk with her?"

"No." Mitch shook his head. "Thank you for letting me know, but this is a family matter now."

"Well, I'm the one who has to live across the hall from her," Phoebe reminded him logically. "It might be better if I talk with her. Keep it between us. She doesn't even have to know that you know."

Mitch, jaw still tight, parked the car neatly in back of the main house and regarded her carefully. Phoebe met his eyes. At least he was considering what she had said.

She pressed her point. "Don't you have enough to do without being referee?"

Phoebe studied his face, her heart slowing to a quiet thud. If she noticed how handsome he was in town, she now saw the integrity etched in his brown eyes as he wrestled with this newest problem.

"You've only been here a week," he said finally as he turned off the ignition, his expression rueful.

"Then, it's time some ground rules were established. It might help us get to know each other," Phoebe said, although she doubted such a positive outcome.

"Okay," Mitch conceded reluctantly. "But Katie can be a handful, so don't take anything personally." He paused and then reconsidered. "No, I should—"

"Believe me," Phoebe interrupted with a small smile. "This is a tiny bump in what may be a long association. If I fail miserably getting through to her, I'll let you rescue me." She opened the car door, her voice cheerful again. "So I'll talk with Katie, agreed?"

Mitch didn't move, still thinking.

Phoebe leaned over and peered at him. "Agreed?"

Finally he looked up. "Yes. Agreed. And Phoebe?"

"Yes?"

"I'm sorry."

Phoebe flashed him her most generous smile. "You're not your sister's keeper."

He got out of the car and muttered, "Until she's eighteen, I am."

CHAPTER THREE

AS IF PULLED BY THE SAME invisible string, everybody, including Carlo, appeared at exactly noon and at 12:05, lunch began. Though delicious, the meal was the usual silent affair, except for the abrupt requests for condiments and the rhythmic clink of silverware. Phoebe had discovered that if one ate fast enough with large enough bites, the mastication rate alone eliminated the need for conversation. The Hawkinses seemed to subscribe wholeheartedly to this theory. Phoebe, who couldn't keep pace without severe gastrointestinal distress, resigned herself to finishing just about the time Katie was done with the dishes.

This lunch, Phoebe broke with tradition and paused to compliment Bess on her good food. Bess appeared flustered at the interruption, giving her a quick and almost unfriendly stare. Phoebe vowed not to let her feelings get hurt and took building a personal friendship with Mitch's mother as a personal challenge.

But she couldn't shake the memories triggered by the awkward meals.

Phoebe had spent the bulk of her adult life trying to compensate for a childhood of strained silences or bitter, ugly arguments, most of which occurred during sporadic evening meals. Sometimes, her family wouldn't eat dinner until two in the morning, when the bars closed. Drunk as a skunk, Audrey would insist on a family dinner, waking her children up with violent shakes, making them get dressed to sit at the table and pretend to eat dinner. Her father showed little compunction in smacking the first kid who drifted off to sleep, usually Tucker who was the smallest.

On her own, Phoebe was always grateful for just a simple, peaceful dinner. But Will had introduced her to a new mealtime concept. Together, they dined with friendly verbal exchanges, hosted many an evening filled with fine wine, friends and lots of laughter—the food itself merely a catalyst for the gathering. Will's family enjoyed fun meals, where the brothers good-naturedly ribbed each other, his parents benignly indulgent of their sons' antics. For two years, Phoebe had immersed herself in that family, soaking up the pleasantry, dreaming of the day she and Will—

Bess got up first, signaling that lunch was

mercifully coming to an end and Phoebe returned her attention to her plate, knowing that her appetite was all but gone. Even the best of food couldn't compensate for the lack of warmth and conversation at the table.

Suddenly, Mitch broke the silence and said meaningfully, "Privacy sure is important around here."

Phoebe's head shot up in horror. Surely, this was not the place for— After a monosyllabic lunch, *this* was going to be the only topic of conversation?

She took a deep breath, and tried to head off Mitch. "I'm sure this can be discussed later."

Mitch ignored her entirely and persisted, his dark eyes sternly trained on Katie. "I'd hate to come home and find that someone had been through my things." His tone was chilling and sent shivers down Phoebe's spine. A flush crept up Katie's neck. "Wouldn't you, Katie?" The question shot out like a cannon.

The stricken look on Katie's face flagged guilt at one hundred yards.

Bess immediately glared angrily at Katie and demanded, her voice on edge, "What have you been up to?"

Katie's face was bright red. "Nothing," she denied, her chin tilted at a defiant angle.

Phoebe wanted to crawl under the table. She

looked at Carlo who nodded at her sympathetically and then helped himself to another portion of potato salad.

"Tell me what you've done," Bess insisted. It wasn't something that she was going to let go of.

"Nothing," Katie said again, her voice less defiant, her eyes welling as she fought to hold back tears. She looked at Mitch and then back at her mother and then down at the table.

"Don't lie to me, young lady," Bess said, the parental command cracking above the girl's head.

"I'm not lying!" Katie screeched with a persecuted wail as she jumped up, knocking over her chair, then bumped the table, causing water glasses to wobble precariously. Four hands reached to steady the glasses. With pounding feet, Katie was gone, her bedroom door slamming behind her, the house reverberating with her outburst.

Phoebe bit her lip and tried to smile.

"Well, that went well, don't you think?" Mitch commented dryly.

Carlo chuckled. Bess started to clear away the lunch dishes, clanking noisily, muttering to herself. A few minutes later, Katie reappeared, eyes red, her temper obviously subdued, not looking at anyone in particular, stealing a glance at Bess who ignored her.

"All I did was straighten up her clothes. It's not like I was stealing anything," Katie said abruptly, explaining herself to no one in particular. She turned a reluctant eye toward Mitch, who frowned but listened carefully. Katie hiccuped and continued, her voice raw, "Her door was open and half her clothes were on the floor, so I picked them up and put them straight on the bed. I'm sorry for being helpful."

"Well, stay out of people's rooms," Bess snapped with her back turned. "We're not that kind of people. You know better than that."

Phoebe cringed. *We're not that kind of people,* echoed in her subconscious, the tone sparking a nerve long dormant.

But what kind of people are we, Momma?

The kind the rich people like to spit on.

But why, Momma?

Because you're trash, little girl. Do you hear me? You're a snot-nosed piece of trash.

Phoebe kept her head down, blinking back the memories, her throat tight. She took a deep breath and looked out the window. It was beautiful Saturday afternoon, clear, bright. She'd give her notice to Mitch this afternoon and she'd begin looking Monday for a new place to stay. Renting a floor was preferable to living in such a volatile household.

PHOEBE RAPPED SHARPLY on Mitch's trailer door. When no immediate answer came, she knocked louder. She knew he was there because she had watched him walk in a few minutes earlier. She wanted to get it over with as soon as possible. She'd give him three weeks to find someone else to take her place. She knocked again, a persistent ten raps.

"Whoa, hold your horses," Mitch shouted. "I'm coming. Can't a guy take a— Oh! Sorry, Phoebe."

"Why didn't you let me take care of it?" Phoebe demanded without preamble.

"Do you want to come in?" Mitch offered, as he opened the door wider and stepped aside. "Or do you want the cows as witnesses?" As if on cue, the cows mooed.

Phoebe clamped her mouth shut and mounted the stairs into his trailer, surprised at how tidy the interior was and how much bigger Mitch appeared in relation to the tiny trailer. His shoulders alone seemed to fill the width of the trailer. Looking around, her eyes were drawn to official looking documents, flagged with yellow sticky notes encoded with neat, almost artistic, script, spread across a small built-in table. Phoebe wondered how hands as big as his could produce such tiny even letters.

"EPA information. You know, waste disposal, nitrates. We've got a ton of forms to fill out," Mitch remarked. "We've got an appraisal coming up. It's pretty routine, but it doesn't hurt to have everything in order. Have a seat."

"I prefer to stand," Phoebe replied, her voice stiff.

"Suit yourself. Do you want something to drink?"

"No." She crossed her arms defensively. "You promised you'd let me talk with Katie—"

"I'm sorry. I thought it'd be best—"

Phoebe gave an unladylike snort. "Best? I find that hard to believe. You must have known what a mess it would be. With you two tag-teaming her, no wonder—"

"Don't say it," Mitch warned, his own voice carefully modulated. They stood staring at each other. "Don't make judgments about things you don't know anything about."

"It's almost child abuse," Phoebe said flatly, knowing that it wasn't, but projecting her own experiences as a child on to Katie.

"We're doing what needs to be done," he

replied, sharp and cool. "Maybe not by your upper-class standards. Maybe where you're from, people don't discipline their kids. In the real world, we teach them right from wrong, even if it means they get a little embarrassed at the supper table. Katie's way too old to not know that going through your things is not acceptable behavior."

"You agreed to let me take care of it," Phoebe said.

"You didn't, so I did," Mitch said flatly.

"You didn't give me time." Phoebe raised her arms in exasperation, fighting to keep the conversation civil.

"How much time did you need?" Mitch asked, his irritation with the conversation clearly evident. "You could have talked to her right before lunch. She was sitting in the living room. But you didn't."

Phoebe stared at him and he met her gaze, his brown eyes pointedly honest. She cleared her throat and muttered, "I was going to talk to her this afternoon."

"Or you weren't going to talk to her at all," he suggested with an arrogant arc of his brow. "You'd give her a break and just wait to see if she did it again."

Phoebe flushed because she had been thinking exactly that and then said with a defensive shrug, "It wasn't that big a deal."

"If it wasn't a big deal, then why did you mention it?" Mitch asked, annoyed. "I'm a busy man. Didn't you think I'd take what you said seriously? We need to keep you as a renter." He added quietly, "And it seems as if you need to stay."

The blunt truth in the statement deflated her resolve. Mitch was right. At this juncture, the possibility of moving was slim.

"I thought so," Mitch said.

Phoebe was silent. Mitch turned his back on her. Tension stretched thinly between them, made more acute by their close proximity and the tentative overtures of friendship that they'd shared earlier. When it seemed as if he wasn't going to say anything further, Phoebe turned to open the door.

"My mother and I are doing the best we can," Mitch finally said, his voice heavy. "It wasn't always like this."

Phoebe paused at the door and met his guarded eyes, struck by the sorrow, a deep wounded sorrow, in their depths that flickered away in an instant. Her heart beat faster and she took an even breath to calm it. Eventually, she nodded and although she wasn't quite sure what she was apologizing for, she said quietly, "I'm sorry."

"Yeah. Me, too." He smiled a crooked smile. "I promise dinner will be better. I'll be on my best behavior."

"I'm going to hold you to that," Phoebe said lightly and stepped out of his trailer.

MITCH WATCHED PHOEBE walk back to the house, his heart slowing from the rush of adrenaline sparked by her visit. He took a deep breath. He hadn't argued like that with anyone in— Suddenly, she paused in the middle of the farm and looked around, as if locating herself. She stared up at the sky, clear and blue and then west into the distant horizon at the far off San Andreas mountain range. Then, she started walking again, entering the house through the back door. He saw Katie slip out the front and head toward the barn and the calves.

With a sigh, Mitch went and joined her. Katie was preparing to feed the calves, her hands working automatically, so used to the job she was.

"Hey, there," Mitch greeted his sister.

Katie gave him a baleful glance, and kept working, lining up several five-gallon buckets, measuring formula from a forty-pound sack.

She had nearly sixty calves in various stages of growth to feed.

"You shouldn't have been in her room," Mitch said reasonably as he turned on the hose and started filling up the buckets. He shooed away the pups, eager for a sample.

"She tell you that?" Katie asked bitterly, filling a large pail with grain. She hauled the grain to the pens, where the smallest calves were kept, slopping a proportionate amount into each calf's dry feed trough.

"No. She mentioned that her clothes had been rearranged—"

"They were on the floor!" Katie said angrily as she spilled some grain. The greedy calves dived at it. The pups scampered out of their way.

"So what? They're her clothes. They can be in the toilet for all it matters to you."

"It's not fair."

"Katie. Nothing is fair. You have to accept that."

"But she's got so much," Katie said in a tearful voice, and hiccuped, her hands breaking their rhythm.

"Yes, she does." Mitch turned off the water and as an afterthought, mixed some powdered antibiotic into the formula, then followed behind her, carefully pouring milk into smaller pails for each of the calves.

"It's not—"

"Fair," he finished for her. "Life is not fair."

"I wish Daddy were here. It wasn't like this before." Katie, now finished with the smaller calves, lined up the five-gallon buckets again, measuring more formula. Mitch handed her an antibiotic packet, which she sprinkled into each bucket. Then Mitch turned on the hose while Katie assembled thirty or so sturdy plastic pans. As Mitch finished filling one large bucket, Katie sloshed the formula into the pans, lining them up just out of the reach of the older calves in the corral. She coaxed their heads into the waist high stanchions, manually locking their necks in, so all could be accounted for.

"I know, but these things happen."

"Why doesn't Mom ever talk about him? Didn't she love him?"

"Too much maybe," Mitch replied as he pushed one calf to the side so another could be caught.

"She burned all his pictures."

"Not all." Mitch remembered Bess's rampage only hours after his father had been officially pronounced dead of cardiac arrest. Mitch had rescued as many of the precious family albums as he could and stored them in a box in his closet in the trailer. Eventually there'd be a time when Bess would want them back. He, himself, never looked at the pictures, but it had never occurred to him that Katie might want to.

"Why can't we be normal?" Katie asked plaintively, putting the small pans full of formula in front of the larger calves. They dove for it.

Mitch chuckled. "I don't know if we'd recognize normal if normal milked one of our cows."

That coaxed a glimmer of a smile from Katie.

"You'll stay out of her room?" he asked seriously. They both watched a couple of the older calves finish their portion of milk before reaching for their neighbors.

Katie nodded and gathered up the small pans. She released the stanchion's lock and the calves all pulled free, waiting for their last feeding. Mitch picked up a pitchfork and started to distribute generous portions of hay along the trough.

Katie stopped short and said suddenly, "I'm sorry."

"I know you are. But you know what, squirt?"

"What?"

"I'm not the one you should be telling this to."

Katie only grunted in response, but he knew he had made his point.

PHOEBE ARRIVED AT HER office by 7:00 a.m. and with a satisfied grin glanced at the clock, pleased with herself and the time she'd made during her commute. She had just missed a four-car pileup at the 101-280 interchange that would have made her wait at least a half hour.

After six weeks, she was actually getting used to her new life, hurtling between personal and professional catastrophe. Katie had stiffly apologized and since that first weekend had been excessively polite, even going so far as to address her as "ma'am." Phoebe had wanted to find a moment to talk privately with her, to ease the tension that bristled between them, made even more uncomfortable by Bess's watchful eye. In some ways, Katie's excessive politeness was even more irritating than her rudeness. At least then she was being more honest. She had, however, stopped filching Phoebe's shampoo and conditioner, but that hardly made for a pleasant living situation.

Phoebe flipped through her organizer and

the almost but not quite forgotten subpoena fell onto the floor. She fingered it and glanced at her desk calendar. She had ninety days to reply to the injunction. If she didn't appear, the court would automatically hand down a judgment against her, but she was in no condition to present her case in court.

Living all the way out in Los Banos hadn't helped nearly as much financially as she'd hoped it would. She grimaced. Her sacrifice of getting up early and commuting four hours a day, was simply a tiny Band-Aid on a gushing wound. Even the extra income from renting out her condo seemed to slip through her fingers between the minimum installments of the bills she did pay and the mortgage.

She shook her head, refusing to be consumed by the financial pressure. What did it matter that her mail was going to catch up to her or soon, some clever collection agency would track her down in Los Banos? Denial was a useful coping tool, she told herself. One needed until her condo sold.

But when Diane tactfully suggested lowering her asking price, Phoebe blanched. If she lowered it too much, she'd owe the bank money and she'd never get out from under this boulder on top of her. Hang tight, Phoebe thought. For a few more months. If by January, nothing was happening, then she'd consider lowering the price. Diane agreed. Phoebe stared at the subpoena. This was something that couldn't wait until January. She glanced at the calendar again. Two more weeks. She'd think of something.

But she'd already liquidated most of the furniture, antiques and collectibles she possessed. She couldn't bear to part with her Tiffany lamp and a silver hair clip that Will had given her. God only knew why. That just left her clothes. The only thing she had left was her clothes. She made a mental note to inquire at a few consignment shops. Perhaps she could get some quick cash for some of her suits. More Band-Aids, her worried conscience scolded her. She squelched it. Her conscience had already done its best to keep her tossing and turning at night. Carlo had gotten used to her joining him for the 3:00 a.m. milkings.

The lull at the dairy her first weekend was apparently a fluke. Since that time, she'd rarely seen Mitch, who, between calf births, inseminations and a particularly nasty epidemic of hoof fungus among the big cows and pinkeye among the calves, had little time to eat, much less converse. The brief conversations they had were short and clipped. *Here's the rent. Thanks. How's it going? Not so good, you? The same.* She would have taken it personally, but Carlo, whom Phoebe regarded as the sanest person at the dairy, had told her the hoof fungus was badly timed to coincide with the dairy's annual assessment.

"The bank, they don't like sick cows," Carlo had said placidly as he milked one morning. Perched on the rail, Phoebe had long given up on sleep. She had to leave for work in a hour anyway and keeping Carlo company was far preferable to worrying.

Once she had learned not to be intimidated by the huge animals, she'd become fascinated by how trained the cows were—each cow automatically going to the empty stall, waiting patiently for Carlo to attach the cups that would relieve its swollen udder.

Carlo opened the gate to let another cow in, using the hose to wash away any mess the cows made. Carlo continued, "Mitch, he needs a good showing. Still got three years on the loans. But keeps having bull calves."

"Sounds like a lot of pressure," Phoebe had said as she watched one cow leave and another take its place. She was impressed with the immaculate nature of the facilities, not unlike the sterile environment of the hospital. She knew that Mitch scrubbed down the area after each milking, using powerful sterilizing products.

"It is," Carlo said matter-of-factly, as he tweaked the teat of a cow to get her to move out of the way of the next cow to be milked. "But he's a dairy man. His dad and granddad were dairymen. He knows disaster is part of the job."

"Disaster?"

"Anything. Bad weather. Sick cows. Dead cows," Carlo muttered and let two cows in to fill vacant spaces.

A sharp rap broke Phoebe out of her daydream. She smiled when her boss entered. When she saw the look on Miriam's face, Phoebe put down her pen and sat back in her chair, resigned. The paperwork making her job obsolete had apparently traveled through the ranks with the speed of light. Two weeks sooner than she had planned. Phoebe shook her head and exhaled. Well, why not?

With the hopes of turning salary savings into profit, the hospital had already severanced three of her administrative peers. While the company line was justified that the cuts directly translated into salary increases for frontline staff, like therapists and nurses, Phoebe had been privy to the conversations behind the memos and knew the current board was simply cleaning house, preparing for a huge merger that would eventually lay off a third of that same front-line staff.

"I was just going to ask you for the morning off," Phoebe joked lightly. "But I guess that's a moot point now, huh?"

"Phoebe," Miriam said helplessly. They had been good coworkers. Never close, but always respectful of each other's talents and abilities. Phoebe was going to miss working with Miriam.

"When?"

"Now. I'm supposed to escort you out of the office before the rest of the staff get here."

"You bring the box?"

Miriam nodded and produced a standard box with handles. "You know you can't touch the computer, of course."

"Be sure to close out the files," Phoebe said abstractly.

"Anything you want me to copy for you?" Miriam asked.

"No." Phoebe glanced at the clock. "At least you didn't make me work a whole day before canning me."

"You know we've put this off as long as we could. But—"

"I know, Miriam. I was there for the meeting. I got the memo."

"The severance is good." Miriam put an envelope on the desk. "And of course, we've got an excellent letter of recommendation for you on file and you can feel free to use our placement services. There might be need at an affiliate hospital."

Phoebe nodded with a wry grin, "I developed the placement services, remember?"

Miriam smiled back painfully, then glanced meaningfully at the clock. "Doesn't Cindy usually get here by a quarter of?"

Phoebe nodded and stood up. It didn't take long to pack a box. Most of the stuff, she'd leave for her replacement. More than likely there'd be no replacement. They'd just assign her workload to an entry-level clerical person who wouldn't be compensated for the intensity of the work. She gave Miriam her keys, took her coffee cup from the staff lounge and walked out the door at 7:40 a.m.

After spending her last dollars on breakfast, Phoebe deposited the severance check in the bank, feeling a little better about her cash situation. At least the hospital was generous. Bolstered by the numbers in her checking account, she stopped at her post-office box and found it stuffed full.

Reluctantly, she pulled out the business sized envelopes, looking around to see if anyone was watching. She flipped over those envelopes that had red printing on the front, separating her immediate monthly bills from the rest of the mail. She spotted the key that indicated she had a package.

When Phoebe inserted the key into the package box and opened the door, she almost fainted. Four large bundles of bills. She slammed the door shut and relocked it, her heart accelerating with her fear. Those would never fit in her stereo box. She tried to leave the bundles there, but the key was stuck in the box and her conscience got the better of her. She walked back to the car, emptied the box that Miriam had given her and took it back inside. Wincing, she filled the box with the bundles and hurried to hide the box in her trunk.

On her way out of town, she passed the Valley Fair Mall, where the stores would be opening in a matter of minutes. She looked around her, the crisp October morning beckoning her. So what if she had just gotten fired? It was a beautiful day. How long had it been since she was able to shop on a weekday? Before she knew what she was doing, she pulled into the left hand turn lane and waited for the signal to change.

Phoebe worked her way through a large department store, sniffing bottles of cologne, peering at engagement rings, posing in front of the mirror in a variety of hats, particularly admiring the jaunty angle of a summer straw hat with a sunny-yellow trim and a big silk peony tacked to the brim. Woefully out of season, it advertised seventy-five percent off the original price. It would be perfect for a cruise or a luncheon on Will's parents' yacht. It was a perky hat. If she focused on this cheerful, perky hat, she wouldn't think about the fact that she'd just lost her job or that her condo was never going to sell. With this perky hat, she could be anything, feel anything that she wanted.

Phoebe put the hat aside and found her way to the ladies room and surveyed herself in the mirror, to make sure she hadn't acquired a tattoo on her forehead that screamed jobless debtor. She didn't look like someone who had just gotten fired. Her suit was top quality, her makeup impeccable, subtle, her hair twisted into a smooth professional knot fastened with Will's sterling silver clip. She didn't look like someone who had grown up broke and hungry. She looked every inch the successful career woman. She exuded confidence, ability.

She gave her reflection a winning smile. No one would ever guess. She went into a toilet stall and rifled through her purse, pulling out the wad of credit cards. She studied the two cards she thought she had some money left on. Which one had she used to wire Stella her rent money? She did some mental math. Then with a deep breath, she picked the one she thought she hadn't used and then inserted it into her wallet, rewrapped the others and walked out—feeling only slightly better.

CHAPTER FOUR

MITCH LOOKED UP as a billow of dust caught his attention. He squinted, pausing from his tinkering on top of the big tractor, trying to identify the midsize car that looked an awful lot like Phoebe's. He glanced at the sun. What was she doing home in the middle of the day? Katie wasn't even home from school yet.

He straightened, as the car slowed and pulled in front of the house. Yes, it was definitely Phoebe. She obviously didn't see him up on top of the tractor, because she rested her head in her hand for a second before she bent over to retrieve a garment bag from behind the driver's seat. With a quick look around, she scurried inside.

He shook his head. That woman could shop. He watched her emerge a few minutes later, digging through her trunk, taking a large brown box into the house. He frowned. She didn't look too happy. About twenty minutes later, now dressed in a pair of snug jeans, a T-shirt, and a light jacket, she came looking for him, stopping Carlo, who pointed in his direction. She approached the tractor and waved standing stiffly as she waited for him to climb down. Before he could say hello, she thrust an envelope at him.

"Whoa. I'm fine. How are you?" he asked. He was right. She wasn't happy at all.

"I got fired today," she announced flatly, not meeting his eyes, looking past him.

"I'm sorry." Mitch wondered what that meant about her tenancy. Then, he opened the envelope and whistled. "What's this?"

"Rent for the next six months," Phoebe said baldly. She crossed her arms over her chest and looked as if she was trying very hard not to cry.

"And why are you giving me this?"

Phoebe's lips tightened and she glanced up at him. "Because I'm not going to have any money soon, so I want to know I have a place to stay."

"I'm sure you'll find a job soon enough—" Mitch said uncomfortably.

"Be sure to cash it this week," she instructed, her tone brusque. "Or you might not be able to get the funds at all." She talked as if he had perfect insight into her babbling.

Mitch was silent for a minute and then watched with increasing dismay as her tight control vanished entirely. Big, round tears spilled over, catching on her lashes. Phoebe turned abruptly, ready to flee toward the house. He caught her upper arm.

"Are you okay?" he asked and steered her back to face him.

"Yes. I'm fine." She averted her face and sniffled. "It's nothing. I'm fine."

Mitch dropped his hand and studied her trembling lips, her flushed cheeks. Her nose was turning red. She wasn't a pretty crier, he decided.

"You don't look fine," he observed.

"Well, it's been a hard day."

"Happens to everyone."

"No, it doesn't." More tears pooled in her eyes. She looked away.

"Sure it does. People get fired all the time. And those very same people find new jobs. Sometimes they get jobs they actually like better than the ones they had."

Phoebe nodded automatically, her voice overly polite. "Yes, you're right. Thank you for telling me that. I feel much better for knowing it." She started to walk away again.

Mitch paused for a minute and walked with her.

"Come on. Let me show you something,"

he said impulsively and pointed to his truck. "Let me take you for a ride."

"What?" she asked, a sob catching in her throat.

"Let's go for a ride."

"Where?"

"A place that always makes me feel better," he said and then added teasingly, "It's not like you have to work, right?"

PHOEBE REGARDED MITCH for a moment, intrigued in spite of the fact that she could feel herself emotionally unraveling the longer Mitch stared at her with those compassionate brown eyes. She watched him stuff her envelope into his shirt pocket. Then, he guided her across the open property to his truck. Reaching over her, he opened the pickup door for her, boosting her up with strong fingers on her right elbow.

"Thank you," she whispered as she clambered in, surprised by his cordial assistance. Mitch didn't speak as he drove down a back road, past the cornfields, one turn left, another turn right onto a progressively bumpier dirt road. She looked over her shoulder and saw the farm as a distant speck when he finally pulled up next to a small grove of eucalyptus trees and stopped. She looked around her, slowly realizing that she passed this grove every day, used it as a distant landmark to let her know when she was five minutes from home.

"Follow me," Mitch ordered and led her into the grove. Phoebe was enchanted. It was a tiny, shady oasis among the flat fields, a perfect place for a complete breakdown.

"What is this?" she asked Mitch as she found a place to sit on a fallen tree. It was like being a million miles away from reality.

"When I graduated from college, my father gave me about twenty acres right over there." Mitch pointed south to east. "He wasn't sure whether or not I was interested in dairy farming, so he thought if I had land to start my own farm, I might be more willing to stay in the area."

"Did you want to leave?"

He shook his head. "I always knew I was going to be just like my father. College only confirmed it."

"College," Phoebe murmured. "Where'd you go?"

"Davis. Got a degree in agricultural management but hated being inside." He shuddered and gave her a quick smile. "I'm allergic to fluorescent light."

Phoebe smiled, then asked, "So you didn't start your own farm?"

Mitch shook his head. "I didn't have the capital or the experience so my dad and I agreed that it'd be best to work his farm until circumstances changed."

"Changed?"

Mitch shrugged. "Either I got the money or got married or something. Either way, I'd have more experience and people would be more willing to invest in that."

"But you never did?"

Mitch's face clouded over. "My dad had just finished expanding the milking area. He wanted to take on more cows so that I'd have some for myself later. But he died." His voice turned flat.

"I'm sorry." Phoebe felt terrible, her problems suddenly seeming trivial. Poor Bess and Katie. She took a deep breath. Well, that explained much. Phoebe now understood the emotional distance Bess had erected around herself and Katie's prickly attitude. Mitch's father must have been loved very deeply.

Mitch spoke quietly, "That's okay. It was a couple of years ago."

"So, why did you bring me here?" Phoebe asked, her voice softening.

"I don't know. I thought you needed it."

Phoebe considered her state of mind. She slowly nodded. "Yes. I think I did. Thank you."

"This land is not tied to the dairy at all," Mitch explained with a far away look in his eyes. "I guess I have it in the back of my mind that even if we lost it all, we'd at least have this. Maybe that's why my dad gave me the property. So if I screwed up too badly, I could still support my mother and Katie."

Phoebe made a noise of protest. "Your dad gave you the property so you could do whatever you wanted to do. I highly doubt it was because he thought you were a screwup. I bet he was really proud of you."

"Maybe," Mitch said noncommittally.

"Well, you're doing fine now, right?" Phoebe asked concerned, remembering what Carlo had told her earlier. "You seem to run a pretty tight ship."

Mitch squatted down and picked up a thin stick that he twirled around and poked into the ground. "We're getting by. Things change fast. Some days, like today, aren't so bad. But even with the most careful—" He stared out into the horizon. Finally, he glanced up at her. "This winter's supposed to be hard."

"Really?" Phoebe looked up into the crystal clear autumn sky. "It's hard to believe, now."

"October isn't January. Even a mild winter is hard. At its worst—" He stood up and threw the stick, watching to see how far it traveled.

"Aren't California winters generally mild?"

"Relative to the rest of the country, but for us, it's all about milk production. Cows give more milk when they're warm and dry, rather than cold and wet. If the rain persists, the ground gets soaked, the cows get stuck in the mud, then they get tired, and if we can't get them out, they die. That's bankruptcy right there. We need every single one of our wet cows to break even." He stopped talking. "Sorry." He gave her a brief smile. "I didn't mean to talk about this."

"That's okay. I don't mind," Phoebe said quickly. "You're right about this spot. It's a place where anything can be said."

"So tell me your sad story." Mitch changed the subject.

Phoebe looked away. "Besides the fact that I just lost my job?"

"No warning?"

"Some," she admitted.

"Is it the end of the world?"

"Well." Phoebe tried to laugh. "I guess not the end of the big world." She looked up at the sky. "The earth is still spinning on its axis.

But the world I knew. Yes, it's pretty much over."

"Seems as if it was over when you moved here," Mitch observed.

Phoebe agreed wryly. "That was the beginning of the end."

"So tell me about this check." Mitch fished the envelope out of his pocket.

"What about the check?"

"Tell me why you're paying for so many months in advance. Surely even if you've just lost your job—" Mitch studied the check. "From this, it appears that you can live just about anywhere you want."

"Does it matter?"

"No. But I'm curious."

Phoebe stared pensively at the expanse of field, parts of it freshly cut and just plowed.

"You know nothing is ever as bad as it seems." His voice was curiously gentle, but Phoebe couldn't be soothed by his confidence. She felt as if she was being crushed under a tidal wave of guilt, but if she dared talk about her debt, then her pact with denial would be violated and the floodgates of hell would open up and drown her in her bad choices. William Holworth III being the worst choice of all.

"Oh, yes. It is," Phoebe said ominously.

"Never. I don't believe it and I can tell you, I've seen pretty bad pretty recently."

Phoebe gave him a speculative look. "Hoof fungus?"

"Botulism."

She couldn't help it. She laughed. But Mitch wasn't amused. "Botulism?" she asked.

"Botulism. Have you ever seen 226 cows die in a matter of hours?"

"No."

"I have." Mitch's voice was grim. "About two months after my father died. Turned out there was a dead cat baled into the hay that I fed the cows. It was a typical morning feeding. By the end of the day, most of the cows had died."

"How awful." Phoebe was filled with horror. "The poor cows."

"A dairyman's nightmare. My father had a registered herd," Mitch said flatly as if that said it all.

Phoebe had to ask, "Registered?"

"It's like dogs. Registered cows are worth about $1500 apiece. In one feeding, I lost everything my father worked for his whole life."

"Could you have known about the cat?"

"No," he reluctantly admitted. "Small rodents get baled all the time. But it doesn't help to know that." Mitch fixed his brown gaze on her and said quietly, "Trust me, Phoebe, when I say that whatever it is that you're hiding from can't be that bad."

"Oh, it's bad." She bit her lip. She could feel her control slip away.

"You lost your job."

"It's worse."

"How much worse?"

"Lots worse. It's so worse that I don't even know how worse it is."

"That makes no sense."

She shook her head. "It doesn't make sense to me and it's my problem."

"So what is it?" he persisted.

Phoebe was silent for a long time. The wind blew softly around her and she felt a chill run down the back of her neck. She watched a *V* of ducks fly gracefully overhead, their only goal to follow their instincts programmed from birth. Phoebe shivered. Was she just following the programming of her birth? Mitch waited, his eyes patient. Finally, she ventured, trying hard to keep her voice steady, "You know those things that I have? The clothes, the stuff?"

"Yes."

"That's just the tip of the iceberg." She spoke quickly. "You once accused me of being upper class. The truth is I'm a fraud. I own a very nice condo, a very nice car but nothing's paid for."

"That's not unusual," Mitch said reasonably. "Most people have mortgages and notes on cars."

Phoebe nodded, her eyes brimming with tears. "But most people aren't getting subpoenas to appear in court for arrears."

"Oh." Mitch's mouth formed an *O*. "So what are you? A couple of months behind on your Lexus payments?"

"No. I actually make those payments." She added, "And the mortgage."

"So what payments don't you make?" Mitch asked quietly.

"Credit cards." Now that she'd started, confession was easier than she thought it would be.

"How much could you owe on a couple of credit cards?"

"I don't know," Phoebe said honestly.

"How can you not know?" Mitch looked at her in astonishment. "I know how much I owe to the penny. And I know exactly when we're going to pay everything off. The cow loans, the loan on the new tractor, everything."

"Well, that's you," Phoebe said defensively, as she felt her face grow hot with shame. "And it's not a couple."

MITCH REGARDED HIS TENANT soberly. She obviously wanted to talk about it or she would have insisted that he take her home long ago. The air was crisp but the sun was warm. Her hair glinted with gold streaks. Even in her misery, Mitch had to acknowledge that Phoebe Douglas was a beautiful woman. Her casual T-shirt and jeans didn't detract from her sophistication. She looked like a famous actress deliberately dressing down for a shopping trip off Rodeo Drive. If a fraud, Phoebe was a good one.

Finally, he asked, "What do you mean not a couple?"

Phoebe laughed weakly, her fingers twisting, her chin trembling. "Let's just say I lost count at twenty-two."

Mitch sat down. "Twenty-two?"

"I lost count at twenty-two. I have more."

"But you didn't use them all, right?" This was mindboggling to Mitch.

Phoebe started to cry, heart wrenching sobs. Mitch pushed a clean hankie in her hand.

"So I guess you did use them. Didn't you get the bills?"

Phoebe wiped her eyes and blew her nose. She looked away, obviously embarrassed.

"I don't check my mail," she confessed. "And when I do I just shove the bills into a big box. Bills, notices, anything that looks threatening. I just ignore them."

"Even subpoenas?"

Phoebe nodded wearily. "Even subpoenas."

Mitch studied her for a long time, then asked, his tone joking, "Do you ascribe to the theory that if you ignore your responsibilities, they'll eventually go away?"

"It's a good theory." Phoebe shrugged, her eyes averted. "It's worked so far."

MITCH WAS QUIET FOR SUCH a long time that, finally, Phoebe was compelled to turn her head to look at him. She was appalled to find him holding back laughter. When he met her eyes, he laughed even harder.

"I'm glad this is giving you a good chuckle," she said tensely, angry that the tears were back. She dashed them away with his handkerchief.

Mitch still smiling, shook his head in apology. "I'm not laughing at you." He took a deep breath trying to control himself. "It just struck me as funny that you think it's worked so far."

"It has," Phoebe insisted.

"Oh? So why did you sneak into the house with that new whatever it was you just bought?"

"I didn't sneak," Phoebe retorted quickly.

"Really, now. Did you pay cash for it or put it on a credit card?"

Phoebe was silent, her hands clenching.

"Ah." Mitch nodded. "I thought so."

"It's just for a few months," Phoebe said defensively. "Until I sell the condo. Diane said I have two potential buyers."

Mitch chuckled and then asked pointedly, "So you sell the condo, then what?"

"Then I pay off all the bills and I start over."

"Until?"

"What do you mean?" She was getting very agitated by his levity.

"I'll tell you exactly what I mean," Mitch said, his tone suddenly sharp, his brown gaze uncomfortably piercing. "Until you grow up and face your obligations, you'll be in the exact same fix in a matter of years. Only then, you won't have a condo to sell. If you know what's good for you, you'll put your pretty butt in that expensive car and take the-whatever-it-was-you-bought-today-and-can't-afford back. Take that crystal bowl, too, the one you bought for your secretary, while you're at it. She'll be perfectly happy with a card."

"You don't know what you're talking about." Phoebe jumped up and dusted off the seat of her jeans. She started to walk toward the truck, indicating this conversation was over.

"Oh, I don't?" Mitch walked with her, matching his long strides to hers, making her furious that he kept up so easily. "You're talking to the master of debt. I'm in bed with debt. Debt taunts me every single day."

"If I don't think about it then it doesn't bother me," Phoebe said shortly.

Mitch stopped short and stared at her with a look of incredulity. "You haven't answered that subpoena, have you?"

Phoebe walked faster, refusing to show him how agitated she was becoming by their conversation, and replied, "It's none of your business whether I have or haven't."

"You know you only have a limited amount of time to get back to them." Mitch was stating the obvious.

"I know what I'm doing," Phoebe repeated, her voice stiff.

"Your obligations aren't going to go away just because you ignore them. In fact, they're probably growing because you don't know—"

Phoebe crossed her arms over her chest, shaking her head. She didn't want to hear this. She stared at him stonily.

"Debt is debt is debt," Mitch said reasonably. "It doesn't matter how it got that way. It's only important that you deal with it."

"Like you're doing so well?" popped out of her mouth. She glared up at him and said pointedly, "I didn't want to bring this up. But it seems as if you're having just as much difficulty dealing with debt as I have."

"Really now?" He looked at her warily. "Why would you say that?"

"Well. Just take one look at Katie."

"Katie has nothing to do with this." His voice was deceptively soft. His earlier friendliness faded.

Phoebe ignored the internal warning sirens blaring in her ear to stop. Everything about her life was crashing around her and the last thing she needed was— "I think Katie has everything to do with this. If you managed better, maybe you wouldn't have to break a thousand child labor laws," Phoebe said ruthlessly. "No wonder she's such a—"

"Don't even think about finishing that sentence," Mitch said ominously.

Phoebe opened her mouth and then shut it again. Mitch fell silent, his jaw tight from his efforts not to say more. The warm almond of his eyes turned frigid, but Phoebe was too angry to care. They stood silently for a long thirty seconds. Phoebe, arms still crossed, stared down at a weed.

Finally Mitch said shortly, "I need to get back to work. Do you want a ride or—"

"I'll walk," Phoebe said haughtily.

"Fine." With barely controlled anger and practiced ease, Mitch swung himself into the truck. Without a backward glance, he gunned the engine and drove off.

The walk back to the farm wasn't so bad, Phoebe told herself as she trudged along the road. Her head ached something awful. She looked ahead, squinting in the sunlight, and pulled her jacket about her tighter. The October wind was a little cooler than she remembered even with the sun shining. She was too numb, too shaken to even think about what she said to Mitch. But she knew she had crossed the invisible line of civility. He knew it, too, because when she got back to the farm, his eyes flickered over her and he nodded his head curtly as she hurried past him on her way to the main house. She was certain the chill in the air had little to do with the season.

Phoebe sat in her room and studied the fine lines of the suit she had just bought. Mitch's observations echoed through her subconscious. She *had* smuggled this latest splurge into her room—breathing a sigh of relief that neither Katie nor Bess was around. Even under the best of circumstances this suit was excessive, from price to color.

She couldn't justify its purchase, even for the inevitable round of interviews as she looked for a new job. Even though the suit was a jazzy, uplifting color and fit as if it were personally designed for her, it was too flamboyant for most hospitals and she would probably never wear it. She just wanted it to feel better.

Phoebe reluctantly hung the offending suit on the closet door. Then with almost frenetic energy, she tore apart her nightstand, putting her Tiffany lamp aside to pull away the slipcover, revealing in its stark brownness the stereo box that contained all her bills. With a deep breath, she found a pair of scissors and cut open the lid.

The sheer mass of envelopes, all bearing some credit card logo, some stamped in red, some more threatening than others, was horrifying to see. This didn't even include the four bundles that she'd picked up earlier. She hastily closed the lid, pulled the slip-cover back over it and put her little lamp on top. Mitch couldn't be right. No good could come from opening any of those letters. No good. She should just take all of these to a lawyer and declare bankruptcy. That'd be easy. Sure she'd be wiped out, but where else could she start except at the bottom.

She lay on the bed and closed her eyes tight, reverting to the tricks of childhood. If she squeezed her eyes and ears shut, she could block out her mother's strident voice and everything would be all right. Now she tried to block out Mitch's laughter. *It just struck me as funny that you think it's worked so far.* She rolled over on her side, and pulled her pillow close to her chest. *Debt is debt is debt. It doesn't matter how it got that way. It's only important that you deal with it.* Her head hurt. She just wished it would all go away. *If you know what's good for you, you'll put your pretty butt in that expensive car and take the-whatever-it-was-you-bought-today-and-can't-afford back.*

MITCH STARED OUT HIS SMALL kitchen window into the darkness of the cornfield. He had to remind Bess to call the silage man to finish cutting the cornfields. He shook himself, his mind not on the forms he had been trying to fill out for the past half hour. He looked over his shoulder to the numbers on the laptop. So far so good. As long as the cows continued to produce six gallons a day, they were fine. He was pleasantly surprised that he had a few reliably producing seven gallons, a lot for a cow, but his conservative nature refused to count on that for long.

He frowned and stared at the row of thick binders, each carefully labeled. The bank might want to look through those and he'd have to make sure his notes were legible. The hoof fungus had been an unexpected headache but Carlo had rigged a pool of medicine in the milking barn that the cows stepped in and out of twice a day. The pinkeye was another matter.

Mitch took a deep breath as a wave of anxiety hit him. Just a half a dozen cows going dry could put the dairy in the red. He glanced at the calendar. Two weeks until the appraisal. He reached over and pulled a binder out, carefully studying his charts, tracking the output of each cow, the age of the new heifers. The weather had blessed them so far.

It's been a beautiful fall.

Mitch heard a feminine voice in his mind. Damn. He sat back. As if he didn't have enough to think about. Phoebe Douglas was an annoying woman. He was almost sorry he'd taken her to his favorite place. Almost. He sighed. She was right. Katie did work too hard and he probably was breaking a thousand child labor laws. But he didn't need her to tell him that. Irritated, he tried to concentrate on the forms.

How can someone lose count at twenty-two credit cards? Amazing. He craned his neck to see if her car was back. He'd heard rather than saw her drive away, her engine revving as she roared down the dirt road. Probably on another shopping spree, piling up the debt, he thought cynically, then felt bad and took it back.

Mitch stood up and heated a kettle of water just to do something. *Put yourself on the line and all the thanks you get is—* A soft knock on the trailer startled him. He glanced at the clock. Nearly nine. He peered out the back window and saw Carlo moving around his house. He listened for frantic mooing, but all was quiet. The knock came again a little louder.

Mitch opened the door and as if his mind conjured up the woman, Phoebe stood in front of him, a tote bag over her shoulder, trying to balance an oversize stereo box on her knee. At a loss for words, he stared at her. She glanced back at him and then looked away, her top teeth pulling at her bottom lip, her demeanor significantly altered from her early defensiveness.

"Hi," she said uncertainly as she hoisted the box again. Quickly, Mitch stepped down and took it from her when he saw it was actually slipping out of her hands. He tried not to show surprise at the weight.

"It's heavy," she said by way of explanation, her hands waving helplessly in the air. Now that she didn't have the box, she didn't seem to know what to do with her hands.

"Did you want something?" he said surprised by more than just the weight of the box. Her driving away hadn't surprised him. She didn't impress him as the type to stick it out during the hard times. But this surprised him. This surprised him very much.

MITCH LOOKED NONE TOO inviting to Phoebe, and she briefly wondered if she should just turn around. Practically speaking, the box was heavier than she'd anticipated and between that and the bundles in the tote bag, she would have to rest before lugging everything back to her room.

But he was holding her box hostage so she was practically committed to telling him what she had come to tell him. She took a deep breath and looked up. She flushed as he stared down at her, his eyes speculative, ready to dismiss her.

"Do you have a minute?" she asked, cursing because her voice came out like a small squeak. She felt her hands waving again and put them behind her back.

He regarded her for a long moment. Then with a slow nod, he indicated that she should continue.

Phoebe lifted her eyes to his and took another deep breath and said, "I'm sorry."

He considered her, his eyes looking darker in the light. Phoebe shifted, then clasped her hands in front of her, trying to keep herself from wringing them. Then she smiled and tried to look sincere. Finally, after a long, interminably long, moment of silence, Mitch asked, his deep voice guarded, "For what?"

Phoebe exhaled with relief and answered promptly, "For what I said in the field this afternoon, for the way I acted. I'm sorry that I said what I said about Katie. I was completely out of line."

"Yes, you were." He balanced the box easily on one hip and they stood staring at each other, stuck at the entrance of his trailer.

"I'm also sorry for reacting so badly to your advice."

Mitch waited.

Phoebe swallowed hard, her face flaming,

and stammered, "Y-you were right. I was wrong."

"Ah." He just nodded.

Phoebe waited nervously. She glanced over her shoulder. The main house was a long way away. If she rested at least once, she could lug that box back home. She hesitated, chewing on her bottom lip. But then she'd have to face all those bills, all that paper, all by herself. She glanced up at Mitch's impassive face, seeing the tired lines under his eyes. He looked exhausted. She had no right to ask this of him. It wasn't as if he didn't have enough to worry about. She cleared her throat and took a step forward to take the box from him. Now that she had completely humiliated herself, there was no graceful way to make her exit. But Mitch stepped backward, holding on to her box.

"And so you've brought me a stereo," Mitch said suddenly, his lips twitching with what Phoebe swore was a smile.

Phoebe looked quickly into his eyes, which twinkled down at her. She grinned with relief. "You don't hold grudges," Phoebe said with new respect.

"Don't have time to," Mitch replied honestly. "Especially when someone apologizes as thoroughly as you do."

Phoebe glanced away.

His voice softened. "I know it couldn't have been easy. So, let me ask you a question. What do you want me to do with this?" He lifted the box and took it into his trailer, placing it on his small breakfast table in plain view. Phoebe made a little sound in protest.

"Nothing," she lied. "I—"

"Did I tell you that you're as rotten a liar as Katie?" Mitch commented. "Or did I just think it?"

Phoebe flushed. "I think you just thought it."

"So, Phoebe, what *are* you doing here?"

CHAPTER FIVE

SHE LOOKED ABOUT TWELVE, Mitch estimated, enjoying her discomfiture. He watched her eye her precious stereo box, shifting from leg to leg. Then she poked her toe into the dirt, drew a line and used the sole of her foot to erase the line. She looked over her shoulder again, almost as if trying to find an excuse to be rescued. The farm was very quiet. Even the cows were still. Finally, she said frankly, "I need your help."

"Really?" Intrigued, Mitch put his hands on his hips. "What could I possibly do to help you?"

"I just can't do it myself."

"Do what?"

"Those bills."

"Bills?"

"In the box."

"In the box." Mitch had no idea what she was talking about.

"Remember I told you this afternoon that I

don't do anything with the bills. I don't even open them. I just slip them in a box?"

"Vaguely."

"And then you laughed at me."

"Me?" he asked innocently.

"Yes, you. You laughed at me because you said that I was fooling myself in thinking that it was working."

"I remember. I laughed because it was funny."

"Well, that's the box," she said flatly.

"That—" he glanced over his shoulder "—is the actual box?"

"Yes, so give me the Golden Oar award," she said with a sigh.

"The what?"

"The Golden Oar." She gave him a glimmer of a smile. More, he supposed, to hide her emotion than a true attempt at humor.

"The Golden Oar."

"Yes. What I need to paddle down the river of denial."

Mitch laughed.

Phoebe appeared half offended, but then she ruefully smiled. "Look in the box," she said with a shrug. "You'll see what I mean."

Mitch stepped inside the trailer and popped open the lid barely held shut with a piece of transparent tape and whistled. He had never seen anything like it. Sealed envelopes. Hundreds of sealed envelopes. He looked at her and then looked back at the box.

"There's got to be—"

"I told you I don't open the bills," she said defensively. She patted her tote bag. "There's more in here." She looked at him and then added, "They wouldn't fit in the box."

"I see." Mitch took out a handful and commented, "It's probably not as bad as it looks."

"Now you're the one who's the liar. I know how bad it is," she said.

"So what do you want me to do?"

She hesitated. Her chin trembled as she said, her voice barely audible, "I can't do it."

"Do what?" he asked softly.

Tears began to well and her lips tightened. She clamped her jaw shut tight, ready to turn around.

"Come on in," he invited her, opening his door widely. "No need to stand outside and freeze."

She stiffly climbed the few steps up.

"Sit down." He pointed to the table.

She obediently sat, taking in a deep breath.

"Now, what is it that you can't do?"

Her tears spilled over. "I can't—" She wiped them furiously away, and accepted the box of tissue he handed to her. "I ca— I can't open them!" She finally got the words out and burst into a renewed round of weeping. "It's so bad. I lost my job. My life is a wreck. I was rude to you after you tried to help me and now I'm bawling and I can't stop." She hiccuped and put her head on the table. She looked up, her eyes all red, and said pitifully, "And you know what's worse?"

Mitch was having a hard time keeping a straight face. She *sounded* twelve now. "What's worse?" he asked as sympathetically as he could.

"I did it to myself. I did it all to myself."

"Not the job."

"No," she admitted. "Not the job, but—"

"Well, at least you opened the box."

"But I can't open the envelopes. They all have nasty letters—"

"Let's see," Mitch said. He reached for a letter opener and slit three envelopes open, then pulled out a letter and scanned it quickly. Before he went any further, he got a paper bag, set it up at his feet and dumped the envelope. He quickly did the same with the other two, saving the three letters.

"Yep. You're right," he agreed. "Two of these say nasty things."

Phoebe let out a moan of distress but she was curious. "What does the third say?"

"It's pitching life insurance. See?" He showed her the letter and then rifled through the box. "Seems like you stuck everything that came from the credit card companies in here. Most of this must be advertising."

"But what about these?" Phoebe asked, as she opened her tote bag and put the thick bundles on the table.

"Those are probably not advertising," Mitch admitted, his eyes scanning through one pile. "But you know what?"

Phoebe peered at him with hopeful, watery eyes. "What?"

"Even if all of these say nasty things, they don't make you a nasty person. You're still the same person whether you open them or not," Mitch said reflectively.

"What?"

"You're still the same person. You're no better, no worse than you were five minutes ago."

"But—"

"But nothing. Here—" he gave her the letter opener "—try it. See if you suddenly dissolve into the Wicked Witch of the West."

She reluctantly took the letter opener. He gave her a handful of envelopes. With a deep breath, she slit one open.

"See? The world hasn't ended. Nothing has

come to a whirling stop. I'm still here. You're still here."

A nervous laugh escaped her. Fingers shaking, she took out the contents of the letter and read it.

"It's an ad for magazine subscriptions," she said with relief and slipped it into the paper bag. With a more steady hand, she opened another letter. She blanched.

"A nasty?" Mitch asked carefully.

She nodded.

"So put it in the nasty pile. Toss the envelope."

He watched while she did as he said. She then opened the next one and cringed.

"After the first ten, they're all pretty much going to say the same thing," Mitch said reasonably. "You don't get multiple punishments for multiple letters."

He handed her a few more. "Open those. Just take the letters out. Don't even read them yet—and dump the envelopes."

That task alone took Phoebe over two hours and she still wasn't done. She had taken a short break for tea but went straight back to her task. Mitch sat across the way at his laptop pushed to one side so he could pretend to fill out the forms he had been procrastinating about. Dressed in her jeans and bundled in her sweatshirt, humbled by her task, she was a very ordinary looking woman with a very expressive face.

Mitch could tell by the grim set of her jaw how much it took to strip away years of carefully constructed pretense, one envelope at a time. She stopped every so often. The break in her rhythm made Mitch look up and study her. He, who had very little sympathy for Phoebe Douglas's plight, was struck by the tears pooling in her eyes, silently falling when she thought he wasn't looking. Then she dabbed at them furiously with a balled up tissue, taking each letter and adding it to the pile, determined to finish.

This surprised Mitch, in fact, awed him a little bit. As a rule, he didn't allow himself to think about women, and he would have never looked twice at this one. Actually, he acknowledged this one would have never looked twice at him. So why was he so conscious of the fact that she smelled wonderful, the traces of a perfume lingering around her, drifting toward him? Roses and, uh, woods.

He frowned at his thoughts, sat up straighter and bent to study his forms, reaching for another binder to make himself look busy. Probably some expensive kind of perfume. Not-paid-for perfume. He frowned even more when he decided he liked it. It stirred emotions he had almost forgotten existed, tripped long dormant alarms. Phoebe Douglas with her red eyes and puffy nose had managed to squeeze through several unauthorized personal gates, setting free all sorts of prohibited feelings.

"Want some more tea?" he asked gruffly, getting up to put the kettle on again.

Phoebe looked up and noticed his frown. She glanced at her watch.

"I'm so sorry," she said hurriedly. "I didn't mean to stay this late. I'm almost done. I'll pack up."

"I wasn't asking you to leave," Mitch said quietly. "I was just asking if you wanted more tea."

She bit her lip. A very kissable lip, Mitch noted with irritation.

She sighed. "I don't want to be a bother. I know that it's very—"

"Do you want more tea?"

Finally, she nodded and said meekly, "Yes, please." She kept her hands busy slitting open envelopes, smoothing open the letters and tossing the debris to one side.

"How are you holding up?" Mitch filled the kettle with water, putting it on the range.

"Pretty good. This isn't as bad as I thought it would be," she admitted.

"No. The bad part comes next."

"Next?"

"You've got to make a list and record all those letters, tally up your totals and then—"

"I can't do that," Phoebe whispered, the tears starting to well again.

"Sure you can," Mitch said. "You've done the hardest part."

"Tomorrow," she said. "It's late and that's going to take a while. I should probably go. I'm sure you need your sleep. I don't want to take up any more of your time or space." She indicated the cramped corner where he had been working. "Thank you for letting me have the table. I know you were working here." She stood up. "I think I'll skip the tea. Thank you for the offer."

"Better the beast you know than the beast you don't." Mitch studied her closely, watched her maneuver around the small space. She shifted past him to take her mug to the sink. He could hear the thudding of her heart, smell that perfume.

He asked the next question quickly, "Have you ever considered bankruptcy?"

He wasn't sure why he was asking that at this moment, when she looked so wrung out.

She peered at him through red rimmed eyes. "Of course."

"And?"

"And I think I've run away enough, don't you?" She gave a strained laugh that almost made it to her eyes, but not quite. Then she shrugged. "I suppose if that's my only option, I will. Is that what you think I should do?" She fixed her hazel gaze on his face, almost as if she were waiting for him to give her the answer.

Mitch shook his head, meeting her eyes. "No. I don't think that's what you should do. I think what you're doing is what you should be doing."

Suddenly, the trailer seemed a lot smaller, Phoebe's skin creamier, more translucent.

He coughed. Where had that thought come from?

Phoebe brushed past him again to start straightening the table, bending to pick up errant scraps of paper. His eyes were unwillingly drawn to her back, the arc of her neck. She looked as if she carried a lot of tension in those shoulders, so slender that with his palm alone, he could probably span the difference between her shoulder blades. "Angel wings," Bess used to call them.

"I'm wiped," Phoebe said as she straightened, pushing the trash deeper into the bag, squashing it down. "I've been up since before the sun. I've driven to San Jose."

"Twice," Mitch guessed.

"You don't miss much, do you? I took your advice."

"My advice?" Mitch feigned innocence.

"I got my butt in the car and took the suit back. I have a court date to take care of that injunction, too."

Mitch felt a wave of respect wash through him. "That must have taken a lot," he responded carefully. "When do you go?"

"In two weeks," she said heavily. Her eyes began to tear again. "I'm not even sure I've done the right—" She stopped what she was doing, averting her face, the tears spilling over again. "I'm such a fool."

"At least you know it," Mitch said gently.

She gave him a ghost of a smile. "Do you mind if I leave this? I'll clean up the mess early tomorrow morning."

"No problem." Mitch resisted the urge to pull her into his arms. She looked like she could use a hug.

"Thanks." Avoiding his gaze, she ducked out the door and ran back to the house, guided by the light Bess had left on.

Mitch watched to make sure she made it

in the back door, just beginning to feel the fatigue of the day pull at his neck and shoulders. When she disappeared into the house, he turned to the table, the remnants of her presence still palpable, her perfume still lingering. The feeling of his heightened senses, reverberating with an alien awareness, wasn't unpleasant. He glanced at the clock, duly noting that he would need to rise in a few short hours, but right now, sleep seemed to be the furthest thing from his mind.

BESS AND KATIE HAD LONG been asleep. Afraid that she would be overheard by Katie, Phoebe sat in the living room and let the terrible feelings of the evening engulf her.

She cried for her job, her condo, her life, the anxiety that had been crushing her. She had been numb for three years, knowing very early on the mortgage was too big and Will was merely using her. But when it got right down to it, neither Will nor Audrey were responsible for her bills, she was. Instead of telling Audrey she couldn't support everyone, she'd allowed herself to be blackmailed, emotionally and financially. Tonight she saw clear evidence of that spinelessness.

She sobbed harder. How could it be so bad? How could she have let it get so out of control? *You're still the same person.* Mitch's voice in that oh-so-practical tone came into her head. She didn't question why she found him to be a such comforting presence. And she didn't know why she braced herself for his blunt comments or why she listened to him or trusted him implicitly. He obviously didn't approve of what she had gotten herself into, but he didn't judge her, either, and he had readily forgiven her for being so nasty to him earlier. *You're still the same person.*

When the tears were finally spent, Phoebe wearily made her way to the bathroom and splashed her face with cold water. She didn't feel like the same person. She lay down on the bed, grateful for the support of the mattress, the mooing of the cows in the background, impatient for their 3:00 a.m. milking. Her Tiffany lamp now rested on the floor and her fingers sought to find the initials Mitch had carved into the bed. After such a rotten day, she discovered her dearest wish. A small sense of peace.

PHOEBE WOKE THE NEXT morning to the vibration of the tractor right outside her window. With a slight panic, she glanced at the clock and flipped on her light, feeling for it high, realizing foggily that it was on the floor. It was nearly five-thirty. She should be in her car. Then with relief, she realized she didn't have anywhere to go. She peered through the slats of the shutters on the picture window, her heart thudding with a peculiar anticipation when she spotted the headlights on the tractor, Mitch's silhouette moving feed around. She turned away, surprised by the fluttering in her chest.

She spied a white envelope on the floor near the door. An errant envelope separated from its brethren. To prove that she had reformed, she reluctantly picked it up, surprised to see just her first name in small neat script. She opened the envelope and with her back against the door, slid down to sit on the floor.

It's not so bad, Mitch had scrawled across the top. She studied in amazement what he had done. Lists. He had created tallies, interest rates, totals. She closed one eye and peeked at the bottom of the third page, the grand total. $53,987.63. She looked at it in surprise. It was big, but it wasn't as big as she'd thought it was going to be. She had guesstimated her total debt nearer to eighty thousand. Why, once she sold her condo, she *could* pay off these bills.

She looked through the other pages. She cringed when she saw how much she owed in interest alone. One table showed what she owed in descending order, the biggest balances on top. Another demonstrated how delinquent she was. Mitch was absolutely right. It wasn't so bad, now that it was here in black and white. She wasn't sure what she was supposed to do with the lists. She certainly didn't have fifty-four grand on her, but she knew this was an important document that she could take to court.

Spurred by a rush of gratitude, Phoebe quickly pulled on her jeans and a sweater with a pair of sneakers and went in search of the tractor that had rumbled past her room.

MITCH HAD TRIED TO SLEEP. But after twenty minutes of tossing and turning, not being able to clear the trailer of Phoebe's perfume and his mind of her presence, he finally gave up. He had long since finished his own forms and didn't feel like starting a new project and he didn't mean to be nosy, but the temptation was too great. Here was a woman, overwhelmed with bills who refused to consider bankruptcy. He tilted his head with new respect. She fought to retain her integrity as tenaciously as he did. Bankruptcy was always an option and many people who didn't need to take it, did. But not Phoebe.

All her bills were there, sitting on the table, almost all the way open. He peered into the box, realizing she only had a couple of dozen to go. Before he knew what he was doing, he was opening them, swearing that he wouldn't read them. He'd just open them and then get rid of the box and the garbage, so he'd have room to move around.

After the box was dumped outside with the garbage, the most natural thing in the world was to start sorting the letters. Surely, there were numerous repeats. She didn't need to wade through all of them. He'd just make sure she had the most current letters. Then he wondered how many credit companies there were.

Forty-three, he discovered three hours later. Some of them maxed-out with exorbitant interest accruing monthly, others with only one or two thousand dollars, but so delinquent that they, surprisingly, were sending the nastiest letters. He noticed that she hadn't started out with forty-three cards. Only a few, but she'd graduated to bigger and better cards, with more prestige and higher credit limits. He also noticed that she was paying the maximum on the interest rates.

Soon, he gave up all pretense and studied the bills avidly as he sorted. She ate out a lot, but that seemed to have abruptly stopped. However, much of the expense was accrued from either the chain superstores or cash advances. Big cash advances, he noted. The latter ones showed increasing charges at grocery stores. He frowned, not certain what she'd been doing. He double-checked, tripled-checked. Yes. All accounts showed that Phoebe had been showing signs of losing everything almost two years ago.

Mitch sat back and tried to figure her out. The numbers clearly showed that she was practically living off her credit cards. He added up her last known payments. She had been valiantly trying to keep up by making hefty payments on several. But then, the cash advances always set her back. In most cases she owed more in interest than what she originally borrowed.

By the time he finished entering her totals on the spreadsheet and printing out a copy for her, it was time to feed the cows. Now on the tractor, he sorely felt the lack of sleep, still thinking about Phoebe and all those bills. He grinned ruefully to himself. He could never resist a financial challenge, especially if it was someone else's. He enjoyed his own challenges much less. He watched the sky begin to lighten. If inventory went quickly this afternoon, he could probably knock off a little early and get to bed. He automatically reversed and almost ran over Phoebe, who neatly jumped out of the way and waved at him to turn the tractor off.

He obliged and smiled down at her.

"You look better this morning," he commented, noticing the glint in her hair, thinking he could smell faint perfume about her. He probably couldn't, but he imagined it anyway.

"I can't believe you did this," she said, getting right to the point and holding up the envelope.

Mitch surveyed her, trying to gauge her state of mind. She didn't look upset at his intervention.

"No problem," he replied noncommittally. Even in the breaking dawn, she was beautiful.

"I can't believe you did this," she repeated. "You must have stayed up half the night."

"About that," he replied, reluctant to let her know that he had stayed up all night.

"And you're right."

"About what?" She looked very earnest.

"It's not so bad."

"Well, not as bad as you thought it would be," he amended. "I wouldn't say it wasn't bad. It's a load of debt to carry."

She nodded. "I know but—" she flashed

him a dazzling smile "—at least I have something to go to court with now." She paused and then said seriously, "I can't let you do all that work without repaying you."

"With what?" Mitch joked, greatly amused.

She silently chewed her lip. Finally, she said slowly, "Work."

Mitch laughed out loud. He couldn't see Phoebe putting in a day's work on the farm. She'd peter out within an hour, either from fatigue or sensory overload.

She gave him a piercing stare. "I'm not kidding," she said, the tone of her voice altering dramatically. It deepened and rang with authority. Mitch studied her and then shook his head. As fun as it might be to have her around, he had a lot to do and could hardly spend the day playing nanny and praising her when she accomplished the smallest little task.

"You wouldn't last an hour," he said shortly. "Don't worry about it. Consider it a gift."

"I beg to differ," Phoebe retorted. She shook the envelope at him. "This must be worth at least ten hours of work on the farm. I'll do whatever you tell me to do." She met his eyes with a calculating look, choosing her words carefully. "You look as if you could use the help."

Mitch blanched, her words needling him.

She obviously knew which buttons to push. He stared out, considering the sunrise, finally uttered gruffly, "Forget it. It wasn't anything."

"It was everything to me," Phoebe said. "And I want to pay you back." She was quiet for a minute and then added pointedly, "Maybe you can give Katie a day off or something."

Mitch shot her a stinging glare and started up the tractor with a roar. "It was nothing," Mitch shouted over the din because it made him feel better to shout. "Use the time to find another job."

PHOEBE STARED AT HIS straight back as he drove away, dumping his load into the feeder and then noisily reversing. She should have been relieved that he didn't want her to work on the farm. Instead of spending a day mucking through dairy waste, he was right, she could start her job search—update her résumé, drive to San Jose and visit her headhunter, check on the progress of her condo.

But instead of feeling relief, she was furious. Steamingly furious. Blindingly furious. *You wouldn't last an hour,* rang in her ears. Her lips tightened and with stunned clarity, she realized that she *wanted* to help him the same way he had helped her. And it annoyed her that he obviously thought what she had to offer wasn't worth taking.

With forced casualness, she turned back and walked into the house, nearly colliding with Katie in the hall.

"What are you doing here?" Katie, still in her pajamas, asked rudely.

"None of your business," Phoebe replied, and then stopped herself. Just because she was angry at Mitch didn't mean she had to take it out on his sister, no matter how much of a twirp she was. Phoebe took a deep breath and paused at her bedroom door. She turned and said directly with the nicest smile she could summon, "I'm sorry. I'm having a bad day."

"It's just started," Katie said warily.

"Some days are like that." Phoebe paused and then said, "I was fired yesterday. That's why I'm still here."

"Oh!" Katie's face turned red. She ducked her head and muttered, "Sorry." Katie turned back toward her own room and Phoebe followed her, standing in the doorway.

"Don't be. I knew it was coming."

"Is that was why you moved out here?" Katie asked, almost in spite of herself.

Phoebe shrugged. "Sort of." She glanced around Katie's room, watching Katie gather her clothes for the day.

"That looks nice," Phoebe commented.

"It's picture day," Katie replied briefly.

"I remember picture day. That shade of blue will really bring out the blue in your eyes."

Katie didn't say anything. Phoebe stepped to one side when Katie pushed past her to get to the shower. Phoebe smiled, ruefully acknowledging that Katie didn't know how to take a compliment any better than her brother.

At six-thirty, Phoebe arrived at the breakfast table. Mitch and Carlo were already seated, Bess was frying eggs, but Katie, dressed in her picture-day best, stood in the kitchen, her posture stiffer than usual, poised to let loose one of her famous screeches.

"I can't believe you don't remember," she accused.

"You didn't tell me," Mitch replied, his voice equally stern. "I would have remembered something so important to you."

Phoebe slipped into her seat.

"I did tell you," Katie insisted. "I told you last week and you said fine."

"Katie, I wouldn't say fine if it wasn't fine. You know we've got the appraisal. Carlo and I need to do inventory all afternoon, so we can't cover for you today," Mitch explained carefully, his tone maintaining his authority. "I'm sorry you're disappointed, but we can't spare you this week."

"But you promised." The plea was truly mournful.

Phoebe's heart went out to Katie, as belligerent as she was.

"All the girls are going. I even found a ride— Mom?" Katie, ever valiant, appealed to her mother who served Mitch and Carlo their eggs and put a plate of toast on the table, her face impassive.

"Tell them you can't make it," Bess said matter-of-factly.

"I can't ever make anything." Katie's eyes filled with tears. "They want to be my friends. They won't ask me again if I don't go." Tears sparkled in her eyes. She looked at Mitch again, and pleaded, "I told you about this party two weeks ago. I reminded you about it last week. You said—"

"Katie, I'm sorry," Mitch said, cutting her off, his voice softening. "I just can't spare you. If it were next week, you'd—"

"It's *not* next week. It's this week. It's today. Picture day," Katie wailed.

"Sit down," Bess intervened. "Eat your breakfast. You'll be late for school."

"I don't care." Katie's tears spilled over.

Mitch looked helplessly at her.

Phoebe cleared her throat, and all eyes turned toward her. "Maybe I can help."

CHAPTER SIX

PHOEBE KNEW EVERYONE WAS looking at her. Mitch glared in surprise, Bess studied her with curiosity, and Katie eyed her resentfully. Phoebe buttered her toast.

"What can you do?" Katie asked, the disdain heavy in her voice.

"Katie!" Mitch admonished. His face exhibiting a range of conflicting emotions as he said to Phoebe, his voice as chilly as ice, "Stay out of it."

"Why?" Phoebe asked levelly. "I live here, too."

"This is a family matter," Bess said, but her blue eyes were darting back and forth between Mitch and Phoebe, speculation growing. Phoebe smiled. Bess wasn't nearly as distanced as she would like people to believe.

Phoebe shrugged. "Doesn't seem like a family matter at all. Seems like a labor issue to me."

"Phoebe." Mitch's voice softened with an implicit warning. His brown gaze challenged her to pursue her train of thought. She met his eyes and then gave Katie a sidelong look.

"Seems like," she said casually as she bit into the toast, "if I helped out today, Katie'd be able to make her outing."

Katie's expression changed dramatically. She sat up in surprise and then asked suspiciously, "Why would you do that?"

Phoebe chewed, noticing that Bess was listening to her answer. She met Bess's eyes, saw her interest. She swallowed.

"Let's just say that I owe Mitch a few hours of work," Phoebe said carefully.

"No, she doesn't," Mitch replied, his tone sharp.

"So, if I worked today, then Katie can go to her party and everybody's happy." She didn't dare look directly at Mitch. She took another bite of toast, and the silence extended. Carlo winked at her.

Katie peered surreptitiously at Mitch. Finally, Katie asked in a tiny voice, "Please, Mitch?"

Phoebe watched him struggle. She knew he wanted to give Katie the day as much as Katie wanted it. He shot Phoebe another stinging glare, and she braced herself for his dislike. With a small smile, she met his gaze directly, although her heart was beating a mile a minute. Then she looked at Bess, who regarded them intently.

Phoebe held her breath and smiled, seeing a spark of life that hadn't been in the older woman's faded blue eyes two weeks earlier. Phoebe bit her lip.

Mitch opened his mouth to say something and surprisingly, Bess settled it by saying gruffly, "Sounds okay to me, if Phoebe does owe us some time."

"She doesn't—" Mitch began.

"I'll start after breakfast," Phoebe assured Bess, who had suddenly become very busy clearing the breakfast table.

"Thank you, Mom," Katie breathed. She jumped up and gave Bess an awkward hug that Bess pulled away from.

"It doesn't mean you'll have tomorrow off," Bess warned.

"I know," Katie said. And for the first time since Phoebe had moved in, she saw a genuine smile from Bess.

Phoebe avoided looking at Mitch. This was worth it. After what Mitch had done for her, even though he didn't like it one bit, this was definitely worth it. He was a smart man. Eventually he'd see that this small concession to Katie was a sound investment in his family.

Mitch shoved his chair back, not bothering

to finish the rest of his breakfast. "Meet me at the barn in ten minutes," he said to Phoebe in a tense, clipped tone. He rose angrily, then got enough of a hold of himself to drop a tender kiss on his sister's head. "You have fun, munchlet."

"I will." Katie fairly beamed.

Phoebe nodded. See? It was working already.

"You," Mitch's voice cracked above Phoebe's head like a whip. "Ten minutes."

"I'll be there," she said. He'd get over it. But as she heard the door slam shut behind him, the house rattling with the barely controlled violence, she doubted he'd get over it in the next ten minutes.

After Katie left to brush her teeth and Bess went to put a new load of laundry in the dryer, Carlo leaned over and tapped Phoebe on the forearm.

Phoebe stared at him startled.

"Mr. Mitch likes things his way," Carlo observed complacently, his voice a conspiratorial whisper. He got up from the table with a slow grunt and gave her a toothy smile. "You'll do fine if you remember that you're stronger than him."

Phoebe didn't feel stronger than him. In fact, the thudding of her heart had been replaced with a thudding in her stomach as she approached the barn. And after a morning with Mitch, the thudding in her stomach was replaced by a persistent ache in her arms and shoulders, as she scoured the milking area walls, with a bucket of soapy water and a rough brush. It was positively medieval. She swore that she'd seen Carlo use a hydraulic spray gun for exactly the same purpose.

As soon as she finished that task, Mitch gave her another, handing her thigh-high boots, so she could slog through the murky waste to help Mitch fix a portion of the corral. Just as she got there, he remembered he'd "accidentally" forgotten to bring the blow-torch. So she had to slog back for the torch, doing battle with the gate with the rusted hinge. Then, he made her run up and down the big corral, identifying cows from one end to the other, wobbling precariously on the stanchions as she sought to find cow number 497 with the yellow tag in her ear. When she swore she couldn't find it, Mitch admitted with a wry smile, "Maybe it was a green tag."

Phoebe fumed because she *knew* Mitch knew all his cows, their numbers, their locations just by sight. She had seen him identify cows from as far away as his trailer. Carlo grinned and gave her an encouraging nod. By

lunch, she was muddy, smelly and ravenous.
She barely had time to take a shower and eat
some food, before Mitch was barking at her
again. This time he set her to the task of im-
munizing the newest calves.

After ten years of hospital work, regard-
less of the fact that it was in administration,
Phoebe refused to be squeamish and grabbed
a squawking calf by her leg and administered
a quick shot. However after fifteen calves,
Phoebe realized the sheer arm strength needed
to subdue their vigorous and physical protests
was beyond her. She sat on a bale to rest.

"No time to sit down. The calves' pens need
to be cleaned and hayed. And then they need
to be fed," Mitch said shortly. He looked up at
the sky. "You've only got a couple more hours
of sunlight. The shots took you a lot longer
than I thought they would."

Phoebe groaned as she pushed herself up to
a standing position. Her butt and thighs ached
terribly and she barely caught the pitchfork,
Mitch thrust at her. But, drawing on some
inner reserve, she systematically mucked out
their pens, putting out clean straw for them to
sleep on. The gloves she wore were too big,
obviously men's sized, and she felt blisters
begin to form on both hands. She stopped to
readjust the gloves and saw Mitch studying

her critically. With gritted teeth, she ignored the searing pain.

"Need to grain them first. Then milk," Mitch said, indicating the next row of calves. He handed her a five-gallon bucket of grain. Her shoulders protested but with two hands, she dragged the bucket toward the calves who greedily ate. Back and forth, back and forth.

"There's the milk. I made them up for you," he said briefly.

The buckets of milk seemed heavier. She tried not to spill any as she carefully poured a portion out for each calf. She knew she was moving slowly. Katie usually had the job done within two hours. By the time Phoebe finished putting down hay in the trough for the older calves, she was working in rapidly dimming light, a distinct fall dusk settling on the farm as it wound down for the evening. Gathering up her supplies, she supposed it was probably near dinnertime. Her stomach growled.

"Not done yet," Mitch said as he flicked on the light. "You need to wash out those for tomorrow. Put all these away." Mitch pointed to the used buckets, big and little. "Be sure to use hot water," he reminded her as he strode past her to go to his trailer.

Phoebe was so tired that she wanted to cry. *You're stronger than him,* echoed through her mind. With grim determination, she shored up the very last little bit of her resolve. Well, she might not be stronger than he was, but she'd lasted much longer than his projected hour. She gave herself the satisfaction of a small smile as she prepared to rinse and wash the buckets.

So far, she had avoided taking the gloves off in Mitch's presence. She wouldn't let him have the satisfaction of knowing that her hands hurt. When she saw Mitch's trailer light come on, she gingerly peeled off the gloves, wincing. Her hands were a mess. She rinsed them under a gentle stream of water and the crusted blood washed away. She looked at them in relief. It wasn't so bad. There was only one big blister the size of a quarter on the lower right quadrant of her right hand and on her left, a nickel-size blister in the valley between her index finger and thumb. She was tempted to peel away the skin, but decided not to. She searched around the sink for some dish gloves. Not finding any, she looked warily at the disinfectant. That would sting.

Well, she shrugged philosophically, at least the wounds would be clean. The sting, however, made her eyes tear, and she wasn't sure whether her hands shook from fatigue or pain. She turned the buckets upside down to drain and straightened the area, checking to make sure she left things just as Katie did. She shook her hands to air dry them. The blisters felt raw. With no moon and no light from Mitch's trailer, it was nearly pitch-black.

Phoebe wearily trudged to the back door. She was definitely late. She could hear dinner in progress, the clinking of forks and knives against stoneware. She took off her shoes on the back porch and entered quietly. However, instead of usual silence, Katie chattered away. Phoebe paused in the laundry room, feeling very vindicated, especially as the sound of laughter came toward her. She allowed herself a rush of joy for the Hawkins family. That's what a dinner table should sound like.

"And then Denise *called* him," Katie was saying, her excitement barely contained. "I could have died. But she just called him up on the phone. Of course, she didn't tell him I was the one that dared her to call. We all talked to him."

"Who's this?" Mitch asked, his voice amused and light.

Phoebe stood in the shadows, her delight fading, feeling oddly bereft, the friendly timbres of his voice contrasting greatly from his coldness to her all day. The table burst into laughter. Phoebe swallowed hard. It had been a long time since she had enjoyed such a meal. Suddenly, her palms stung. She looked down and realized she had clenched both hands. She relaxed her grip and bit her lip, hovering on the outskirts of the family space. Reminding herself that she was history as soon as her condo sold didn't seem to help the loneliness washing over her.

"Stinky Whitfield."

"Stinky Whitfield? Jay's brother?" Mitch asked in amazement.

"The same," Bess remarked dryly.

"Well, I'll be. I thought he would've outgrown that nickname by now," Mitch said.

"And then," Katie continued, talking over Mitch and Bess. "Then, he talked to me and said that he thought I looked nice today."

"You did look nice," Mitch responded affectionately.

"But he said I looked *nice,*" Katie emphasized.

"Oooh. *Nice.*" Mitch nodded in understanding. He laughed and asked, "What's Stinky's real name?"

"Leslie." Katie took a big bite. "He's trying to make everyone call him Lee, but even the teachers call him Stinky," she said with her mouth full.

Phoebe tried to duck past them unnoticed.

"You're late," Bess commented, rising to get another plate.

Mitch pulled out a chair for her, his eyes meeting hers.

"Sorry," Phoebe said with a forced smile, the lump in her throat growing as she walked past. She waved to Bess to sit down. "I'm going to skip dinner tonight. I've got a shower and a bed calling me." She surveyed the table quickly, her gaze skittering past Mitch, and took heart from Carlo's sympathetic nod.

"You have to eat something," Mitch said sharply. She looked at him briefly, not wanting to see if his expression matched his voice. "You haven't eaten since lunch."

"Thanks, but I'm fine," Phoebe assured him as she turned quickly, willing herself not to cry in front of everyone. She felt his gaze follow her down the hall.

She sought refuge in the bathroom. She ran as hot a shower as she could stand and stepped in, relaxing immediately as the hot water streamed over her scalp, ignoring the sting in her hands as she washed away the grime of the afternoon. Still wet, she shivered while the tub filled, her mind churning with emotions from the day. But after she sprinkled her favorite bath salts liberally in the tub and lowered herself in the steaming water, the need to cry passed, the heat taking away much of her tension and physical ache.

She inhaled deeply, her spirits returning. She had nothing to be ashamed of. As much as Mitch resented her intrusion, he couldn't find fault with her efforts. She carefully kept her hands out of the water, balancing her elbows on the edge of the tub and sunk deeper into the water. Oooh, that felt good.

The ache wasn't so bad, she thought reflectively. She had a great respect for the work Mitch did every day. She only had to do it once. This was his life. *It could be yours* flashed into her head. She shook the thought out, but it persisted as she drifted into a sedated lull, reminding herself that there were worse ways to make a living—like working for a hospital that offered no job security and didn't appreciate or compensate the talent it exploited.

She smiled sadly, feeling unappreciated, as more laughter wafted toward her. She took a cleansing breath, deeply satisfied with the levity. Yes, that sound was worth every torturous minute. It was worth Mitch's wrath, even if he couldn't get it through his thick, stubborn head that laughter was exactly what this house needed.

MITCH WAITED FOR PHOEBE to emerge, but after all the dinner dishes were done and put away, there was still no sign of her. He made her up a plate of food, ignoring the inquiring look from Bess. He wrapped it in plastic wrap and put it in the refrigerator. Rather than retreating to his trailer the way he normally did after dinner, Mitch hung around the living room and watched Bess quilt as Katie did her homework. When Bess asked whether it was cold enough to start a fire, Mitch's throat tightened. Katie sent him a look of delight. Bess hadn't wanted a fire since his father died.

After the fire was crackling in the living room, he became impatient, watching Katie stare into the dancing flames. Finally, he strode down the hall and found Phoebe's room dark and vacant. Steam that smelled an awful lot like fresh cut roses and musky woods escaped from under the bathroom door. He smiled involuntarily, inhaling deeply. She certainly didn't waste any time transforming back into her real self.

He tapped at the door.

"Just a minute," she croaked groggily.

He heard the splashing of water.

"You okay?" he called.

There was silence. And more splashing.

He cleared his throat and rapped on the door again. "You didn't drown, did you?"

"No," came a muffled response. "Tell Katie, I'll be out in a second."

"Katie's doing her homework. I need to talk to you."

There was a long pause. Finally, the door cracked open, Phoebe freshly scrubbed in a high-necked green flannel nightgown, pressing a washcloth in each hand, a towel wrapped around her hair, peered cautiously at him. "Yes?"

"Uh—" Mitch was at a loss for words. Her face looked so bright, flushed from her bath, her eyes a translucent green-gray, made greener by the color of her nightgown. His eyes trailed down the delicate line of her cheek, perfect for kissing. "Mom made up a dinner plate for you," he lied. "It's in the refrigerator."

"Thank her very much, but I'm pretty tired. I think I'm just going to get into bed," she said evasively. As she started to shut the door, Mitch deftly slipped his foot in the crack.

"Not until you eat something," he said firmly.

"I'm not hungry."

"Too bad." He gave her what he hoped was

an uncompromising look. She stared back, exasperation written all over her.

She heaved a sigh, still clutching the wash-cloths. "Okay, I'll eat the dinner later. Thank you."

Mitch persisted. "I'll set a place for you at the table."

"Thank you, but I'll eat in my bedroom," she said, then in response to his skeptical expression, added, "Look at me. I can hardly go out like this."

Mitch surveyed her modest flannel and laughed. "Don't worry, it's just pajamas. Come on," he said in his most persuasive voice. "You can't tell me you're not hungry. I'll even sit with you."

"You don't have to do that," Phoebe said hastily. "You probably have a lot to do. Entering all that inventory into the computer or something."

"That'll wait."

"I'm really tired," Phoebe said again.

"Come eat," he commanded. Taking her slender elbow, he guided her down the hall. She reluctantly allowed herself to be led, obediently sitting at the table, watching him set her a place, while the plate heated in the microwave.

"Why are you doing this?" she asked warily.

"Sometimes people need to be taken care of."

"Missing a meal won't kill me."

He paused and admitted, his voice wry. "No, I suppose it won't. But I figured you were probably hungry after the day you had."

"I'm more sore," she retorted and Mitch smiled at the belligerence in her tone as the microwave dinged.

He put the plate in front of her and asked with his most gracious host voice, "What would you like to drink? Milk, soda, water?"

"Water, please," she said. Then, washcloths still in hand, she worked the plastic off the plate. "This smells delicious," she admitted. When he put the water glass down before her, she smiled. "Thank you."

"Need anything else?"

Phoebe shook her head. She paused and said frankly, "You don't have to stay. I'm sure you want some sleep or something. You were up half the night."

"A few minutes more won't hurt me," he assured her. He had no intention—no intention at all—of leaving.

PHOEBE STARED AT MITCH, who sat across the table from her and looked determined to supervise every bite.

"You know, I eat better if you don't watch me," Phoebe commented, feeling very self-conscious.

"Well, to know that you'd have to eat something first," Mitch replied evenly, an easy smile on his lips.

Phoebe smiled back, and awkwardly picked up her fork.

"You can put those washcloths down, you know," Mitch observed, reaching for them. "Here. Let me take those, so you can eat."

"That's okay. I like them," Phoebe said. "I've become attached." It wasn't a lie. They had been pressed into her hands so long that she knew her blisters had welded themselves to terry cloth.

"Don't be ridiculous." He took her hand.

"Be careful," Phoebe warned, trying to pull her hand away from his.

"Phoebe," he said impatiently as she tugged.

She looked down at her hand still captured in his warm, strong fingers. She, then, looked up at him. "Please, wait. Let go of my hand and you can have the washcloths," she promised.

He stared at her expectantly and then released her hand. With a deep breath, she slowly opened her right hand and carefully peeled away the cloth, wincing when some of the skin went with it. She grimaced. Heartened that the worst was done, she peeled the left cloth from her hand. This one went much easier. As the stinging waned, she gave Mitch a quick glance and saw his eyes glued to her hands, his lips rigid, his jaw tight.

"It's not so bad."

"Then why were you hiding it from me?" Mitch said grimly.

"Because I didn't want you to think that I couldn't handle the work."

"What?" Mitch narrowed his eyes. "How could I possibly think that after all you did today?"

Phoebe shrugged. "These just confirm what you thought about me. That I wouldn't last an hour—"

"This didn't happen after an hour of work," Mitch said. He took her hand and opened up the palm, studying the blister, carefully tapping around the perimeter of the wound. "It happened because I gave you gloves that didn't fit properly. I'll put something on it."

"That's okay. I'll take care of it before I go to bed."

"No. These things are very serious. Infection is not fun. Eat. I'll be right back." Mitch got up and disappeared down the hall.

Phoebe didn't feel much like eating. She

pushed the food around on her plate and waited. A few minutes later, Mitch came back.

"This shouldn't hurt." He gently took her hand, and Phoebe watched, fascinated at how tenderly he treated her wound, carefully cutting away the excess skin, softly rubbing salve across the raw surface, then fashioning a bandage out of gauze and taping it down. He took her left hand and did the same thing. "There." He looked at her hands and then up at her. "That should hold you. I'll change it tomorrow."

"Thank you." Phoebe examined his work, trying to flex her hand. "It feels much better."

She ate and Mitch sat, his eyes watchful. She chewed slowly, savoring Bess's dinner. She felt even more wonderful now that he wasn't mad at her anymore.

"I'm sorry," Mitch said in a low voice.

"You have nothing to be sorry for," Phoebe said. "I knew what I was getting into."

"I doubt that very much," Mitch said with a shake of his head. "There's no way you could."

She fell silent.

"I guess I should thank you," Mitch finally said.

Phoebe looked at him expectantly, her heart beating. "For what?"

"The work you put in today."

She nodded, a little disappointed. She ate a morsel. "I hope it helped."

"It did help." Mitch paused and looked at her. "In many ways." He gave her a piercing stare. "But I think you knew that already."

Phoebe leaned forward and whispered because Katie was just in the other room. "Anyone with eyes could see Katie needed to go to that party."

"I didn't."

"You're personally involved. Your eyes don't count." Phoebe swallowed and reached for the glass of water. "I know exactly how Katie feels. Exactly. So much so that it's kind of scary. Except I didn't have an older brother who cared for me the way you care for Katie."

"You turned out okay," Mitch said.

"No, I didn't," Phoebe said honestly. "I don't think I turned out okay at all or else I wouldn't be here now."

"But you're not going to be here for very long. Pretty soon you'll have a job, your condo will sell. You'll pay off your debts. You'll be right back on top. Things can only get better."

Phoebe smiled again. "So they say."

AFTER PHOEBE HAD RETIRED, Mitch said goodnight to his mother and sister. The brisk night air felt good as he walked slowly back to his trailer. He took the long way around, so he could pass by her window. The shutters were closed but the room glowed with a low light.

Phoebe had finished her meal at her own pace and Mitch suddenly realized how much she had adjusted to life with his family. She was a delightful dinner companion. He found himself talking about nothing in particular, trying his best to make her laugh. She was easily tickled, he discovered and paid close attention to what he said, obviously listening, learning as he talked about the farm.

Mitch inhaled deeply, his walk extending around the perimeter of the corral. The last vestiges of summer gone completely, the wind added its chill to the crisp evenings. Soon the rains would come. But right now, worrying about potential disaster seemed to be a waste of energy, when he needed to understand why his heart had started to pound, just at the thought of Phoebe Douglas.

He shook his head, denying the feelings that had just begun to simmer. He had no use for such feelings. He had casually dated before his father died, but when things had taken a turn for the worse, he'd had too much to do. And frankly, he didn't miss it, the complications, the courting games. Except when it peered at him with clear hazel eyes, its face freshly scrubbed, pink from steam and smelling like woods and roses. Then he wondered.

"She's something, ain't she?" Carlo said quietly.

Startled, Mitch turned, having to look to spot the milker reclining on a bale, staring up at the stars. Mitch stared up, too.

"Who?" Mitch asked, distracted.

"Phoebe."

"Yes. If you like that type."

"Good heart. Hard worker. Pretty, too. Okay type. Seems as if you could've made it easier," Carlo observed.

Mitch didn't say anything. Seeing those blisters on her small hands pained him. He had just wanted to see what she was made of. He'd never thought she'd push herself to the point of injury. He'd expected her to quit long before the afternoon.

"Haven't heard Katie laugh like that since your dad passed on."

Mitch nodded reflectively. "Nice, wasn't it?"

"Seems the day off did her a lot of good."

"I guess."

"Your mom looked happy."

Bess *had* looked happy, Mitch admitted to himself.

"Guess your Phoebe's pretty responsible for it all."

"She's not my Phoebe," Mitch protested, trying to subdue the lurch of his heart at the remote possibility.

"Then that's a problem," Carlo chuckled. "Wouldn't you say?" Still chortling, Carlo stood slowly and headed toward his home.

Mitch wondered what Carlo meant. Phoebe wasn't by any stretch of the imagination *his,* even if he wanted her. She was destined to be on the arm of a banker or lawyer, someone who could keep her in the manner she had grown accustomed to. Not some dairyman up to his pole barn in debt, one infection away from bankruptcy.

Dairymen didn't get the fragile flowers that smelled of woods and roses. Those flowers wilted. He glanced back at the house, saw the glow of the light in Phoebe's room click off. He silently wished her a good night and sweet dreams. Fragile flowers wilted, but Phoebe hadn't. She hadn't even come close to wilting. Not even close.

CHAPTER SEVEN

PHOEBE WOKE EARLY AS usual, the noise of the tractor rumbling past her window. She didn't feel so bad, she thought, until she tried to sit up. Her muscles, having had the entire night to tighten, refused to move as she reached to flick on the light. The back of her legs were especially stiff. Her shoulders still ached.

Groaning, she pulled herself to a sitting position, allowing her muscles to readjust to the fight against gravity. She carefully peeled off Mitch's wrapping and examined her right hand. It looked okay. The skin, though an angry berry color, was already healing. The salve he'd put on it had softened the skin around the blisters and kept the edges from cracking. She gently poked at it and winced. Still tender. She would need to keep the bandage on for a day or two as long as the sores were as open as they were. She couldn't imagine trying to do anything that would stress them.

She gently rewrapped her hand. The tractor reversed and she stood up stiffly to peer out the window and watch Mitch at his morning tasks, his strong arms working the tractor with practiced ease. She noted his flannel jacket and black knit cap, pulled down over his ears. She hoped he was warm enough. Phoebe turned away, her face flushing. Why should she care whether he was warm enough? All he'd done was fix her hands and make her laugh at dinner. Then, he'd left abruptly, wishing her a good night.

When Phoebe arrived for breakfast, the tone of the table seemed ever so slightly altered, but Phoebe wondered if it were just wishful thinking. Mitch wasn't there and Phoebe tried not to be disappointed. But Katie made up for her brother's absence by talking animatedly to her mother. Bess actually listened, having softened just the tiniest bit. Phoebe gave a general greeting and sat down with a smile. Bess gave her a small tube of ointment.

"That should help," she said briefly.

"Help what?" Phoebe looked at the tube in surprise. It was the first time that Bess had actually initiated an act of kindness.

"Mitch told me about your blisters. This should help if they hurt too much during the day."

Phoebe felt a rush of emotion. "Thank you,"

she said. "That's very thoughtful of you. I'll return it."

"No hurry." Bess, embarrassed by the amount of conversation, turned abruptly to fix the eggs, then said offhandedly, "I do jeans and blues in the morning. You may as well add yours to the pile. It won't make much of a difference."

Phoebe was touched, knowing how much that gesture of friendship meant. "Thank you. I went through two pairs yesterday."

"That's a slow day," Bess said and Phoebe swore she caught a glimpse of a smile.

But Bess said nothing more, continuing with breakfast as if there hadn't been a conversation to begin with. Carlo soon joined them.

"Where's Mitch?" Bess asked.

"Said he ate early, and that he'd be by after breakfast."

Katie ventured, "Mom, do you think I can go to the outlet mall on Saturday with Denise and the rest of girls?"

Bess frowned. "No. You have work to do."

"But," Katie protested. "Everyone is going. Denise got a new car for her birthday and it's just to Gilroy."

"I said no," Bess said.

"But *why?* It's a Saturday."

"You already went to one party this week. That's enough."

Katie sat silently.

"Uh," Phoebe interjected quietly. "I'm free on Saturday—"

"Good," Katie said tartly. "Then you go with Denise."

Phoebe laughed. "No, I was thinking that I could probably do Katie's work, Bess. That is, if you don't mind."

Katie shot her a look of disbelief, then looked hopefully at her mother.

"What are you going to do about money?" Bess asked her daughter.

"I've saved some of my allowance. I'm not going to spend a lot. I'll just look." She assured her mother, then gave Phoebe a sidelong look. "Though Denise has her own credit card."

"Credit cards are just trouble," Bess said shortly.

Phoebe gave a silent amen to that.

Bess regarded both of them and finally said, "I'll think about it."

Katie was quiet, knowing not to push her luck.

"You don't mind working?" Bess asked Phoebe suddenly.

Phoebe looked at Bess in surprise. "No,"

she answered, her voice honest. "I actually enjoyed it."

"It's probably not what you're used to," Bess commented cautiously.

Phoebe realized they were having a conversation and answered slowly, "I grew up on a farm."

"So this is like home?" Katie asked, her curiosity getting the better of her.

Phoebe shook her head, regretfully. "No," she replied honestly. "This is nothing like home."

After a long silence, Bess said in a clipped voice addressing Phoebe, "Well, if you don't mind doing her chores, I guess she can go on Saturday."

Katie gave Phoebe a look of awe. And Phoebe smiled to herself as she ate her breakfast. Halfway through, she dared to look at Carlo who was grinning at her.

The door banged open and Mitch entered. All eyes turned to him. He didn't smile as he scanned the breakfast table. Finally, his gaze settled on Phoebe who felt dread scurry down her spine.

"Ten minutes," he said shortly. "The barn."

Even Bess looked startled by his tone.

"Okay." Phoebe nodded, swallowing the last of her juice.

"Ten minutes."

Before she left, Bess pushed a pair of leather gloves in her hands.

"These should fit better."

Phoebe gratefully took the gloves, gingerly pulling them over her bandaged hands. Bess was right. They did fit better, and Phoebe braced herself for the workload. Even though she was stiff, the kinks would eventually work themselves out. Or maybe not. She stifled a groan as she maneuvered down the few back stairs. Walking was proving to be enough of a task. Once at the barn, she found Mitch talking soothingly to a newborn calf, still damp from the womb.

His beaming smile startled her, and a pleasant shiver replaced the one of dread. His eyes crinkled at the corners. "Don't look as if you're coming to face a firing squad," he said lightly. "I thought you'd like to see this."

Phoebe cautiously approached him, her eyes studying the calf. "It's so cute. Is it a boy or a girl?"

Mitch double-checked. "A girl. Thank goodness. We've been having a run of bulls lately. I wondered if we were ever going to get any girls."

"Girls are good," Phoebe observed.

"If you're a dairy farmer, girls are gold.

These girls are getting better and better," Mitch said proudly. "She's my second generation."

His hands examined the calf who was squirming to get free. He laid her gently on the hay and then backed off. Together they watched her wobble to a stand, then dip down, her front legs trying to compensate for the weight of her head.

"You need to separate her from her mother?" Phoebe asked a little wistfully.

Mitch nodded. "The mother's at her milking peak. That's why we feed the calves formula."

"What happens if you have a boy?"

"Bull," Mitch corrected.

"What happens if you have a bull?"

"He gets sold at auction."

Phoebe watched the little calf, having already mastered gravity, take a few steps. Mitch ushered her to a clean pen.

"Thank you," Phoebe said, her voice sincere.

"You still owe me two hours of work," Mitch said suddenly.

Phoebe looked down at her gloved hands and then met his eyes with a defiant tilt of her chin. "You're right," she said, her voice firm. "What do you want me to do?"

"You won't need those," Mitch replied, indicating her gloves and then laughing. Almost as if he couldn't help himself, he ran a finger down the line of her cheek.

Phoebe shivered from the intimacy of his touch, then exhaled. "Thank God. I was dreading it. Though I wouldn't mind helping out after the blisters heal." She asked curiously, "So what do you want me to do?"

"Follow me." He strode off to his trailer.

Phoebe trailed behind him, curious about the task he had for her. Maybe he wanted her to input all the inventory information they'd compiled yesterday.

"I'm very computer literate," Phoebe volunteered. "Just show me what to do and I can input almost any data you want."

"Can you do financial plans and projections using a spreadsheet?" he asked.

"Sure," Phoebe said as she climbed the steps to his trailer, wincing as the muscles in her thighs protested. "I did it at the hospital all the time."

"Good. Then I think you have everything you need." Mitch flipped open his laptop, then pulled out a binder and handed it to her.

"Great. What am I supposed to do?"

"Sit down in front of the computer first."

She obediently sat and felt Mitch's large

presence loom behind her. He reached around her to enter a quick password.

Phoebe became acutely aware of him as he scrolled through files. She could smell hay and soap and some masculine shampoo. She could hear the slow thud of his heart beating right behind her ear. When she ducked out of the way, the soft flannel of his shirt rubbed lightly against her face.

"Ah. There it is." Mitch said with a satisfied grunt.

Phoebe looked at the screen expectantly, surprised to find her name in the header. "What's this?"

"Your finances."

"What?"

"I want you to spend the next couple of hours creating a reasonable payment plan. Projecting your expenses and the most reasonable payments that you can manage—"

"But I thought I was going to help you—" Phoebe protested.

"Didn't you say you had a court date soon?" His voice was firm, his brown eyes steady.

"Two weeks."

"Then this is exactly the kind of information the judge will want. The more prepared you are to answer his questions, the more likely he'll decide in your favor. You'll need to show him a detailed outline of your current financial state as well as a projection of payments made over the next several years. Also factored in will have to be when you expect to be employed again, how much you reasonably think you'll make and how much you can pay back, what the total debt you owe is. The judge needs to see signs that you're trying to recover, not digging further into the hole. Have you cut up your cards yet?"

Phoebe was silent. Finally, she heaved a large sigh and said honestly, "I'd rather slog through cow sludge."

Mitch laughed and she felt another pleasant shiver run down her back. "Consider this slogging through your personal waste. But the first step is to commit to honesty and stop charging cold turkey."

"Waste." Phoebe felt slapped. The truth hurt. She looked over her shoulder and met his eyes. "You know," she said softly, "that this is a lot harder for me than what I did yesterday."

Mitch regarded her, his eyes sympathetic. "I know. But you're going to feel much better once you get this done. You'll also need to create a letter to send to your creditors."

Phoebe nodded, her resolve growing. "I know. I know what I need to do."

"Then do it. I'll come check on you soon."

"Promise?"

"Promise." He turned to walk outside, the trailer moving with his weight. "Help yourself to whatever you can find in the kitchen. And Phoebe?"

"Yes?"

"Thank you for Katie," he said quietly.

Phoebe nodded, a lump in her throat. "You're welcome."

PHOEBE STARED AT THE documents streaming out of Mitch's printer. She looked up, her neck stiff, realizing with surprise that it was dark. Mitch had for the most part left her alone. He'd brought her a plate of food at noon and then after a few minutes of chitchat left her to her task. It wasn't exhilarating or productive work. It wasn't like yesterday where at least calves got fed or the fence got fixed or cows were counted. It was work that brought to the surface all her waste, her terrible judgment with money, with people. All those cash advances for Audrey and her sister and Will. What did she have to show for it?

Mitch had meticulously organized all the dunning letters, indexed the amounts owed. She had spent the morning juggling numbers and came to the depressing conclusion that she wouldn't have enough money to pay even the minimums on each of her forty-three charge cards. It didn't matter how many times she juggled the numbers around, how many times she reworked the different scenarios. She was stuck until she sold the condo.

Earlier in the afternoon, she had desperately called Diane. The agent had been sickeningly optimistic. When Phoebe pressed her, she remained unruffled. Be patient. The housing market was turning. If she was patient, she could get just about what she was asking. The likelihood of selling the condo before her court date seemed unlikely.

The door to the trailer rattled noisily. Mitch poked his head in. "Dinner," he announced.

Phoebe shook her head. "I'm not hungry."

"Mom isn't going to accept another skipped meal. Come on. Take a break."

Phoebe stared at him, her mind not on dinner at all. "This is terrible."

"Yes, it is," he agreed, his voice matter-of-fact. "But that doesn't mean you'll be forced to eat only moldy bread and water."

"I'm going to have to declare bankruptcy."

"No. Bankruptcy is not an option," Mitch responded firmly.

"Oh, yes, it is," Phoebe said, her anxiety

rising another notch. "It's not a great option. But it is an option."

"No. Bankruptcy is not an option," he repeated. "Come on. Let's go eat. We'll think of something."

"I've thought of everything."

"Until we think again." Mitch held his hand out. "Come."

Phoebe stared at his outstretched hand and took it. He squeezed her fingers gently, careful of the bandage on her palm. She let him pull her out of the trailer into the night air, studying his face, which had become increasingly familiar. *We'll. We.* Words of partnership. Never in her life had she dreamed that— She shivered, not from the cold, but said anyway, "I didn't know it had gotten so chilly."

"Here." Mitch took off his flannel jacket and draped it over her shoulders, his arm resting casually on top of his jacket. He slowed his long stride to match hers.

"Thank you," Phoebe whispered, her heart fluttering at his proximity.

"Don't give up. There are always options," he said quietly, misreading her thoughts, his voice next to her ear. "Always."

While she couldn't be sure, she swore he kissed her on the side of the head. Reflectively, they walked to the main house. At the back door, Phoebe slipped off his jacket. Mitch put it on again and they entered the house, the smells of Bess's cooking assaulting them.

"It's about time you two got here," Bess fussed. "It's six-fifteen."

"I had to drag Phoebe away from the computer," Mitch joked.

Katie looked at them suspiciously. "What's she doing on the computer? You never let me use the laptop" she accused.

"Phoebe's got some business she needs to attend to, squirt," Mitch fended off his sister easily.

Phoebe looked at him in amazement. Apparently, he hadn't told anyone about her financial state. He gave her a private wink.

"Did Mom tell you that I'm going with Denise to the outlet mall this Saturday?" Katie asked quickly, glancing at Phoebe, daring her to back out. "Phoebe said she'd feed the calves again for me so I could go."

Phoebe reddened when Mitch shot her a piercing look. She helped herself to a pork chop and mumbled with a helpless shrug, "All the girls are going. You know, Denise got a car for her sixteenth birthday. That's all."

THAT'S ALL. Mitch couldn't grasp the generosity of the woman who sat across the table from him, slowly eating her food. The family lapsed into its usual silence, but the aura had changed significantly. Even Bess, who normally seemed tightly wrapped, ready to jump from one task to the next, relaxed, her eyes more focused than they'd been in a long time.

"Phoebe, do you want to go for a walk?" Mitch asked after dinner, ignoring the look Katie gave him.

Phoebe glanced up, suddenly drawn back to the present. When her hazel eyes met his, he saw a flash of anxiety before she shuttered it away. She hesitated for just a fraction of a second before she said with a forced smile, "Sure. Okay. I could use a stretch."

"Can I go, too?" Katie piped up.

"You've got homework," Bess said firmly, her eyes speculatively dancing between her son and Phoebe.

"It's done," Katie retorted.

"Of course you can." Phoebe's tone was equable.

Mitch frowned slightly. This wasn't quite what he'd had in mind. He wanted to talk to Phoebe privately. He wanted to *be* with Phoebe privately.

"Let me go grab my jacket," Phoebe said rising from the table.

"Don't go until I finish the dishes," Katie begged.

"I'll help," Mitch volunteered, his eyes following Phoebe down the hall.

Katie turned on the water, impatient for it to get hot. "This tap is so slow," she complained, as she began rinsing the dishes. She accepted the plates Mitch handed her, as he started to put away the leftovers. Phoebe returned with her jacket on and joined them, picking up a dish towel. She passed the dry dishes to Mitch and the three worked in amenable silence, finishing the task quickly and effortlessly.

"I'll be right back," Katie said in a rush. "Don't go without me."

"We won't," Phoebe promised, glancing over her shoulder to make sure that Katie was out of earshot. She moved in close to Mitch, honey colored wisps of hair hiding her expression as she looked down. She thrust a bundle into Mitch's hand with the merest brush of her fingers against his skin.

"What's this?" Mitch asked quietly.

"Look," Phoebe said with a small smile. She gazed up at him, her hazel eyes now bright olive-green, big and trusting.

He opened his palm and saw a wad of credit cards. A big wad of credit cards.

"All forty-three of them," Phoebe said in

such a low tone that Mitch had to bend his head to hear her. The action caused him to catch a deep whiff of woods and roses. He straightened quickly, disconcerted.

"Why are you giving them to me?" He sought to meet her eyes.

"I want to cut them up." She shrugged a slender shoulder. "I knew I had to sooner or later. It probably would have been better to have done it sooner rather than later." She laughed softly and then put her small hand over his. "I figured if I gave them to you, you'd keep me honest."

Mitch looked down and whistled softly. "All forty-three?"

"All forty-three. I haven't matched them to your list, but I counted. And they're all there."

Katie came pounding back into the room. "What's that?" Katie asked curiously, her sharp eyes missing nothing.

Mitch slipped the wad into his jacket pocket. "None of your business, squirt," he told Katie. "Did you get a flashlight?"

She ran out of the room at the same moment Carlo came in.

"Two calves coming," he announced.

Mitch grimaced as Katie returned with a flashlight. "Sorry, ladies. I'll need to take a rain check."

"Why?" Katie fairly wailed.

"Calves."

"Oh." Katie looked downcast. "I guess we don't need this." She gave the flashlight a look of dislike as if it had caused the calves to be born at just that second. She put it on the table.

Phoebe gave Mitch a sympathetic look at Katie's obvious disappointment but asked quickly, "Do you mind if I do a couple of hours of work in your trailer later?"

"No. Not at all." He started to follow Carlo out, then paused at the door. "If you guys are still going," he instructed, "be sure to take the light."

PHOEBE TURNED TOWARD the completely defeated Katie and asked quietly, "Is there a problem with the calves?"

Katie gave her an impatient look. "No."

"Mitch is always careful with births," Bess said. "You can go watch if you like. The cows do all the work."

Phoebe smiled and this time Bess smiled right back. Phoebe picked up the flashlight and said, "I think I will. Katie, do you want to go, too?"

Katie shrugged. "It's nothing new."

"It's new to me. I'd like to go see," Phoebe said cheerfully as she headed out the door.

After a moment of hesitation, Katie followed. "They're probably over in the back corral," she said, walking quickly so that Phoebe's muscles protested as she tried to keep up.

"They don't take the cows into the barn?"

"Only if they're sick. Usually, the cows just have the babies wherever."

"Oh." They fell silent, and Phoebe inhaled deeply. The clean, crisp autumn air felt wonderful, clearing her head, making her money worries seem a universe away. Phoebe looked up. More stars than she had ever seen in the city glittered in the night sky.

They were almost to the back corral, and Phoebe could see Mitch and Carlo standing back, letting the dogs keep the rest of the herd at bay. She could hear the murmur of their voices, the moos of the cows when Katie stopped in her tracks, turned, and asked bluntly, "Why are you being so nice to me?"

Phoebe masked her surprise. Then she smiled at the young woman. "Am I being nice to you?"

"Well, you worked all yesterday so I could go to the party."

"Sounds as if you had a good time at the party."

"And you're going to work for me on Saturday so I can go to Gilroy."

"Well, I don't have to," Phoebe teased.

"No, no. I didn't mean that," Katie said hastily, her voice less rough. "I just wondered, that's all."

Phoebe thought about her answer. Then she finally said, "Maybe I know how hard it is to be fifteen."

Katie's face was full of suspicion.

Phoebe hastened to reassure her. "I'm not making fun of you. Fifteen was a particularly trying year for me."

"Why?"

Phoebe stared at Katie, tempted to lie, but then said quietly, "I ran away when I was fifteen because it was so hard."

"Ran away?" Katie looked shocked. "Why?"

"Well, when I was growing up in Michigan—"

"In Michigan?" Katie asked with the wonder of a native Californian.

"Yes, Michigan," Phoebe said with a smile and continued. "We lived on a deserted farm because it was cheap. My dad was gone most of the time. My mom was stressed out a lot. I missed a ton of school because I was taking care of my sister and brothers."

"You have brothers and sisters?" Katie gave Phoebe a look of surprise. "You act like an only child."

Phoebe was silent. "I feel like one now."

"Have you talked to them?"

Phoebe looked away and said evasively, "I've talked to my mother once or twice."

"Don't you miss her?" Katie asked with the innocence of a child.

Phoebe shook her head. "I used to, but not anymore. We don't really get along."

"It's probably because you're rich and they're still poor."

Phoebe smiled slightly. How perceptive the young are. "Maybe. We're just different."

"There's no one?"

Phoebe shook her head. "No."

Well, there was one. But Phoebe wondered if Tucker was even in Michigan. Audrey's last numbers had been useless. Facebook and numerous internet searches had netted nothing.

"Don't you miss them?"

Miss Stella or Todd? Phoebe grimaced. But she did miss the little boy who had been her constant shadow, who had clamped his mouth shut to not cry when she slipped away— Phoebe cut off those thoughts.

"Maybe," she said evasively.

"The holidays are coming up," Katie said,

her tone helpful. "Maybe you'll want to go visit. At least, call."

Phoebe gave a sad shake of her head. "I don't think so." She almost called her munchkin.

A shout rang out and Phoebe and Katie looked up. Mitch was waving them over.

"Let's see the calves," Katie said with new excitement and took off at a run.

Phoebe followed along, a well of anticipation bubbling up inside of her. She was looking forward to seeing the start of another new life, just like the wobbly one she had witnessed this morning with Mitch. But she stopped short, a gasp caught in her throat, as she surveyed the scene before her.

One cow was down, the other was in the throes of heavy labor, the tail and a leg of the newborn dangling from its mother, a breach birth. Carlo was trying to calm the distressed cow as she experienced another powerful contraction. The loud moan was chilling.

"Mitch, we need you," Carlo said urgently.

Mitch, kneeling by the downed cow and cradling something, looked up and saw them.

"Katie, call the vet," he barked sharply. "We need more light. Phoebe, go turn on the big lights."

Phoebe ran to the end of the corral where

the switch was as fast as she could. When she returned, Katie had hung Mitch's jacket on a post, while she talked frantically into his cell phone.

"Phoebe, come here!" Mitch ordered.

"Mitch!" Carlo shouted. "Help!"

Shedding her jacket, putting it on top of his, Phoebe climbed into the corral and walked quickly to Mitch.

"Hold this. I need to help Carlo or we're going to lose another one."

Phoebe obediently knelt next to him, thinking that she was going to hold a newborn calf, when he carefully placed a wet sticky, bloody mass in her arms. She saw the newly born calf a few feet away, lying unnaturally still. "Watch her hooves," Mitch warned. "She may kick."

She realized with growing horror that what she held was the dying cow's uterus. She fought the impulse to throw it away and held firmly on to the weighted mass, the stench of blood and death almost choking her, as the cow moaned, too weak to do anything.

Phoebe tightened her resolve and just waited, holding the uterus, trying to stay optimistic. But her hopes began to sink as she watched Mitch and Carlo work to assist the birth of the breach calf. With a loud moan and thud, that cow went down as well. The dogs barked in the distance, continuing to keep the other cows away.

Mitch shook his head in frustration.

Katie joined them, her jacket off as well.

"The vet's on his way," she said out of breath.

"Katie. Come here," Mitch barked. "We need your arm."

Katie immediately went to his side.

Phoebe watched in amazement as Katie, without a blink, got on her stomach in the wet muck and stuck her arm up the bloody canal, her cheek resting on the cow's rump. Mitch had a tight hold on the back hooves that twitched perilously next to Katie's head.

"I think I can get the other leg out," Katie said, her arm completely disappearing. She shifted around and the cow moaned and thrashed. Mitch couldn't hold on and her hoof narrowly missed Katie. He recaptured the leg and put himself between it and Katie.

Terrified, Phoebe looked on, feeling the wet, sticky ooze seep through her shirt and turtleneck onto her skin.

With a triumphant yelp, Katie pulled and the entire rump emerged followed by the rest of the calf. The cow moaned again and tried to stand. Mitch and Carlo, working in unison, heaved together and got the cow upright.

"It's a girl!" Katie shouted.

Carlo walked the cow around, and Mitch gave Katie a quick hug of approval. "You did great, squirt," he said. "Will you clean it up?"

Katie nodded, having already started on her task. Mitch came over and knelt next to Phoebe.

"You okay?" he asked.

"I should be asking that of you," Phoebe replied, her voice shaking.

"I've had better births," he admitted.

"I'm really sorry."

"I don't want to lose this cow, too."

"What are its chances?"

Mitch placed his hand on its head, looked into its eyes. He shook his head. "I don't know. Can you hang on? I'm going to see if the vet's here. Carlo will wait with you."

"Okay," Phoebe said and watched Mitch walk away. Katie had installed the small calf in a clean pen and returned. She had rinsed her hands and forearms but she still picked up her coat gingerly.

"I'm a mess," she said. "Do you want me to take your coat in?"

Phoebe nodded and looked back at the cow.

She felt it dying, as its breathing became more shallow.

Finally, the headlights flashed past the front driveway and Mitch came back with the vet.

"You can go get cleaned up. This might take a while," he said shortly, kneeling next to her, taking the burden.

"I'll wait," Phoebe said as she backed up to give them room.

"You want to get that blood off. It'll stink to high heaven," Mitch said, ever practical.

"Okay," Phoebe said reluctantly.

Mitch's attention was already gone, he and the vet in deep urgent conversation.

"Good luck," she whispered before she made her way back to the main house.

Bess met her at the door with a robe and gestured at her blood stained shirt and jeans. "You'll want to take those off here. I'll see what I can do, but I don't think I'll be able to get the blood completely out of those clothes." she said briskly.

Phoebe shook her head wearily as she stripped, noticing her undergarments were also stained, and wearily pulled on the robe. "That's okay. I have more."

"Well," Bess conceded. "You'll be able to use them for farm work. That way you won't have to ruin your good jeans."

"If the cow dies, is it terrible for the farm?" Phoebe asked, her voice low.

Bess looked at her and said slowly, "It's not good, but that's part of dairy life. It evens out in the end. Some die, some are born. It'll hurt but we'll survive."

"It didn't look good."

Bess shrugged. "It never does."

In the bathroom, Phoebe carefully peeled away the bloody bandages that covered her blisters, an injury now minuscule in the light of what had happened. Then she stepped into the shower, let the water run over her and whispered her hopes for the cow, for Mitch, for his farm.

CHAPTER EIGHT

IT WAS JUST PAST MIDNIGHT when Mitch kicked
off his bloody boots and wearily climbed the
short steps to his trailer, only thinking of a hot
shower. Even after all their efforts, the cow
had died. He'd used the tractor to move the
massive animal out of the corral to the side
of the road.

Bess had promised to call the animal disposal people in the morning and had given
him an awkward pat on the back murmur-
ing, "This isn't so bad. These things happen."
Katie had just stared at him, her grief for the
cow and her calf apparent in her red-rimmed
eyes.

In many ways, at these times he felt like
Katie. Although each cow represented a
chunk of revenue, they also had personali-
ties. He liked some better than others. This
one tonight, he'd liked. He swung open the
tinny door to the trailer and Phoebe, clean,
her hair not quite dry from her shower, sat at
the table, her binder of bills spread out before

her. She gave him a worried look of greeting and asked, "How is she?"

"Dead," Mitch replied briefly.

"I'm sorry."

They stared at each other. Phoebe got up and went to the kitchen. "Would you like some tea?" she asked, poised to put the kettle on.

"Yes," Mitch said slowly, surprised after the evening he'd had, he *did* want tea.

"Why don't you take a shower?" Phoebe suggested. "I'll have the tea for you when you get out." She looked at him, then bit her lip. "Would you like me to leave?"

Mitch studied the woman who stood in his kitchen, not ten feet away, and who in the past two days had seemed to make his small trailer hers. Phoebe Douglas seemed perfectly at home, as if she was supposed to be waiting for him after a particularly rotten evening, willing to make him tea. Did he want her to leave?

"No," Mitch said. "I don't want you to leave."

She smiled gently. "Take your time. If you hand your clothes to me, I'll take them up to the house."

"Don't worry. I have a pile."

"Okay." She filled the kettle with water and put it on the small stove and then turned. "Oh yeah. Katie accidentally took your coat to the main house, so I put it on your bed."

"Thanks," Mitch said. He disappeared into the bathroom and noticed with a small smile that Phoebe had angled her back to him to give him some privacy.

He was tired, bloody, and he found immense comfort in her presence. He wasn't sure why she was here, but he was glad she was. Twenty minutes later he emerged, clean, in a fresh pair of jeans and a button-down flannel shirt, feeling the fatigue, but in much better spirits.

"You look exhausted," Phoebe said as she handed him a cup of tea. He took it and sat on the couch across from her, studying the lines that creased her forehead.

"Thank you." He tried to look reassuring as he took the tea, wanting to ease her worry. "That's dairy life for you."

"Maybe I should leave so you can get some sleep." She started to rise.

"No," Mitch said quickly, gesturing for her to sit down. "Please. Stay for a little while, if you don't mind."

She hesitated, then shook her head and sat back down. "I don't mind."

They were silent for a minute.

Finally, she asked in a low voice. "Is this

really bad for the farm? You had talked about being on the edge. Is this going to put you over?"

He regarded her carefully, feeling her genuine concern for his welfare. "It's not good," he admitted. "It would have been better if either she or the calf lived. But it's not going to affect the bottom line that much. Our margin isn't that close."

Phoebe breathed a sigh of relief. "That's good. I was worried."

"Don't be." He gave a tired laugh. "It's just stressful, that's all."

Phoebe laughed with him, nodding her head in vigorous agreement. "You're telling me." She shook her head. "I can't believe how quickly Katie acted, just like she and you were one. She did what had to be done as if it wasn't anything."

Mitch smiled proudly. "That's Katie for you. She knows the farm better than anyone. When I came back from college, she was probably only six or seven, but she taught me the entire farm schedule and introduced me to all the cows."

"She's a good kid."

"Yes. She is." He grinned at Phoebe. "Though she doesn't act like it sometimes." He paused and then deliberately changed the subject. "It's nice that you're going to work so she can go with her friends on Saturday."

"Are you mad?" Phoebe asked with a smile.

He shook his head. "No. Though I have to admit I don't like that plans are being made without me. Do you remember what to do?"

"We'll see," Phoebe said self-deprecatingly. "I'll have Katie give me a thorough review."

"And I'll be there," he added, not knowing why that seemed important to say.

Phoebe gave him a shy smile. "I was sort of counting on that." She looked away and then added, her tone turning brisk, "Anyway, a day with the girls will be good for Katie."

Mitch nodded and they lapsed into silence again. He sipped his tea and watched her, his pulse increasing slightly as she got up and came to sit next to him on the couch. She pulled her knees up to her chest and rested her chin on her knees. "Can I ask you a personal question?"

"Sure." Mitch grinned faintly. "But I don't guarantee I'll answer."

Phoebe smiled, then ventured, "How did your dad die?"

Taken by surprise, he avoided looking at her, but answered simply, "Just a plain ordinary heart attack."

"Do you have a picture of him?"

Mitch started. It was such an innocent question to be so hard to answer. After a long moment of deliberation, he finally said, "Yes."

"Can I see?"

Mitch just stared at her, several emotions welling up inside him. Regret, loss, but something deeper, more fundamental that caused his heart to pound rapidly, his breathing to alter. His eyes were riveted to her clear, now very green eyes, his earlier fatigue forgotten.

"I haven't looked at a family picture since he died," Mitch admitted slowly.

"If it's too much, I understand. You've been through a lot this evening," Phoebe said, her voice calm, soothing. "I just couldn't help thinking how much you must be like him, and then I wondered if you looked like him." She cleared her throat. "I also noticed there are no pictures in the house at all."

There was a reason for that, but he wasn't sure he wanted to tell Phoebe what it was. He concentrated on sipping the tea, still hot, feeling the warmth down the back of his throat as he swallowed.

"I don't have any pictures of myself from when I was growing up, either," Phoebe said suddenly, her voice wistful.

"Really?" Mitch was intrigued. It seemed as if Phoebe's parents would have photographed her from the beginning, starting with the silver spoon in her mouth.

Phoebe shrugged. "My mother wasn't the picture taking sort. I have a couple of school pictures, but we couldn't afford to get the copies most of the time."

"Couldn't afford the school pictures?" Mitch looked at her in disbelief. Here, she sat perfectly manicured and garbed despite the work clothes, despite the bandages on her hands.

She chuckled, her laugh low, and wagged her finger at him. "I told you I was a fraud. I was poor, not-enough-food-at-the-end-of-the-month poor."

And Mitch heard the hurt amid her laughter.

"They're not hard to find. If you want—" Mitch looked at her uncertainly.

"The pictures?"

Mitch nodded.

Phoebe said gently, "I'd love to see them."

Mitch put his cup down and went to his closet, wondering why he was digging through his past, why it seemed so important for Phoebe to see the pictures. Maybe he wanted Phoebe to see Bess smiling, wrapping hugs around him and Katie. Maybe he wanted to see that himself. He searched through the box, looking for the least charred of the bunch.

"What happened?" Phoebe asked as she took the album from him. Her hands skimmed around the burnt edges.

It still smelled of smoke, he noticed. "My mother tried to burn them after my dad died."

"Thank goodness she didn't succeed."

"Well." He paused, not knowing why he was admitting this to Phoebe. "She thinks she did. I just tossed bundles of newspapers in the fireplace to make her think she'd burned the albums. I saved most of them."

"She doesn't know you have these?" Phoebe's eyes were brightly observant.

"And I would prefer her to not know."

"I understand," she said, then she gave him a hard stare before adding, "If this is too, uh, personal—I don't need to see these."

Mitch met her gaze, feeling closer to Phoebe than he ever had to anyone else. He replied, his voice equally low, "No. I want you to."

Phoebe took a deep breath and opened the album. An adorable baby Katie peered up at her. A teenage Mitch, with much longer hair, parted in the middle, bangs falling into his eyes, held the infant awkwardly, an older man standing proudly behind the both of them.

"Is this your dad?" Phoebe asked.

Mitch nodded, his eyes fixed on the photo, aware of how much his chest had tightened against the wave of pain. He had forgotten his father's smile, how his huge hand would clamp down on his shoulder. There was Katie on her first birthday, her fist in the cake, Bess grinning ear to ear. As Mitch talked quietly, offering Phoebe the story behind each picture, he became conscious that she had shifted closer to him, so now her arm rested lightly on his, the album across both their laps.

He also realized her genuine interest in his family had eased the ache he'd come to associate with his father's death.

PHOEBE COULD SEE JUST from the pictures how much Peter Hawkins's death had devastated his family. She blinked her tears away. Then she smiled at Mitch and said the first thing that came into her mind, "You're very lucky."

Mitch raised an eyebrow. "Am I? I don't feel lucky."

"It's because you were so well loved," Phoebe observed. She remembered that same love within Will's household. His parents had thousands of framed pictures of their sons. "Your dad's death was probably hardest on you."

Mitch's voice was cautious. "Why would you say that?"

"Absence is most felt when you've had something wonderful. Your family was something wonderful. And then it was gone."

Phoebe closed the album and placed her hand on top of his. "When your dad died, you felt the loss as much as anyone, but somebody had to be sane while everyone else went insane. That's hard work, you know." She fixed her eyes on his, searching, surprised to see a vulnerable soul peer back at her.

Mitch gave a short laugh and looked away. "What do you mean?"

"I mean being sane," she observed with a hint of clairvoyance. "Trying to hold everything together—the farm, your sister, your mother, yourself—because there's no one else who can and no one to talk to about how hard it is, when all you want to do is fall apart with the rest of them."

Mitch was silent. He put his hand to his forehead and rubbed.

Then, with his voice deep in his throat, he asked, "Would you mind if I kissed you?"

Phoebe's heart stopped with his simple query. She stared as deeply as she could into his brown eyes, inexpressibly moved by the emotions behind them. As he moved toward her, she whispered, "I don't mind at all," the lump in her throat making her breathing shallow.

She waited an eternity, it seemed, for Mitch to lean over, one large hand supporting her neck, and very gently, almost experimentally, place his lips over hers. Phoebe wanted to cry from the tenderness of the kiss, and instinctively moved closer to him, wrapping her arms around his neck and pulling him to her. He pulled away slightly after a while and she gave him a very strong hug, burying her face in the crook of his collarbone, feeling the worn softness of his flannel shirt, smelling his clean, masculine scent.

"I am so sorry about your father and the cow," she whispered.

Mitch's arms went around her and tightened in response.

She pulled back and gazed into his eyes, which seemed to have somehow grown several shades darker.

Then she kissed him, placing several featherlight kisses on his eyes and forehead, her own urgency to soothe his tired soul something deeper and more profound than she'd ever thought possible.

After a moment, she pulled back and smiled at him. "I should go."

"You don't have to leave," Mitch said, both disappointed and relieved that she was going, and unsure how to explain the intensity of everything they'd shared this evening.

"Don't get up," she murmured and leaned over to give him a light kiss before standing up.

"No, I'll walk you to the house."

"It's just a couple of yards."

"That's okay." Mitch smiled at her. He grabbed his jacket and helped her with her jacket.

The chill of the air was a stark contrast to the cozy warmth of the trailer and they both shivered. Mitch put his arm around Phoebe, and they slowly walked to the main house. The lights in the milking area were bright, the hum of the machinery in full gear, the pups probably asleep in the barn, their father up with Carlo. Mitch shoved his hand in his pocket, feeling the big wad of credit cards Phoebe had given him after dinner. He had forgotten about them. Dinner seemed a thousand miles away.

They stopped at the back door, where Bess had left the light on, and lingered, both reluctant to part.

"Thank you," Mitch said. "I appreciate

what you did tonight. You didn't have to get involved."

"Of course I did," Phoebe said, her voice low. "Anything that helps you helps me."

"We should probably talk about…this," Mitch whispered, changing subjects. "About what's happening here."

She nodded. "I know." Then, she lifted up on tiptoe and gave him a quick peck on the cheek. "But let's not talk about it too much," she said with a wink, before she slipped into the house.

Mitch took a deep breath and turned around. A second late night in about as many days. He only had two hours or so to sleep before the cows needed to be fed, but he didn't feel tired at all. As he walked, he pulled out the credit cards and studied the large wad, running his finger over the imprint of Phoebe's name, honored that she had entrusted him with the task of keeping her honest.

Once in the trailer, intent on crashing for a couple of hours, Mitch unloaded his pockets on top of his dresser, dropping the credit cards on the nightstand. But sleep eluded him, and he found himself getting up, shuffling through the credit cards, looking at her name. Then he counted the cards, surprised to find only forty-one. She'd told him forty-three. He counted again, thinking he had made a mistake. He tried to brush off the questions that rose in his mind but he couldn't. Had she saved two just for emergencies? Disappointment washed over him, though he wanted to give her the benefit of the doubt. Taking a flashlight, he ventured outside into the cold night again to look for the missing cards where he had hung up his coat. Maybe a couple had slipped out of the rubber band. There'd been a ton of commotion. He slowly waved the beam of light over the ground, hoping to see the metallic bank logos glint up at him. Nothing.

He stared up at the starry sky and then at Phoebe's darkened window. Like a blow to the solar plexus, Mitch was reminded how very much of a liability she was. He couldn't afford to indulge in something like love. He had his mother and Katie to consider. He closed his eyes tightly, his heart squeezing. He couldn't—no, he *wouldn't* be responsible for ruining another life, especially Phoebe's.

AT BREAKFAST, BESS GAVE Phoebe a full, shy smile, and Phoebe smiled back, realizing that slowly, she was being enfolded into the Hawkins family. Bess's acceptance made last night even more special. The only puzzling thing was that, even after all they had shared the night before, Katie had reverted back to avoiding her. Phoebe shook off a sense of foreboding. After all, Katie was a teenager. Her moodiness was legendary. Phoebe's heartbeat accelerated when she heard Mitch and Carlo talking and laughing as they came in through the back door.

"Good morning, ladies," Mitch said with forced cheerfulness. Carlo nodded his greetings as they sat down.

Phoebe tried to meet Mitch's eyes but he glanced at her quickly and then shifted his eyes away. Her heart skipped a beat as she studied his face.

Bess bustled around and said briefly, her hand resting a millisecond on her son's shoulder as she gave him an awkward pat, "They'll get the cow this morning."

Mitch nodded, obviously surprised by the physical contact Bess offered to him. He grinned up at her and took a large helping of scrambled eggs. "Thanks." He turned and addressed his younger sister, "Katie."

Katie's head shot up guiltily. Her face bright red.

"What?"

Phoebe observed her carefully. Why did Katie act as if she'd just stolen the crown jewels?

"I just wanted to thank you for last night."

Katie averted her face, looking down at her breakfast. She pushed her eggs around. "It wasn't anything," she muttered.

"I think you were incredible," Phoebe added, giving her hand a friendly pat. "You just got in and delivered that calf. I—"

"It wasn't anything," Katie said loudly, snatching her hand away from Phoebe as if her touch burned. "I wish you'd quit talking about it. I'm not perfect, you know." She pushed her chair away from the table with a noisy clatter. "I've got to get to school early. Denise is coming to pick me up." She hurried down the hall.

"Puberty," Mitch muttered under his breath.

Phoebe chuckled and settled into the rest of the meal.

"Are you going to do some work in the trailer today?" Mitch inquired. Did his voice sound cool? Or was she just imagining it?

"Yes. I thought I'd finish up what I started yesterday," Phoebe replied in a perfectly natural voice, her heart pulsing in her throat. She added, "If that's okay with you."

Mitch nodded, still not really looking at her. "No problem. Carlo and I are going to finish up the inventory, so I won't be in the trailer."

"Thanks," Phoebe said, ducking her head, aware of Bess's speculative glance.

After a few moments, Phoebe ventured another look at Mitch and this time found him studying her intently, his brown eyes unreadable. Phoebe swallowed. What could have changed? A couple of hours ago, he was like… well, he wasn't like this. Her thoughts were interrupted by a sharp honk from Denise's horn as Katie, with her backpack and jacket in hand, flew out the front door.

AFTER BREAKFAST, Mitch waited for Phoebe in the trailer. He had a million things to do today, but he needed to talk to her first, to stop this budding relationship before it turned into a full-blown something he could no longer control. He could barely look at her at breakfast, her face shining so brightly at him. He heard her laughter and the jiggle of the trailer as she climbed up the steps and pushed open the door.

"Oh!" she said startled and then gave him a big smile.

"Phoebe, we need to talk," Mitch said without preamble, guilt swirling around his stomach.

"Okay," Phoebe replied agreeably. "Let's talk."

"You might not like this," Mitch warned, shifting his body away from her.

"What?" She asked carefully, her voice neutral. "Is this about last night?"

Mitch stared out the kitchen window. "Yes and no."

"Should I sit down?"

"Maybe you should."

"That's never good." She stared up at him, trying to study his face. He kept it averted so she wouldn't see his indecision. "I hope this isn't one of those, 'I like you a lot but I shouldn't have kissed you last night' conversations." She laughed nervously.

Mitch cleared his throat. "I don't regret what happened last night," he began, hearing an odd tone in his voice, "but this morning, I discovered something that made me reevaluate—" He hated the way he sounded. He hated the stricken look on her face, the wariness in her eyes. He hated having to lie to her. But this was for the best.

"DISCOVERED SOMETHING?" Phoebe asked, a cold shiver running down her neck. Reevaluate? Terrible, terrible words. "What did you find?"

Mitch was silent for a moment and then said abruptly, "These."

He gave her the wad of credit cards.

"What about those?" she asked, puzzled, her mind whirling, trying to find a reason for his sudden change of heart. Last night had been wonderful. Wonderful. What did he need to reevaluate?

"You said you gave them to me to keep you honest," he said, then looked directly at her. "Did you really mean what you said?"

"Yes, of course, I did. What's this about?" Phoebe asked, her anxiety level rising even more.

"It's about financial recovery, Phoebe," Mitch said. "Cold turkey isn't cold turkey if you hold back, especially with credit cards. If your balance isn't going down, it's going to go up."

"Hold back?" Phoebe shook her head not understanding at all. "I have no idea what you're talking about. None."

"I counted the cards, Phoebe. There's only forty-one." He gave her a half smile. "That's better than none, but it means that you're still keeping two for emergencies."

"Forty-one?" Phoebe echoed in disbelief, her heart racing, her stomach churning. "No. That can't be. I gave you all forty-three cards. I have no more cards."

Mitch shrugged. "Well, they're not all there."

A long silence followed while they stared at each other, then down at the cards she held in her hands. Phoebe took off the rubber band and rapidly counted the cards, frowned and then counted them again. She looked up helplessly. "I don't know what happened. I gave you forty-three."

"I counted twice," he said.

"And they never left your pocket?" she asked.

"No."

"Not even with all the commotion last night?"

He shook his head. "They were all wrapped in the bundle in my coat pocket when I walked you back to the house last night. I just can't imagine—"

"Maybe two fell out," Phoebe suggested, feeling a little desperate, searching his face for a sign that he believed her.

He stared out the window. "I thought of that," he admitted. "So I scoured the area this morning, but I didn't find anything."

"I *know* that—"

Mitch stood up. "Phoebe, I'm probably the last person who should be telling you what you need to do. But I do know that committing to honesty is a fundamental step for financial recovery." He added gently, "For relationships, too."

"What does that mean?" Phoebe looked at him, her heart sinking.

"It means this has made clear to me that what happened between us last night needs to be an isolated incident," he said, his voice tight with tension. "As wonderful as it was," he hesitated, then rushed forth, his voice shifting imperceptibly. "It was a mistake. For both of us."

"No!"

"I take full responsibility," Mitch said stodgedly.

"I don't want you to take full responsibility," Phoebe said, with a vehement shake of her head, trying to ignore the fact that the walls were closing in on her. "I want to know why last night was a mistake. Did you just wake up, count the cards and say she's a liar—it was a mistake to kiss her?" Phoebe winced at the baldness of her words.

Mitch was silent, an emotional wall going up around him as she watched.

"No," he denied finally, but Phoebe felt little relief, her new sense of security rapidly crumbling.

He continued, "It reminded me how both

of us are in questionable financial circumstances right now. Even if I wanted to, I can't start anything with you, Phoebe. This dairy's barely hanging on. I've got Katie and my mother to support."

Phoebe thought about what he was saying. Then, she swallowed hard and asked, "Is that all?"

Another silence. "No."

"What else?" She didn't want him to say what she knew he was going to say.

Mitch tried to be tactful. "I—you, er, your financial situation, would really stress our business." He paused. "We can't afford to—"

A financial liability. Phoebe heard Will's voice. She stepped back feeling Mitch's intention as fully as a slap. She stared at Mitch who finally looked at her. Her voice shook as she said in the most polite voice that she could muster, "I see. Well, then, I understand." And the sad part of it was that she did understand. Mitch didn't need any more burdens. He had enough. She tried to hold back her tears.

Mitch patted her awkwardly and made a move toward the door.

"Mitch," she called.

He stopped at the door. "Yes?"

"I just wanted you to know that I did give you forty-three cards."

He looked away, and Phoebe's heart burned when she could tell that he didn't really believe her.

"Feel free to stay as long as you like," he said gruffly. "I know that you have a lot of work to do."

Unsettled, Phoebe watched him leave, her chest aching. She stared at the bundle in disbelief. How could there only be forty-one cards? She had counted forty-three herself yesterday. She brushed away the tears that spilled over. She hated those cards, the debt that openly displayed her fiscal irresponsibility. A financial liability. Mitch hadn't said as much, but she knew he was under some heavy financial pressure himself. Even though it hurt like hell, she didn't blame him for backing out, better now than before they had invested more time in the relationship, before they were actually in love with each other.

She sat at his table and unbundled the cards again, laying them all out in rows. Then she found the list he had made and carefully matched each card to the master list to find the two missing. She counted the cards again. It didn't make sense. Surely, there was an answer. She'd go back through her purse and wallet. Maybe she hadn't...

But trying to make sense of this didn't help.

She stared out the window and watched Mitch work side by side with Carlo. It was too late. She bit her lip in an effort not to cry. There was no way she could *not* love him.

PHOEBE WORKED nonstop the whole morning, making sure to be finished by the time Mitch was ready to clean up for lunch. Rather than humiliate herself further, she wanted to be gone before he returned to the trailer. In her room, she tore apart everything searching for the cards. She looked in her car. She looked behind the bed, in the closet. She had no explanation, and all she could remember was the disappointment in his eyes.

For two days, Phoebe managed to avoid any close contact with him, working in his trailer only when she knew he was busy outside. When she saw him returning, she would quickly straighten up, shut down the computer and be gone before he reached the steps. She could give him a quick greeting in passing; she just didn't like how she felt around him, her heart aching, while she pretended everything was fine.

She would have liked to have avoided talking to him altogether, but the numbers that she faced were dismally clear. If she were ever going to get herself out of her financial mess, she needed Mitch. Finally, on the third evening after he'd severed their relationship, she rapped on the trailer door. When he opened it, glasses perched on his head, she said abruptly, "May I talk with you?"

MITCH SURVEYED PHOEBE cautiously and indicated that she should come in. He noticed how she avoided him, being ever polite, her earlier ease with him all but evaporated. Mitch ignored the distinct twinge of regret and the renewed sense of loneliness. He'd done what was best.

"Yes?" he said, his voice more formal than he'd intended it.

"I need that check back. The one I gave you Monday," she said badly.

Monday? Had that been just five days ago? She'd been a virtual stranger then.

"The rent check?" he asked.

"Have you cashed it yet?"

Mitch shook his head and with one hand flipped through a file and retrieved it. He smoothed out the crease from where he'd folded it. "Here. May I ask why you want it back?"

"I'm completely broke," Phoebe explained, taking the proffered check. "I haven't even started to look for another job, and I need the money to send at least good-faith payments.''

"So what are you going to do about rent?" Mitch asked, with an arc of one eyebrow.

Phoebe was quiet for a full minute.

"I thought we could exchange my rent for labor," she said finally, her voice flat.

"No," he said immediately.

"You need someone anyway," she argued persuasively, her face reddening with embarrassment. "It's not like the amount of rent I pay can really impact that heavily on your—"

"No," Mitch repeated.

"Okay. Then I'll have to move," Phoebe said desperately, near tears. "Consider this my two-week notice." She turned to leave.

Mitch leaned over and caught her sleeve. "Phoebe, let's not overreact."

"Mitch, this isn't overreacting." She whirled suddenly, her eyes glistening with tears. "This has nothing to do with us. This is reality and it's not easy for me. I have very few choices right now. If I use this check and divide it up among my creditors, do you know how much they'll get? About eighty-five dollars each. Eighty-five dollars. If I give them all just a proportional amount of what I owe in total, some of them get about twenty-two cents. Do you understand me? Twenty-two measly cents. So I don't think I'm overreacting."

Phoebe took a deep breath and said, her voice rational once more, "I can learn to do anything you want me to, and you can set the hours. If you want me to feed the calves, I'll feed the calves. If you want me to input inventory, I'll input inventory. If you want me to work all day, I'll work all day."

Mitch regarded her carefully.

He thought for a while and then said against his better judgment, "Okay. If you feed the calves five days a week and then give me a few floating hours, we could call it even."

"Thank you," she said stiffly. "I'll start on Monday morning. I'll need to go to San Jose on Tuesday. Would that be a problem?"

"I don't see why it would. I'll talk to Katie. We can make Tuesday one of your regular days off, if you like," he offered.

"Thank you." She was very polite. "That will work out fine because my court date is on a Tuesday as well." She nodded, about to leave, but paused at the door. "Thank you for the use of the office. I left the empty binder on your desk. I really appreciate your help."

Without another word, she fled the trailer.

CHAPTER NINE

THE NEXT TEN DAYS PASSED quickly and before Phoebe knew it, she was dressing carefully in a plain suit, her financial recovery plan and the documentation carefully stored in her lambskin briefcase. She had made small payments on every one of the cards, but not enough time had passed to know whether or not the embarrassingly small checks had been accepted. Diane called with the good news that there was an offer on her condo, and for Phoebe, given the circumstances at the dairy, a sale couldn't happen soon enough. Between that and sending out two dozen résumés, some to hospitals more than four hours away, she resigned herself to the idea her life on the Hawkinses' farm was only temporary. Katie still kept her distance, which Phoebe could not understand. After all, even though she and Mitch had had the fight, Phoebe had still worked that Saturday so Katie could go shopping in Gilroy with her friends. But Saturday night when Phoebe tried to ask how her day went, Katie just shut herself in her room.

For Phoebe, it was normal to not understand the mood of one of the Hawkinses. She had adapted more easily than she'd anticipated to the farm routine, quickly learning the quirks of the job, no longer bothered by the pups, who had gotten into the routine of following her from task to task. She had never done such physical labor before, but her blisters had healed and thanks to Bess's gloves, no new ones ever appeared. She also began to notice more muscle definition in her arms and shoulders, which she wryly admitted, she'd never achieved even with the hefty health club fees.

Mitch, fortunately, had been pleasantly detached, not above giving her a pointer or two, sharing information that would help her. He was preoccupied because his farm review coincided with her court date. Yesterday, she'd made sure to thoroughly clean the calves' pens and put down new straw, so that when the appraiser looked around Mitch would have a good showing.

She, too, was as ready for her court appearance as she could be. She arrived an hour early, but if she expected a private meeting with the lawyer and the judge, she was sorely mistaken. The docket was full and the courtroom, inside and out in the hall was chaotic and noisy as sets of people negotiated settlements. As Phoebe waited nervously for her turn, she played the mental game of trying to figure out who were the lawyers and who were the unfortunate souls like herself, ready to be humiliated. Prepared to wait for a while, she was dismayed by how rapidly each case was disposed of. It seemed that it took only a few minutes between having one's name called and leaving, looking shaken or relieved. Then she heard her name.

Her nerves pounded as she faced the judge, who studied the documents Phoebe had handed her. Phoebe tried to block out the background noise of papers shuffling, the courtroom door opening and closing, people whispering about their own predicament, but was unsuccessful and looked up distracted when she realized the judge was addressing her.

"So you can't afford to make even the minimum payment for this creditor?" she inquired, staring down at Phoebe over her glasses.

"No, your Honor," Phoebe said respectfully. "As you can tell, I have many obligations and this is a relatively small one."

"I notice you've also sold your possessions?

Is this an accurate estimate of amount you've received?"

"Yes, it is." She crossed her fingers behind her back since she still had the Tiffany lamp.

"You say here that you've already received this amount for your jewelry. Is this accurate, as well?"

"Yes, your Honor." She *had* sold Will's silver hair clip.

"Then, it seems you should have enough to pay the plaintiff."

"But I don't have a job right now," Phoebe explained. "The money I've gotten so far has been needed for my basic living expenses. Here's a list of the people I've sent my résumé to. As soon as I get a new job, I'll be able to pay more."

"Do you still possess credit cards?"

"No, your Honor," Phoebe said truthfully. "When I lost my job two weeks ago, I stopped using them. I know that doesn't seem like a long time, but I'm trying. I've cut up the cards."

Phoebe pulled out a gallon sized zip top freezer bag from her briefcase and held it up.

"They're all here, if you'd like to count," she offered and was relieved to see the judge smile.

"Your Honor." The attorney for the plaintiff rose. "While Ms. Douglas has presented herself very well, I have evidence that she has been less than forthright with the court."

"What is it?" The judge turned her attention to the attorney.

"My investigator looked into her card activity and discovered three purchases that were made in Gilroy ten days ago amounting to more than three hundred dollars."

"That's impossible," Phoebe protested as the lawyer handed both Phoebe and the judge a document.

The lawyer continued, "I find it hard to believe that she's sincere in her request to pay us back over time. While she has the money available, I would like a judgment in full or—"

"Thank you, counselor. I know exactly what you want." The judge addressed Phoebe. "How do you explain this?"

The judge waited while Phoebe studied the content of the document.

"How do you explain this?" the judge repeated.

Phoebe looked up helplessly. "I can't."

"Did you make these purchases?"

Phoebe reddened and then said firmly, "No, I did not."

"You realize that you are under oath?"

"Yes," Phoebe said, her eyes returning to the form, as she tried to remember what she'd been doing on the date of the purchase. Then, she remembered. It'd been a Saturday. She'd worked for Katie that day. Her second day of feeding calves. The day after she'd asked to exchange rent for labor. "Your Honor?"

"Yes, Ms. Douglas."

"I was working that day."

"I thought she said she didn't have a job—" the attorney protested loudly.

"Please explain, Ms. Douglas."

"I'm renting a room from a dairy farmer, who has agreed to exchange my room and board for some chores around the farm until I'm employed again. During that time, I was feeding calves." Phoebe looked up earnestly at the judge and continued, "Your Honor, I have nothing right now but huge bills. I understand why you might think I would lie. But as you can see, I'm still trying to sell my condominium. When it sells, I'll be able to pay back all the obligations you see before you in full. I just need time to get back on my feet. I did not buy anything in Gilroy."

"Do you have a phone number for this dairy farmer?"

"Yes." Phoebe wrote Mitch's number on the slip of paper.

"Just a minute." The judge got up and retired to chambers.

While the judge was gone, the attorney approached her.

"Give us half and we'll dissolve the debt."

"Half?" Phoebe looked at him in surprise.

"Half is better than eighteen cents a month if she rules in your favor."

"I'll take it," Phoebe agreed quickly.

"Send us a cashier's check by the end of the working day tomorrow. If we don't receive it, we'll see you back in court."

The judge returned shortly. "Ms. Douglas, Mr. Hawkins has confirmed your story."

"Your Honor—" the attorney stood up respectfully "—we've just settled the matter."

"Thank you for showing good sense," the judge said with obvious satisfaction. Then she said to Phoebe, "I appreciate your organization here, but I would like to caution you that you have demonstrated that you cannot handle credit reliably, and any further use of the vehicle will put you in a much worse situation than this one."

"I know, your Honor. Thank you," Phoebe said, her face burning.

"Next!" The judge banged the gavel and Phoebe gathered her things to make way for the next person on the docket.

The attorney came up to her. "By the end of business tomorrow."

"You'll have it," Phoebe assured him.

Once he was out of sight down the hall, she slumped against the cool marble wall of the corridor. It was over. She had faced one of the worst demons created by her debt. And it was over. With a settlement, no less. She took a deep breath of relief. Mitch had been right. She could get through this. Thoughts of a three-hundred-dollar shopping spree in Gilroy filtered into her head. Phoebe shook them away. She would first get a cashier's check made out to the collection agency followed by a call to Diane, and then on her way home, she'd think about Gilroy.

"Please, Diane," Phoebe begged. "Give me good news."

"I don't want you to get your hopes up," Diane said cautiously, her voice all smiles. "But we have a firm offer and we're going into escrow. Maybe you'll get a nice Christmas present."

Phoebe laughed out loud. December. She would be free in December. She could last until December. She picked up her mail from the post-office box. Just three letters from collection agencies. She immediately opened those first, relieved to find that two companies had accepted her offers and another one hadn't and would be starting legal action. Well, she could deal with legal action. She smiled feeling freer than she had all year.

"Gilroy." Phoebe tussled with her doubts down Highway 101, through two traffic delays, the turnoff at Leavesley, past the Gilroy Outlet Center. Phoebe looked at the complex willing it to give her the answer. Then, bang. *Katie.* Three hundred dollars worth of new clothes. Every instinct told her she should take her suspicion to Mitch, but what would she tell him? And would he believe her? And what would happen to Katie if he did believe her?

Poor Katie. Poor Mitch. When could Katie have gotten the credit cards? Of course, the night the cow died. Phoebe slapped the steering wheel, feeling a little more than angry. Katie had taken the coats into the house. That girl— Phoebe took a calming breath, trying to put herself in Katie's shoes. It was surprisingly easy. The young woman obviously thought— Phoebe shook her head. How tempting the stack of cards must have been. After all, Denise had her own credit card. She glanced at the car clock. If she hurried, she could get to Katie's high school just before it let out.

Nervously, Phoebe waited at the entrance, the feelings of high school wafting over her. All high schools smelled the same. She studied the teenagers, varying in height, weight. Some of the girls looked like women, others still looked like girls. Phoebe immediately recognized the popular group with the nice clothes, clustering around new cars and smirking at those who took the bus or walked. She felt a twinge of envy, remembering all those times she'd shrunk out of their way, conscious that they were snickering because she wore the same clothes every day.

Phoebe blinked away those memories, almost missing Katie who took a wide berth around this group. Still, one young man made a rude comment and Katie and her friends clustered together more tightly, hurrying toward a much older car. Phoebe blinked. The serviceable twill jacket Katie had worn this morning had been replaced by a snazzy brown leather jacket with fringes on the sleeves. Phoebe looked down at Katie's feet—brand new cowboy boots. Ahh. That would total about $300.

"Katie," Phoebe called nonchalantly, her

posture casual, as she quickly walked to intercept them at the car.

"Phoebe!" Katie looked stricken and exchanged glances with another friend.

"Nice jacket," Phoebe commented. She looked up at the sky. "I hope you've weatherproofed it. It looks as if it's going to start raining any day now." She looked at Katie's friend and saw the car keys. Phoebe gave her the most winning smile she had.

"You must be Denise," she said with adult authority. She held out her hand and Denise shook it weakly. "I remember when I was finally able to drive."

"What do you want? Is anything wrong at home?" Katie asked, a tinge of desperation in her voice, sounding as if she almost wished something was wrong at home.

"Something is definitely wrong, but it's not at home," Phoebe said. She put her arm around Katie's shoulders and started to guide her away from her friends. "Let me take you home."

"I can't go home," Katie muttered, balking. "I left some stuff at Denise's that I need to go pick up."

"Is that how you've done it?" Phoebe asked curiously. "Denise keeps your new things so your mother doesn't know what you've bought?"

"Those are mine," Denise said quickly. "I've just let Katie borrow them. Her mother wouldn't approve of her wearing these clothes."

"Really?" Phoebe raised an eyebrow, then studied Denise's feet. "You look like you wear about a size six shoe?"

Denise shifted uncomfortably.

"So you always buy your boots three sizes too big?" Phoebe asked innocently. "Also this jacket would probably swim on you." She nodded, looking approvingly at Katie. "Seems as if it fits Katie perfectly."

"I need to go home. It's my day to feed the calves," Katie said.

"Yes, it is," Phoebe agreed. "Why don't I drive you?"

"What about my clothes?"

"You can pick them up tomorrow. Let's go show your mother and Mitch your new things."

Katie paled and then whispered, "You know I can't go home like this. My mother would kill me. Mitch would kill me."

"Well, you might have thought about that before you took those cards."

"I'll pay you back. Mitch gives me some

money from the bull calves. I just didn't think you'd notice—" Her voice cracked. "You have so many cards. I just wanted—"

Denise and the other girls backed away, waiting nervously, definitely wanting to be somewhere else, but hanging in as only true friends would.

Phoebe lowered her voice, her tone sharp and unforgiving. "That's stealing. It doesn't matter if someone has more than you have. It's still stealing."

Katie burst into tears.

And Phoebe gasped, appalled at how much she sounded like Audrey, her heart squeezing at the frightened look on Katie's face. Gosh, she had been just Katie's age when she'd left home. Had she looked that young and vulnerable? She took a deep breath, disturbed by the feelings that were beginning to overwhelm her, shaking her head to bring herself back to the present. This wasn't Michigan and she wasn't Audrey.

The right thing to do was just go straight to Mitch. Let him take care of it. That was the right thing, the adult thing. She glanced at Katie again, who stared at her like a small animal about to be slaughtered. She could have been looking in a mirror and the insecure bravado of a fifteen-year-old girl hitchhiking across the country stared back at her. Back then, she had wanted more than anything in the world for adults to be allies—not enemies.

Finally, she blinked and gave a rueful laugh, admitting slowly, "You know what, Katie? You're absolutely right, if I hadn't been embarrassed in court today, I would have never noticed the missing cards."

Though Mitch had, her heart complained. Phoebe shook those thoughts aside and asked Katie, "Do you know the reason why I went to court?"

Katie shook her head.

"Because I can't pay my bills," Phoebe said flatly. "I bought all of this stuff that I can't pay for, so my creditors are taking me to court. I had just told the judge that I hadn't used the cards for weeks, but lo and behold the attorney against me had done his research and said I had purchased three hundred dollars worth of goods ten days ago in Gilroy. The judge had to call Mitch to confirm my alibi, just to check to see if I was lying. It was humiliating."

Katie's tears spilled over again. "I didn't know."

Phoebe nodded. "That's exactly right. You didn't know. You couldn't know. So all this time when you were thinking that I had all sorts of stuff that you don't have, that I'm rich and you're not, it wasn't true. And here you are, starting out doing the exact same thing I did. Trying to make yourself better by using money that's not yours."

"I can take the jacket back," she whispered. "I can't the boots, but I can the jacket. Just don't tell my mom or Mitch."

"Okay." Phoebe regarded the young girl, clearly dissolving in front of her. She thought for a minute. "We'll take back the jacket, but you'll keep the boots and pay me back from your allowance. I want the cards back."

Katie nodded, eager to cut a deal. "You'll get them."

"Good," Phoebe said.

"What about my mom and Mitch?"

Phoebe frowned, looking around her, seeing the schoolyard had cleared completely. What about them? He'd probably be furious with Phoebe if he found out. But he already thought the worst of her, covering for Katie would only be one more infraction. Finally, she said seriously, "I guess I'll leave it up to you to tell them or not."

Phoebe gave a friendly smile to Denise and said, "I'll follow you to your house so Katie can pick up her things. Katie, do you have the original bags these came in?"

She nodded.

"Good. We'll pick them up and I'll bring them into the house," Phoebe said. "You'll get the boots for Christmas. Your mother or Mitch will never have to know. But Katie—" Phoebe gave her a hard look "—do we have an understanding?"

Katie, much subdued, said simply, "Yes."

MITCH LOOKED UP WHEN BLUE barked to announce Phoebe's arrival. As usual, her entourage of pups eagerly crowded around her car. Mitch pushed back the small tingle of pleasure to see her, then grimaced. Obviously, his hypocrisy knew no boundaries. He was the one who'd halted their relationship, yet when the bank had given him their stamp of approval, Phoebe was the first one he'd wanted to tell. He walked toward her, but stopped frozen when he saw her pull out the shopping bags from behind her seat.

He couldn't resist asking, unable to temper the sarcasm in his voice. "Bad day in court?"

Phoebe looked up startled. "What?"

"Bad day?" He gestured toward the shopping bag she held in her hand.

"Uh, no." Phoebe stammered, obviously

taken off guard. She gave him a quick glance and said with a forced laugh, "Actually, I was able to settle for half of what I owed the company."

"And so you thought you'd celebrate?" He couldn't help it. The disappointment washed through him, even though it confirmed what he suspected. Phoebe was a compulsive shopper.

"Not exactly."

"Then what exactly?" Mitch inquired.

"An early Christmas present," Phoebe said flippantly. She saw he wasn't smiling and started to say something, but then stopped, her mouth set. "How did your review go?" she asked instead.

Suddenly the good news he'd wanted to share with her evaporated, his chest hurting.

"Fine," Mitch said shortly, his eyes studying her purchases. "We've been approved for another year."

"That's wonderful," Phoebe said with genuine happiness. She glanced up into the sky, which had begun to darken with thunderclouds. "Just in time. It looks as if the rain has finally reached us."

"Yes," Mitch said, but didn't add anything more. They stood and stared at each other.

"I guess I should go in," Phoebe said uncertainly.

"Okay." Mitch started to turn away, but couldn't control the impulse to say, "I wasn't kidding when I said that committing to honesty is the first step."

"I know you weren't," Phoebe replied. She looked uncomfortably at the packages she held, then muttered, "This is different."

"No, it's not."

"I'm doing a favor for Katie."

Mitch picked up the bottom of the plastic bag that was draped over the jacket and peeked in. He gave a low whistle. "Leather. That's quite a favor."

"Oh, I'm going to take this back—"

"Good," he said, his voice light but the gleam in his eyes sober, serious. "What else did you get? Shoes."

"Boots."

"Take those back, too. Get her a card."

"I can't," she said helplessly.

"Or you don't want to." He gave Phoebe a piercing stare, which she met with a disconcerting honesty. He didn't want her to look at him that way, vulnerable, pleading, especially when she was simply digging herself further into the hole. Mitch asked sharply, "Did you pay cash for it?"

Phoebe recoiled as if shot, but kept her lips tightly shut, her gaze breaking away from his.

"I thought not." He paused, trying not to let his disappointment in her bother him too much. Instead, he said, "I hope you realize you're not going to get Katie to like you any better by buying her off."

Phoebe flushed. "I'm not trying to buy her off."

Mitch nodded abstractly, his mind deliberately shifting toward next year's grain crop to keep himself from shaking Phoebe to force her to understand that there were better ways to gain Katie's acceptance. Finally, he said, "Well, I hope you get your money's worth and your condo sells soon."

He started to walk away.

"Mitch," Phoebe called.

He paused. "Yes?"

"Sometimes things aren't what they appear to be," she said quietly.

He nodded gravely. "I'm beginning to realize that."

PHOEBE WATCHED MITCH walk away in despair. *Commit to honesty.* The words haunted her. She wanted to run after him and tell him that she had committed to honesty. She hadn't held back from him before, but when she looked over her shoulder and saw Katie staring at her from the driveway where Denise had dropped her off, Phoebe knew she couldn't betray a teenage trust. This was between the two of them. It was none of Mitch's business.

Phoebe took in a deep breath and reassured herself that as soon as she found a job and sold her condo, she would be out of this mess, off this farm. She glanced back at Katie who gave her a grateful nod before hurrying into the house. Phoebe followed at a much slower pace, wondering if she had made the right decision.

Later, when she saw Mitch ruffle Katie's hair as they worked together to feed the calves, Phoebe reminded herself that she was only temporarily on this farm and family peace was worth the price of Mitch's thinking less of her. And she almost believed it.

As NOVEMBER PASSED, Phoebe fell into her tasks on the dairy. The routine was comforting, though she realized how spoiled she'd become with the dry weather, because when the first of the rains hit Los Banos with a vengeance, the working conditions turned awful. The rusty hinge on the gate that was merely annoying during dry weather, became burdensome in wet. But Mitch had bigger worries than a stuck hinge.

Stuck cows were the worst, but Phoebe had learned quickly how to harness them and tie sturdy knots with numb fingers frozen from cold and wet, to lead them out, although she, herself, could barely get her footing. Mitch was never really very far away, often there to assist her. She clung to his strong grasp as he pulled her up and out of the mud several times. Once, he even needed to pull her and a cow out with a tractor. She quickly became used to living thigh-high in mud. On her Tuesdays, she shifted her mind back to her alternative world where she continued her job search, driving to various parts of central California to interview with several hospitals. But every time she was told that decisions wouldn't be made until after the New Year. Her Tuesdays kept her sane, reminding her that she had life beyond the farm. Wednesdays through Mondays showed her just how much she loved the farm and the farmer who didn't love her back.

She spent her mornings in Mitch's trailer, contacting and negotiating with creditors who were often less than cooperative. She did find several of her largest creditors to be very supportive of her efforts, even lowering her interest rates to help her cause. In between those calls, she tried the numbers Audrey had given her for Tucker, checked the internet and Facebook page, ever vigilant about getting information about Tucker. Audrey pressured her for money at every turn, but Phoebe had stayed firm, offering her condolences for their troubles, but explaining that she was tapped out. It wasn't a lie.

Mitch made a special effort to stay out of her way. She made a special effort to not let her work spill into his, gathering up all her materials before lunch, making sure his desk and work area were as tidy as he'd left them.

In the afternoon, she and Mitch worked well together as long as they avoided conversations of a personal nature. Mitch didn't talk about her finances and she didn't bring it up. True to her word, Katie surreptitiously gave back the credit cards and had since made a concerted effort to be pleasant. They slipped away one afternoon after the calves were fed, working as a team to return the jacket. She felt Mitch's disapproving stare on her, as if she were a bad influence on Katie and tried not to feel awful about it.

The family dinners of the fall were just about gone, because of the weather. The cows, as predicted, produced less milk and the incessant labor demands of the dairy took their toll on tempers and good will. Surprisingly, it was Bess who rallied the spirits of her children.

PHOEBE KNOCKED on Mitch's trailer.

"Yes," he inquired shortly, glasses perched on his head.

"Bess wanted me to bring you this." Phoebe held a basketful of laundry. She hadn't been in his trailer at the same time he was since she'd come to ask for her check back. She painfully noted that Mitch seemed intent on not breaking the streak as he bent over and took the basket, his body blocking the entrance.

"I think she thought you might be low on jeans and shirts," Phoebe added.

"I am. Thank you." He made a move to go back into his trailer. She saw the glow of the computer screen behind him.

"How are you?" Phoebe asked quickly, even though she knew she was interrupting. She longed for the conversations they'd had when she'd first arrived on the farm. She squinted, seeing if she could read the numbers on the screen, but realized they wouldn't mean that much to her anyway.

"Okay." He regarded her warily.

"The numbers coming out okay?"

"They could be worse."

"Or better," she added perceptively.

"Or better," he agreed. "The rain's been hard on the cows. Milk production has dropped a little lower, a little quicker than I thought. I figured we'd average five gallons at least through January."

"The weather's probably not going to let up," she commented, allowing a tiny bit of worry to infiltrate her voice. "Are we in danger of flooding? I've been hearing a lot about ground saturation."

Mitch smiled involuntarily and Phoebe felt a rush of their old camaraderie return. He replied, his voice dry, "Ground saturation can be a problem."

"There are some canals pretty close by," Phoebe said, glancing around.

"The canals aren't going to be the problem," Mitch said seriously. "If you want to worry, worry about the creek bed, we're in the direct path. But there hasn't been a flood in twenty-five years."

Phoebe nodded. "Okay. I know you know best." She turned to go.

"Phoebe?"

"Yes?" She turned back, her heart pounding.

"Thanks for bringing the laundry out."

She smiled nervously, and waved it off. "No problem."

They stood silently for a moment and then as she started to leave, Mitch cleared his throat and asked casually, "How's the job hunt going?"

"Couple of nibbles, but nothing solid. I've got an interview next week in Santa Rosa."

Mitch nodded. "Santa Rosa. Nice country."

"It's a change," Phoebe agreed. "It's a much smaller hospital. Privately owned."

"Santa Rosa's about three hours?"

"Closer to four, I think," Phoebe said. She smiled gamely at him. "I'll find out on Tuesday, won't I?"

"You're going to do it in one day?"

She grimaced. "I have to. It's not as if I have the money to spend the night anywhere. It'll be okay. The interview's at eleven. If I leave by six, I should be there in plenty of time. I'll also have plenty of time to get home."

"Any news on your condo?"

Phoebe made another face. "I've accepted an offer, and we're in escrow. Diane said she hoped to have a true Christmas present for me."

"Are you doing okay?"

"Money wise, you mean?" Phoebe asked, glancing at him, hoping to find some sort of personal subtext, disappointed when she didn't find any.

"Yes."

"Yes," Phoebe said slowly and realized that for the first time she was actually telling the truth. "I can definitely say I am. I've got payment plans. I've negotiated with most of the creditors. There's one or two stubborn ones, but I'll win them over, I think. Why?"

"I'm sure you will," Mitch said. "No reason. I was just curious."

Phoebe nodded. "I'm doing pretty good."

"I'm glad." Mitch began to back up into the trailer. "Well, I guess I should get back to work."

"Okay." Phoebe waited.

"Okay. I'll see you tomorrow."

"That you will," Phoebe assured him. She looked anxiously at the sky. "I hope it clears up soon. I'm getting tired of this rain."

"You and me both." Mitch agreed with a heartfelt laugh.

"Good night, Mitch," she said softly.

"Good night." He disappeared inside and shut the door.

Phoebe tried not to feel bad about her exile. Not ready to go back to the house, she found herself in the barn, one of her favorite places. She sat in the dark, curled up on a bale, enjoying the feel of hay sticking into her back, the pups at her feet.

"Nice to have a break from the rain," Carlo said.

Phoebe smiled. She had gotten used to his sudden appearances. He sat next to her, and she shifted over to make room.

"Are we going to flood?" she asked.

"We might," he admitted.

"What happens?"

"Everybody pitches in. The dairymen in the area are very supportive. If there's time, they'll come with trucks and trailers and move the cows to higher ground."

Phoebe brightened. "Really?" She felt better already.

Carlo nodded. "Really."

She sobered. "Why is it that I always think of the Hawkinses as being so solitary?"

"They've kept to themselves since the papa passed on."

"It seems as if it would be easier to have the support of the community."

"It's there. They'll just have to ask." Carlo nodded. He patted her knee. "Don't worry. If trouble comes, there will be help for Mr. Mitch."

Phoebe smiled at him. "Thank you, Carlo."

He smiled back, then gently tapped her

shoulder with a blunt, stubby forefinger. "You and me. We're a team."

"A team?"

"I help with their dairy. You help with their family." He winked and walked away.

CHAPTER TEN

MITCH CLOSED THE DOOR to his trailer, bringing in the laundry. Just Phoebe's mention of the possibility of a flood had made concrete what he had been avoiding thinking about since the rains began. It had been a long time since he'd had more than a passing relationship with his father's friends. The community had rallied around them when his father died, several of his father's oldest friends, the Whitfields in particular, helping to keep the farm going. But one by one Bess had severed all ties, first quitting church, then refusing to attend social functions, finally, flying into a rage at any show of generosity from the neighboring families.

When the botulism hit, Bess was so engulfed with unbearable grief she staunchly refused any help from her husband's former friends, convinced that they were somehow responsible for the botulism, for her husband's death.

Now, Mitch felt the isolation his mother had

created. He wished that Bess— He started when another soft knock sounded on his door. His heart pounded unexpectedly. Was Phoebe back? He looked around, quickly clearing a place on the couch for her to sit. This time, he'd invite her in rather than making her stand outside in the drizzle. He'd make her a cup of tea, ask if she'd like to sit down and stay awhile. They could talk about the rain. Whether he wanted to admit it or not, he liked being around her.

Maybe that's why he pretended to supervise her when she fed the calves, even though she was far beyond needing help anymore. She accepted his direction easily, demonstrating how adept she had become with the vaccination schedule, reminding him when he needed to place another order with the vet, reporting any differences in the temperatures of the calves.

He liked to watch her when she thought she was alone because she chattered nonstop with each of her calves. He was envious of the attention they received, even though he himself had deliberately rejected the same attention. He opened the door with a ready smile.

"Katie," Mitch said covering his surprise, annoyed at the twinge of disappointment at the sight of his sister. "What are you doing here?"

"I've got an idea," Katie said slightly out of breath, ducking underneath his arm to come inside. She turned around with an excited gleam in her blue eyes, a fine mist of drizzle settling on her light hair.

"About?" Mitch couldn't help but give her an indulgent smile. It had been too long since his sister had looked this excited about something.

"About a Christmas present for Phoebe."

"I thought Mom was making her a quilt." Mitch sat down, surprised by her animation.

"Mitch." Katie heaved a very grown up sigh. "That's one thing, but I think we should get her something else."

"What?" His tone was practical and he was more than a bit suspicious.

"It's just a little one," Katie said, barreling onward, ignoring his question. Mitch smiled. She obviously wasn't going to let him dampen her enthusiasm. "And it doesn't really cost anything," she added pointedly.

"Okay, squirt. What is it?"

"Let's find her family and have them call her on Christmas. I saw an ad on T.V. for a company that finds anyone you want for forty dollars. They look it up on the internet or something. All you need is a state and a name. I've got both."

Mitch frowned, considering Katie's brainstorm, and then shook his head decisively. "No. That sounds way too personal."

"But I think she really wants to hear from them."

"She'd call them herself if she did."

"I think she's afraid to. But I bet she'd be really happy to get in touch. People are always looking for lost loves." Katie continued, her voice sweet, "I just need you to call the service. I'm too young and I need a credit card."

Mitch looked at his younger sister and said reasonably, "Katie, listen to me. I know you want to do something nice for Phoebe. But this is not it. If they don't talk, then it must be for a reason that we don't know."

"It's just a phone call," Katie said flippantly. "If they don't want to talk to her they won't call, right? So will you do it?"

"No." Mitch shook his head. "I won't do it and I won't let you do it, either. Don't try to fix her life."

Mitch grimaced inwardly. Goodness knows, he had tried that already. He looked out the window, realizing that despite her fragile appearance, Phoebe was quite capable of fixing her own life.

"Tell me why you want to do this for

Phoebe," Mitch said suddenly, his voice sharp and paternal.

Katie fell silent for a long time, some of her initial enthusiasm fading. Mitch nodded. That was a good sign. Finally, Katie said guiltily, "I—uh, she's cool. Much better than I thought she'd be. That's all. Kind of like a sister."

Mitch leaned toward Katie and said very slowly, so she would know he was serious, "Be a good girl and forget about calling."

Katie stared at him, mutiny in her eyes. Without a word and without a promise, she flew out of the trailer.

THE DAYS OF DECEMBER sped by. Reports giving thunderstorm and flash flood warnings inundated the radio waves. Bess kept the radio on twenty-four hours now. But Phoebe found for every pelting storm, there was a lull. When the sun emerged, the water was swallowed by the earth and the normally dry brown mountains turned a clear emerald-green. This was how her love for Mitch felt, ebbing and flowing, back and forth. She knew he wasn't nearly as immune to her as he pretended.

It was in this month that Phoebe learned the topography of the dairy farm, where the water puddled, what parts of the mud were akin to quicksand and which parts she could actually lead cows through with sure footing. Even though the water and mud levels grew to what Phoebe at first thought of as being abnormally high, she realized that water was temporary, eventually it would pass, just as the seasons eventually pass, and she supposed she would, too.

As December advanced, Diane had become even more optimistic about escrow closing. But now, ankle-deep in mud, even knee-deep in mud, Phoebe found herself drawn to the dairy's cycles from the daily routine of the truck picking up the milk to the longer one of grain delivery. She loved that this work made her pay attention to rhythms she'd never noticed before, from the week to the month to the season, as she shifted calves from one corral to the next to make room for the new ones being born daily, the by-product of Mitch's steady work to rebuild his herd. Despite the emotional distance he'd put between them, Phoebe could not control the flutter of her heart when he was around, the reassuring "feeling" that she could see him at any time.

Sometimes, if he finished his work early, he'd help her with the calves and at those times, Phoebe tried as hard as she could to show him her competence, asking all the questions she could think of, just to be able to hear the pleasant tone and rumble of his voice. Their talks, while never personal, satisfied Phoebe immensely, gave her a distinct sense of connection to the farm, to the farmer. She found she had developed an invisible radar that quickened her pulse whenever he was around. It didn't matter when escrow closed. Her heart was going to break when she had to leave.

CHRISTMAS MORNING, Mitch and Phoebe were up early, trying to beat the next storm that threatened to arrive by midmorning. They worked side by side laying down planks, fashioning a make shift ramp from the milking barn to the main road, the last of several paths Mitch had created to give the cows some sort of footing, so they could be loaded onto trucks in the most expedient way possible. The dogs had long retired to the barn, preferring the dry hay to the wet air outside. Carlo had left a week ago for a long overdue visit to his family in Portugal.

Mitch rested with Phoebe against the fence, both of them damp from the scattered showers that drizzled down on them. Wrapped head to toe in a yellow slicker, Phoebe didn't look as if she felt the December cold, except that her cheeks, exposed to the wind, were bright pink along with her lips. She inhaled deeply, obviously drinking in the smell of the dairy and the crisp, wet air, and Mitch knew exactly how she felt. He took a deep breath as well. Despite the rain, the past month had been, well, fun.

Phoebe brought wonder and delight to things he had long forgotten were wonderful or delightful. He loved the way she openly talked with her calves, giving them positive messages to grow healthy and strong, to give lots of milk, to enjoy their lives. He loved her sense of fun and the absurd, even in the most awkward or compromising positions. And he loved the fact that she listened, her large hazel eyes masking nothing, looking at him with admiration and respect, making him feel as if he were the most capable man in the universe.

"Didn't think you'd spend your Christmas day mucking through the mud to get this done, I bet?" Mitch smiled down at her.

Phoebe shrugged. "I don't mind. It's not like I had anything else to do." She looked anxiously toward the west. "Doesn't look as if it's going to clear."

Mitch nodded grimly. "Once this lull passes, there's another series of storms backed up across the Pacific. The weather service said to expect heavy rains through New Year's."

"It'll be all right, won't it?" she asked, worry on her face.

"Well, it will have to be, right? We don't have much choice," Mitch said and then gave her playful smile. "Don't look so worried. We'll be fine as long as we have breaks between the storms."

"I can't help it. I keep my ears open for the sound of rushing water from the west."

"Why west?"

"It's where I imagine a flash flood would come from."

"The water would probably come from the south, to flow toward the slough. That's something we're definitely in the direct path of."

"Creek bed," Phoebe muttered.

Mitch smiled. "Yes. The creek bed."

"I wish I knew."

Mitch regarded her for a minute. "Sometimes knowing isn't much better. Come on. Let's finish this off and we can go in."

"When is Carlo coming back from Portugal?" Phoebe asked as she staggered around to help him move a heavy bracing plank.

"Three days."

"I'd feel better if he were here."

"I would, too," Mitch said with feeling. The 3:00 a.m. milkings on top of everything else was wearing. "But he needs time to visit his family, too. I hope he's enjoying better weather."

They continued to work in companionable silence. Finally, Phoebe cleared her throat and Mitch felt a tiny twinge of dread.

"I got some news the other day," she began offhandedly.

Mitch stopped what he was doing and watched her, realizing yet again how beautiful she really was, even with just the oval of her face showing in her sea of yellow plastic.

"Good news, I hope?" He tried to calm his beating heart.

Phoebe shrugged, looking up at the sky. "I guess so."

"You sold the condo," Mitch guessed, keeping his voice deliberately light.

Phoebe shook her head. "Not yet. We've got two weeks left on escrow."

Mitch paused, his gaze following hers, then said, his voice even, "You got a job."

Phoebe nodded.

"In San Jose?"

"Santa Rosa."

"Is it a good job?"

She bit her lip. "It's an excellent job. I'd be making more than I made in San Jose. It's actually a promotion of sorts. Nice benefits package, no immediate plans to sell." She grinned wryly. "I asked."

"When do they want you to start?" Mitch asked casually, glancing up at her.

Phoebe searched his eyes for a minute and then glanced away. "They said they'd prefer sooner rather than later."

"But?"

"But I haven't accepted the position yet."

Mitch was silent. He shifted a plank with his foot and then squatted down to move it into place with his hands. "Why not?"

Phoebe was silent. Then she cleared her throat again. "I guess I wanted to talk to you about it."

Mitch took a deep breath. Those were words that he wanted to hear, but also didn't want to hear. He forced himself to smile and said briefly, "What's there to talk about? It sounds great."

"It does," she admitted.

"You won't have to feed calves anymore."

"I guess not."

"You can't commute," he said, straightening.

"No, of course not," she replied quickly, then flashed him a smile. "Though I've pondered the possibility."

MITCH GAVE PHOEBE A DISTANT look that made her heart sink and said, "Seems as if the answer's pretty straightforward."

She berated herself. It wasn't as if Mitch had done anything in the past few months to make her think he wanted her to stay—except help her cut through all her layers of pretense to reveal a person she could respect. That and share with her his most personal hopes and fears about his family and the dairy farm. That's all. She studied him as he stared at the horizon and then gave her an inquiring glance when she didn't say anything.

"Is it really?" Phoebe probed.

"Yes." He shifted his gaze away from her. Phoebe tried to read his face, the lines around his eyes, the roughness of his jaw, now stubbornly set. He squinted, closing himself to her even more. He had told her he didn't want her life to become his business, but she wanted that anyway.

After all, his life had become her business. Katie was her business, Bess was her business, and the cows, whom she had gotten to know personally, had become her business. Everything that touched and affected Mitch had somehow become her business, from worrying about the possibility of flood to whether he had clean clothes. She shook her head and wondered when it all had happened. He certainly hadn't encouraged it.

Phoebe replied vaguely, "I told them I'd give them an answer after the first."

"Why the delay?" Mitch's voice was very practical.

Phoebe shrugged. "I don't know. I have a couple of other options closer to Los Banos that I'm waiting for."

"Seems as if you'd want to get away as far as possible," Mitch observed.

"Really? Is that what you think?" She couldn't control the disappointment that leaked into her tone.

Mitch looked at her startled. "No. Not the way it sounded. I just thought you'd have had enough of farm life."

"I love it here," Phoebe said frankly.

"It's not an easy life," Mitch replied.

"Nothing worth having ever is," Phoebe reminded him, wondering why she was about to cry.

MITCH STARED AT PHOEBE who looked away, her lips pulled tight. He could read her like a book. But how was that possible? He'd spent his whole life with Bess and Katie, who still befuddled him with their emotional mood swings. How could he know so much about someone he hadn't even met four months ago? The answer came to him suddenly—Phoebe was uncomplicated and straightforward. With her, he didn't have to walk on emotional eggshells, wonder whether his jokes would go awry and hurt her feelings.

Never.

Phoebe didn't leave things unsaid. Instead, she asked directly and bluntly for answers, explanations. She kept him honest. Just like now.

He said gently to her back, "It seems worth having when you know you can leave. But it's different when it's your life."

Phoebe turned to face him, giving him one of those sharp looks that had become so familiar. "Are you saying I'd feel different if this were my life?"

Mitch shrugged, careful to articulate his thoughts. "Yes, I guess I am. I'm saying that it's one thing to play at being a dairy farmer and another to *be* a dairy farmer."

"So what I've been doing is playing?" Phoebe looked offended. "I thought I'd done some valuable work."

Mitch smiled. "You have and we certainly appreciate it."

"But…"

"But it's temporary work—and someone

else will do the work that you did when you're gone. It's like the dishes that get dirty all over again. There's no end, no completion. It just is."

"It's the life you chose."

"It's the life I was born into," Mitch corrected her. "You, however, have endless choices and you'll have even more when you sell your condo."

"What if I choose to make your life my life?" she asked finally.

Mitch looked away, silent.

"What if I choose to make your life my life?" she repeated. Her eyes, clear and cogent, tried to make contact with his.

With an effort that took all the emotional strength he had, he met her eyes, trying not to drown in the depths, now a vivid green-gray, almost an exact replication of the sky above them. He could actually see the clouds move across her irises. He inhaled sharply, steeled himself against the impulse to tell her that he would like nothing more than to have her life be his—he wasn't going to be the one to ruin her life. He had already done that to his mother and Katie. He finally replied, his voice hard, "That's one choice you don't have."

"Why not?"

"Because I won't let you."

"Why not?"

"I won't let this dairy farm do to you what it's done to my mother and Katie."

"Don't you think that should be my choice?"

He shook his head. "No. It's mine," he said flatly. "We don't need you, Phoebe. You may think we do, but we don't. We did fine before you came and we'll do fine after you're gone."

Phoebe gave a short laugh, as if her throat was so tight she couldn't even laugh fully.

"What?" Mitch asked, annoyed by her amusement.

"How ironic," she said thoughtfully. "I said the same thing to you once and you laughed. You found it funny that I thought what I had been doing worked fine. I guess I can make that same observation." She looked around. "Are we done?"

Mitch stopped and looked around, too. "Yes."

"Well, then. I think I'll go in now," she said and tried to open the gate, but was unsuccessful. Mitch shoved hard and the gate swung open.

"You should really fix that," Phoebe observed distantly as she slipped through and started to walk away. "Katie's probably anxious to open her presents and get Christmas started."

"Phoebe?" Mitch called.

"Yes?" She stopped but wouldn't turn around.

Mitch didn't know why he'd called her. He just didn't want her to walk away from him on such a tense note. He opened and closed his mouth and finally mumbled, "Merry Christmas."

She smiled sadly over her shoulder as she hurried back to the house. "You, too, Mitch. Merry Christmas."

EVEN THOUGH MITCH HAD just shattered her heart into several thousand pieces, Phoebe didn't want to let it ruin Christmas day. But as hard as she and Mitch tried to pretend to be normal, the tension between them was almost tangible. On top of that, Katie was downright despondent to receive her leather boots. Phoebe saw Mitch, ever observant, thoughtfully gauge Katie's reaction, then look at Phoebe. Phoebe ignored the clear question in his gaze and forced herself to be enthusiastic, telling Katie to try on the boots.

"That's too much," Bess protested, shaking her head. "Katie can't accept them."

"Too late," Phoebe said cheerfully. "They're bought and can't go back. Since they won't fit any of us, Katie may as well enjoy them."

"It's amazing how you got those boots to fit so perfectly," Mitch commented, his eyes still on Phoebe. "It almost looks as if Katie has tried them on before."

Katie gasped and slipped the boots off. "Thank you, Phoebe," she said hurriedly. "I like them very much." She looked around and pulled a large box from under the small tree. "Here, Phoebe. This is for you from all of us."

Phoebe looked at it, tears welling. "Thank you. I never expected— You didn't have to—"

"Open it," Mitch encouraged her, sitting forward.

Phoebe carefully unwrapped the gift, gasping at the intricately designed lap quilt. "My goodness. I've never had anything this special before," she said, her voice tight.

Bess colored and replied gruffly, "You said you liked those colors."

Phoebe ran her hands over the tiny stitches. "I love these colors. Thank you."

"It's a gift from everyone," Bess said in a voice filled with quiet pride. "Mitch special ordered the fabric. Katie did all the cutting and piecing together. I did the quilting."

Phoebe felt a lump in her throat. This was from the man who said her life was none of his business. She gave him a quick glance, but found him staring pensively into the open fireplace.

"Here, I got you guys something, too," Phoebe said as she quickly distributed two more gifts.

Bess shook her head. "This is too much," she repeated, deeply embarrassed. "What you got Katie was more than enough for all of us."

"Well, they're just little things," Phoebe said with a smile. Darting a look at Mitch, she said, "I paid cash for them."

Bess opened hers, carefully, making sure she didn't rip the paper.

"What is it?" Katie asked, peering over her mother's shoulder.

"It's an old book of quilt patterns," Bess said as she flipped through it. "Oh my, I haven't seen some of these designs since my mother—" She looked up at Phoebe, her eyes misting. "I don't know how to thank you."

"What did you get, Mitch?" Katie asked.

Mitch hefted his brightly wrapped gift. "It's heavy."

Phoebe hid her smile, making her face as bland as she could. It had taken a long time to find a gift for Mitch, one that was neither too sentimental nor too distant.

He opened the box and studied the contents. Then he lifted his eyes, and Phoebe bit her lip to keep down her laughter. Humor danced in his smile.

"What is it?" Katie asked impatiently. "What'd you get?"

"A cow pie."

"What?"

Mitch held up the object. Bess actually laughed.

Katie studied it with a wrinkled nose. "Eew. That's gross. What are you supposed to do with it?"

"It's a paperweight," Phoebe told her. "It just looked so real. I couldn't resist."

"You're not actually going to put that on your desk, are you?" Katie asked aghast.

"Well, at least it'd label the paperwork that I least like to do, won't it?" Mitch gave Phoebe a quick wink and said, "Thank you, Phoebe. I don't believe I've ever gotten anything quite like it."

Phoebe laughed, feeling the sparkle of a connection between them. She was an optimist. Hearts could not possibly stay shattered, if they shared such moments of fun. She sighed with deep contentment, relishing the familiar Christmas songs playing in the background, the wrapping paper strewn across the floor, the warmth of the roaring fire. This was a perfect family Christmas.

The rain began to fall with a reassuring patter against the window. Phoebe studied the quilt, doubting she would ever use it to warm her lap. She would find a place to hang it, display it as the art it was. She looked up and found Mitch staring at her, his brown eyes unreadable. Despite themselves, Phoebe felt the bond between them continue to grow as if unaware it would never have the chance to become fully mature.

THEY WERE HALFWAY THROUGH a lively Christmas dinner, when the phone rang. Bess looked up in surprise.

"Oh my. Who could that be?" she asked.

"Why don't you answer that, Phoebe? You're closest," Katie asked gleefully, shooting an I-told-you-so look at Mitch.

Phoebe glanced at Katie and then at Mitch, puzzled. With three people watching her, she swallowed her bite of turkey, went to the phone and picked it up. "Merry Christmas, Hawkinses' residence," she answered cheerfully.

"Phoebe, pumpkin? Is that you?"

Phoebe's smile faded, as her heart caught in her throat. Audrey was drunk. She quickly turned her back to the Hawkins, but could tangibly feel Katie's delight fade. The urge to flee almost overpowered Phoebe, her embarrassment making her face hot.

"Momma," Phoebe replied, her voice cordial. "How did you get this number?" This was a nightmare.

"A stranger called us and left it on the answering machine," Audrey snapped. "If I didn't know better, I'd think you didn't want to have anything to do with us."

"I've been busy," Phoebe said defensively. She took a furtive look over her shoulder and caught Mitch's concerned gaze. She averted her eyes, feeling tears begin to well. She didn't want them to hear this, but there was nowhere else to go. She crossed her arms tightly against her chest.

Audrey's voice switched from hateful to sugar sweet. "We've had so much trouble, Phoebe."

"I can't talk—"

"Stella's pregnant again," Audrey interrupted, her voice slurred and teary. "Todd's in solitary—"

Phoebe couldn't help asking. "Have you heard from Tucker?"

Audrey's voice turned sharp. "It seems as if that's all you care about. Finding Tucker. Where's Tucker?" She mimicked Phoebe.

"He's not your only brother. It's not like you've ever done anything for him or anyone—"

Phoebe felt her stomach curl, unable to extricate herself from this conversation. "You know that's not true, Momma."

"Phoebe, we need help. Things are bad around here," Audrey pleaded. "If you wire us some money, maybe I'll be able to get Tucker's—"

"No," Phoebe said shortly. "I've sent you enough—" She lowered her voice, knowing that her conversation was being attentively listened to. "There's no more money to send. Now, Merry Christmas, Momma."

"Wait a minute. You need me to find Tucker—"

"No, I don't," Phoebe whispered furiously.

"We just need two thousand—"

"No."

That was apparently the wrong thing to say, because her mother started shrieking vulgarities Phoebe knew the Hawkinses could hear. With a trembling hand, Phoebe carefully hung up the phone to stop the onslaught of abuse. Humiliation burned through her. She glanced at Katie, whose stricken look told Phoebe all she needed to know.

"Well," she said brightly, pressing her hands together. "What an unexpected surprise." She fought to hold back her tears, she wasn't going to cry in front of them. Instead, she gave a weak laugh and said seriously, "You might want to change your phone number tomorrow."

The phone rang again. Phoebe stared at it in terror. Bess, with a look of compassion, quickly stood up and answered it.

"Hello?" Bess greeted in her most clipped tone. "I'm sorry, you have the wrong number. There is no Phoebe here."

She hung up the phone. It rang a few seconds later. This time Bess picked up the receiver and without speaking into it, gently placed it on the counter, allowing Phoebe's mother to rant and rave. Bess gave Phoebe a sympathetic smile and tentatively patted her hand. "It'll be all right. You can't help it."

Mitch finally spoke. "Are you okay?" he asked softly.

"Yes. Fine," Phoebe said brightly, every screech from the phone causing her to flinch. She stared at her plate, trying to control the nausea that threatened to overwhelm her. "Excuse me a minute—" Without another word, she shot out of the kitchen and through the back door.

Mitch rose to follow her, but Bess stopped him. "Give her time alone."

"I'm sorry," Katie whispered, her face pale. "I thought it was a good idea. I thought she would want to talk to her mom."

"I told you, Katie—" Mitch exploded. He got up to look out the window, watching Phoebe run toward the barn.

"Mitch—" Bess tried to intervene.

"Mother, I told Katie to leave Phoebe's family alone." He shot a look at his sister. "How did you do it? I thought you needed a credit card."

"Denise's mother called for me. I gave her the money…."

"I told you—"

"I just wanted to get her something special." Katie's voice broke before she finished speaking.

"She loved the quilt. The quilt was very special," Mitch said, his face full of anger.

"Mitch, it's Christmas," Bess said, jumping to Katie's defense. She wrapped an arm around her daughter's shoulders and Katie, protected by her mother, began to sob louder.

"I'm going to talk to her," Mitch said tightly, slamming the door behind him.

CHAPTER ELEVEN

MITCH FOUND PHOEBE in a small corner of the barn, a rocking ball in the dark. The protective pups barked when he switched on the light. He scattered them with a crisp command.

"Phoebe."

She looked up at him, her face impassive. "Didn't you say my life was none of your business?" she asked him, her voice dull. "What I want to give you, you throw away." She shook her head. "I don't understand why you had my mother call me."

Mitch knelt down next to her. "I'm sorry, Phoebe. Katie's enthusiasm for getting you a nice present got out of hand."

"Katie?" Phoebe blinked in confusion.

"She wanted to reunite you with your family."

Phoebe digested the information for a moment and then asked tearfully, looking away, "Did you know about it?"

Mitch was silent for a long time. Finally, he reluctantly nodded. "Yes."

She lifted her face, not bothering to wipe away the tears. "Why did you let her call?"

"I didn't *let* her call." He kicked himself for not following up on his discussion with Katie, especially since she hadn't promised not to pursue her idea. But that conversation had seemed like such a long time ago and Katie had been so quiet that he'd thought she'd forgotten it. Not that it mattered. He was responsible. *You're not your sister's keeper. Until she's eighteen, I am.* He cleared his throat. "I'm sorry."

"You couldn't have known," Phoebe absolved him suddenly. "I mean, I didn't know until about ten minutes ago."

"What didn't you know?"

"That I hate my mother."

"That's not a crime," Mitch said quietly, his gaze searching her face.

"Really?" She didn't seem convinced. "I've always thought it was." She looked away, and said, her voice wistful, "You know…"

"What?" Mitch asked softly.

"All I ever wanted from her was—" Phoebe stood up. "Actually, I'd rather not talk about this. Let's go in."

"Phoebe, you don't have to run away. You're safe here."

"I'm not running away," she denied.

"Well, you're not staying put. Talk to me."

"And tell you what?" Phoebe looked as if she wanted to cry again.

"Tell me what you wanted from your mother."

"Just news about Tucker."

"Who's Tucker?"

"My youngest brother." Phoebe began to pace. "It was all Will's idea." She stopped and interrupted herself in explanation. "Will was my rotten boyfriend. Expensive taste, no money." She laughed but there was no humor in her tone. As seconds passed she grew more agitated. Finally she said quietly, "I didn't want to think about them at all. I deserted them like they were nothing."

"Who?"

"Stella, Todd and Tuck. I promised them I'd come back and get them. But I never did. I never went back at all. After I hitchhiked to California, I just sent postcards and money when I had it." Phoebe was far away, struggling with something that had haunted her for the past twelve years. She was silent for a long moment and then said painfully, "The only person I really cared about was little Tucker. But I wouldn't go back even to get him. Even when I could afford it, I didn't go back."

"How old were you when you left?" Mitch asked. He couldn't imagine her—

"Fifteen."

"Fifteen?" Mitch paled at the thought of a young Phoebe crossing half the country with strangers. "You were a baby, no older than Katie. Why did you leave?"

"I just needed to be safe," Phoebe said quietly.

"From what?"

"From Audrey, my father, her boyfriends—"

"Were you…"

Phoebe shook her head. "No. But I was terrified." She gave him a look of pure pain. "Let's put it this way. I felt safer hitchhiking than I felt at home. I was very lucky to have made it safely to California. Once I got here, I couldn't go back, even for Tucker."

"But short of kidnapping him, what could you have done?"

"I don't know!" Phoebe sat on the ground and wept, her thin shoulders heaving with her distress. "I could have done something later. Instead I pretended that everything was fine—until W-Will." Her voice choked. "I tried to build a relationship with Audrey but all she wants is money. I thought—" She broke off, swallowed, gasping for air. "I thought that if I gave it to her, she'd tell me where Tucker was. But she just gave me bad phone numbers."

Everything started to make sense to Mitch, he now knew the reason for all those cash advances. "Are you still sending them money?"

Phoebe shook her head. "No. Not since I lost my job. I can't do it anymore. But my sister, Stella, is with a guy who beats her and she's pregnant again. Todd, my other brother, is in jail for involuntary manslaughter. And I still don't know what happened to Tuck. He could be dead for all I know. And it's all my fault."

Mitch touched her arm and she flinched.

"How can any of that be your fault?" Mitch asked, making his voice hard to push past Phoebe's tortured teenager to find her rational self. "You weren't there. You didn't cause your sister to get pregnant or your brother to kill someone."

"Don't you see?" Her bottom lip trembled. "If I'd stayed, if I had been stronger—"

"They would have turned out just the same," Mitch interrupted, "and you would have been sacrificed, too."

"I was the oldest."

"YOU WERE ONLY FIFTEEN!"

Phoebe looked at Mitch in shock, the haze behind her eyes finally clearing for just a moment. Then she broke down and cried harder.

With awkward arms, Mitch pulled her tightly against his chest and then simply rocked her.

WHEN HER SOBS FINALLY stopped, Phoebe found herself encircled by Mitch's strong arms, the warmth of his entire body swaddling her in a protective circle. She allowed herself to accept the warmth, knowing that even though he couldn't promise her a future, he proved that he could accompany her to the murkiest hallows of self-disgust. In the past three months, this man had taught her how to pay attention to the present, to organize her life in such a way that she wouldn't have to worry about the future and could free herself from the past. Amazing things from someone who didn't want to share her life.

From the circle of his arms, she heard the cows moo, saw the pups creep closer, concerned. The rain sounded especially loud here, as the drops clattered against the roof. She took a deep breath, and Mitch's arms automatically tightened, and Phoebe realized that whatever emotions the conversation with her mother evoked, no matter that the horrible truth about herself had been exposed, she had survived it—without buying new clothes or needing her plush condo with its champagne-colored carpet. She had survived it on the dirt floor of a barn in Los Banos in the arms of a particularly dear dairyman, who had declared over and over that what she did with her life was none of his business.

She moved and Mitch released her. She gave him a watery smile and shivered, suddenly cold.

He gazed at her solemnly. "Are you okay?"

She thought for minute and then nodded with a wry smile, "Besides the pounding headache?"

"Those are pretty heavy feelings to be carrying around with you," he observed.

"They're yours now, too."

He smiled and said thoughtfully, "I guess they are."

Phoebe stood stiffly and dusted herself off, staring at her dirty hands, twinges of guilt searing through her, the images still burned into her memory. She had always hated dirt, hated even the color brown. That's why her carpets and the walls in her condo were all light. That's why she was drawn to hospitals.

There'd been no getting away from the dirt on the dairy farm. How many times had she tried to scrub the faces of her siblings, wash their clothes, just so they wouldn't look so poor? But now she realized she'd been wrong.

Dirt was just a way of life on the dairy. It wasn't poverty.

Mitch watched her warily.

Phoebe gave him a relieved smile, as if a heavy weight had just been lifted from her shoulders. She shook herself and then said quietly, "Thank you for not getting involved with my life."

Mitch was silent for a long time, his dark eyes studying her face, then he closed the gap between them and hugged her, warming every part of her body. She buried her face into his flannel shirt, smelling his clean scent. He whispered in her hair, "Any time."

She pushed back from him, comforted by his strong arms, which were still securely wrapped around her waist, and looked up, her hand tentatively reaching to cup his cheek. He turned his head to kiss the palm of her hand, dirt and all. They stood silently for several moments. Then Phoebe hugged him back, suddenly feeling as if she had been away from the beating of his heart for far too long. His arms tightened around her, and she rubbed her cheek against the top of his chest. He fit her so perfectly.

"Thank you," she said again.

It was such an easy thing to do, Phoebe realized with wonder and awe, to move so close to someone and feel as if his heart beat with hers. As she raised herself onto her tiptoes and put her arms around his neck, she felt his reserve crumbling just a little.

She kissed him, and after a moment, he kissed her back, with gentleness that caused her knees to go weak.

"No," Mitch muttered, still kissing her.

"Yes," she said softly. A fog of contentment washed over her and she tried to snuggle deeper into his arms. But before she could protest, he let her go.

"Phoebe." His voice carried a very different quality to it, vulnerable, unsure.

"Yes?"

"You're leaving in a month."

Phoebe refused to let his words dampen her feelings. She gave him a shy smile. "Maybe I don't have to leave. That's what I'm trying to tell you. I love you, Mitch. I love this farm. I love Bess. I love Katie. I care about what happens to you and everything that affects you. I love you, Mitchell Hawkins. You're my family."

"No." Mitch's voice was hoarse. He took another step back and then ran his hand through his hair, rubbed his neck and turned away from her.

Phoebe laughed, relieved, greatly relieved

that it was out. Now, he couldn't possibly make her leave, make her take a job so far away from him. She gave him a beaming smile, joyous in her heart. "You can't tell me no. It's what I feel."

"You just met me."

"I think I've known you a long, long time." She smiled benignly at him.

MITCH LOOKED OVER HIS shoulder at Phoebe, who stood watching him, her head tilted at an inquisitive angle. Her face shone, glowing with the depth of her emotion. His heart skipped a beat. She loved him. His throat constricted. She loved him. But he had no time to love anyone, especially Phoebe. The farm took all of his time, his energy, sapped every bit of strength from him. It left very little for love.

Mitch steeled himself. His life would never be fair to Phoebe. After all, he didn't even know if they would survive this winter. He had enough stress trying not to lose Bess and Katie's livelihood. Ruin Phoebe's life, too? He would never do that.

"I don't love you back," Mitch said tensely.

Phoebe blinked and stepped back as if he had slapped her.

"What?"

"I don't love you," Mitch repeated, turning away, not able to bear the hurt in her eyes.

She stepped closer.

"I think you're lying," she said, her voice trembling.

"I'm sorry if I've somehow misled you," he said woodenly.

"But you kissed me." Her disbelief was obvious.

"You kissed me," Mitch reminded her. "I just responded. I'm sure you realize that you're a very pretty woman, especially when you're distressed. What guy wouldn't respond? So okay, I'm a jerk."

"So that was just a mistake?" she asked with a raised brow.

"Yes," he said firmly. "A mistake."

She looked down at her feet. Then she pulled herself up straight and met his gaze. "Are you sure I was a mistake?"

He couldn't waver now; she'd see right through him. While his chest ached horribly, he said in as firm a tone as he could, "Yes. I'm positive."

She began to pick microscopic particles of dust off her jeans. "How embarrassing," she said carefully. "I'm sorry that I put you in such an awkward position. I'll be sure not to make that mistake again. Thank you for your help tonight. I really appreciate it."

Mitch watched Phoebe pull herself together. She gave him one last look and then walked out of the barn. When he was alone, he finally allowed the barrage of conflicting emotions to wash over him, never realizing that a heart could simultaneously feel disappointment, self-disgust, sadness, relief and simple heartbreak.

"I'm so sorry, Phoebe," he whispered.

As she walked away from Mitch, Phoebe knew two things. Her head ached terribly and Mitchell Hawkins was a big fat liar. She didn't believe for one second Mitch didn't love her. Of course he loved her. She knew that not from his kiss, but from the fact he'd followed her after her mother had called, that he always took care of her. This was all very clear. But he was a stubborn man. She allowed two tears to slide down her cheeks. If she accepted the position in Santa Rosa, she had one month. Could she make him see that he loved her in a month?

The first Monday of the new year, Phoebe called the hospital in Santa Rosa to accept the job. The storms continued to sweep through the valley, giving Mitch ample reason to be distant as their work became more grueling. Phoebe found that even though Mitch told her he didn't need her, he actually did. He needed everyone. Even Bess was outside, working with the cows, pulling them out of mud, letting them walk on the pavement to regain their strength.

The cows were definitely feeling the burden of the continuous rain. She had talked with Carlo, back from his vacation, and found out that the cows were giving twenty-five percent less milk than they had in the summer. Mitch's financial cushion had become thinner and thinner.

At night, Phoebe fell into a deep sleep, but her dreams were as relentless as the pounding of the rain on the roof. Every morning the welcome rumble of Mitch's tractor next to her window reminded her that her days were ticking away.

When Diane called with the news that she had waited so long to hear, Phoebe was oddly bereft.

"Escrow's closed. Everything's signed and sealed. You'll have a check by the end of the week."

"End of the week?" Phoebe echoed. "That fast?"

"That fast," Diane said, her voice congratulatory.

Phoebe didn't feel the flood of relief she'd thought she would. All selling her condo meant was that she had even less of a reason to stay. She could pay the remaining balance on her mortgage, right herself with the credit card companies and establish a place for herself in Santa Rosa. She was free. But at the same time, Mitch, Bess and Katie were falling behind week after week.

A LOUD RAPPING WOKE Phoebe out of a deep slumber.

"Phoebe," Bess said urgently.

"Yes," she roused herself groggily. "What time is it?"

"Get dressed. We need you. It's a flash flood."

She sprang out of bed, hastily pulling on her pants, and her slicker.

"I'm coming, Bess. I'm coming."

OUTSIDE, THE RAIN CAME down in sheets, driven by furious winds that stung Phoebe's face as she stepped out into the night. Katie was right behind her, and they both watched in silent horror, the foot-high wave of water coming directly at them. The cows floundered, some stuck to their knees, moaning as the water engulfed them. Trucks were rumbling far away, but all Phoebe could hear was the rush of the water, the rain, the howling wind, the distressed moans of cows.

"Get the calves," Mitch shouted from the tractor. Even in his slicker, and boots, he looked drenched.

Shocked into motion, Phoebe plunged after Katie into the water, knee-deep, her feet feeling for the planks they had laid at Christmas. Wading against the rushing current was more difficult than she expected. When she slipped, Katie turned and grabbed her by the arm and pulled her to the corral, where they clung to the iron fence, using it as a guide to reach the calves.

The calves bleated piteously. Phoebe and Katie grabbed at the smallest ones barely able to keep their heads above water. Carlo had backed the trailer next to the pens, and Bess stood inside as Katie and Phoebe worked frantically to transfer the wet, frightened calves up to her, to safety.

Phoebe didn't stop to think about anything. She just moved as quickly as she could, still feeling as if she was in slow motion, the water inching up past her thighs. She grabbed at another calf and tottered to the truck. Bess pulled it in, and Phoebe went back, helping Katie get her footing. Past them, Mitch and Carlo shouted directions to each other as they worked to get the big cows and midsized heifers to higher ground.

Adrenaline pumping, Phoebe went to find another calf, dimly realizing that she could no longer see them. She fell forward into the water, sputtering. The water had risen another foot.

"Get in the truck!" Bess bellowed. "Get in the truck."

"But there are more—"

Katie grabbed Phoebe to keep her from going back. Bess dragged her into the trailer. Katie crawled in after her. The calves they'd managed to save were huddled, noisy and frightened, as the wind howled and screamed, shaking the trailer with each powerful gust. Water slowly seeped around their feet.

"If it gets too high, get on top of the trailer," Bess ordered, her tone brooking no argument.

Phoebe nodded wearily, praying as hard as she could. The water rose a few inches more and then miraculously the rain halted and the wind died down. The water continued to creep up and then stopped. Bess, Katie and Phoebe stood and waited. Phoebe strained to hear Carlo or Mitch shouting. But it was eerily quiet.

"Do you think they're all right?" Phoebe asked, trying to keep her teeth from chattering.

"They're fine," Bess said, her voice strong.

"I think the water's going down," Katie said hopefully.

By dawn, the water had receded almost completely, gone as quickly as it had come. Phoebe climbed down from the trailer, shaking her head.

"It's the wetlands," Bess explained briefly.

"The wetlands?"

"Just north. They absorb water like a sponge."

Bess looked at Mitch and Carlo a half a mile away, up on a high spot. "Go to the milking area and see if you can clean up for Mitch and Carlo," she said sharply. "The cows missed their 3 a.m. milking. They'll need to be milked as soon as possible. Go now."

Katie and Phoebe, cold and shivering, moved as quickly as they could to the milking area. Katie got there first and moaned. While the water had receded from the area, it hadn't taken with it the thick six-inch layer of mud.

"We'll never get it clean," Katie said defeated.

Determined to do what she could, Phoebe handed Katie a stiff broom and went to see if the hose still worked. She looked at the drains, hoping they weren't plugged. Thank goodness—someone, probably Mitch—had covered the drains.

"Let's just sweep." Phoebe tried to make her voice as encouraging as possible.

Together, they swept as much of the mud out of the area as they could, then Phoebe ran the hose, which coughed first but then sprayed clean water. She washed off all the milking equipment, Katie following behind sweeping out the excess water. Then they cleaned out the grain trough, finally the walls. It wasn't sparkling , but it was functional. Phoebe pried open the drain covers, and the remaining water danced away.

"Incoming!"

Phoebe and Katie got out of the way as Mitch led the cows, with udders so full they looked ready to burst, down from the main road, using the ramp to the milking barn. Phoebe had never been so happy to see so many cows, mooing impatiently for their turn at the machine.

The two men worked quickly and silently,

the generator for the milking equipment sputtering before eventually starting. Carlo attached the cups to the first few cows, while Mitch put out the grain to feed them. It was a wonderful sight.

"Go in and get cleaned up," Mitch ordered. "After we finish this, we'll take care of the calves."

"But—"

"Go on."

Exhausted and relieved, Katie and Phoebe walked toward the main house. Bess met them in front of the barn.

"The house looks fine. The carpet in the living room is damp, but that's all. Mitch's trailer is fine, too."

"How about the other calves?" Phoebe asked, trying to look behind Bess.

Bess's faded blue eyes were sad. "It's pretty bad," she said. "Mitch doesn't know yet."

Phoebe pushed past Bess and Katie followed quietly. The joy at seeing all the big cows, safe and milked faded as the three women surveyed the corral. Usually, the calves came to the fence, bleating as they greeted Phoebe or Katie. Now it was silent. Somehow, Phoebe forced herself to look around the pen at all the dead calves.

"They drowned."

Phoebe didn't know who said it, but she couldn't talk. She went up to one calf, knelt down just to make sure it was gone and then turned away. Tears choked her. This was awful. Poor Mitch. All his work. All his careful planning.

"How many?" she hiccuped.

Bess cleared her throat. "I couldn't count them all. I think about forty. We saved maybe fifteen."

BY THE END OF THE DAY, they'd all had hot showers, the rugs had been cleaned, the barn swept out, a pup rescued from a rafter in the barn. Most importantly, the cows had been milked. Phoebe was surprised how quickly everything reverted back to normal. The dairy schedule marched on. The only thing that wasn't normal was a death toll of fifty-seven. Forty-three calves. Ten heifers. Four cows.

"This isn't so bad," Bess assured her. "We'll do fine. We've taken worse hits."

"But what about all of Mitch's work?" Phoebe was still dazed.

"He'll be fine. We'll start again," Bess repeated stubbornly, with new resolve in her eyes. She started to put on her coat. "Katie and I are going for pizza. I don't feel like cooking."

"Pizza?" Phoebe asked puzzled. "How can they make pizza?"

"Phoebe, the town was fine," Bess said quietly. "It was just us and three other dairies."

"Just us?" Phoebe echoed. "How can that be? There was water everywhere."

"We were just in the path. It was a fluke." Bess shrugged. "What kind of pizza would you like?"

Phoebe shook her head, indicating that she'd take anything. She wasn't very hungry, she was still shell-shocked, unable to comprehend how Mitch was feeling. She watched him working nonstop as he and Carlo used the tractors to pile the casualties onto the side of the main road. He drove with stoic resolve, obviously fighting extreme fatigue but refusing to quit until the grim task was done.

THE NEXT FEW DAYS DAWNED clear and bright. In fact, the weather felt unseasonably warm for January, as if Mother Nature was taking pity on them, giving them a special sunlamp to dry out the drenched area.

After feeding the calves one afternoon—a job that now took less than an hour—Phoebe started looking for Mitch. He'd grown distant with each passing day, his face becoming gaunt, the stubble of his beard rough and dark. Having had no luck finding him around the farm, she knocked tentatively on the trailer door.

When there was no answer, she knocked louder and listened attentively for movement. As she turned away, she noticed his truck was gone.

"He probably went into town to wash it," Bess said. "It's still so muddy around here. Oh, I put your mail on your bed."

Phoebe nodded and wandered outside again. The sun felt reassuring on her face so she started to walk. She knew exactly where she wanted to go, but wasn't quite sure how to get there. Two questionable turns and thirty minutes later, she was rewarded by the sight of Mitch's truck, haphazardly parked in the eucalyptus grove.

As Phoebe got closer, she slowed and scanned the area for Mitch, finally spotting him under a tree, his back toward her, his head buried in his hands. He started when she quietly sat down next to him.

"What are you doing here?" he asked gruffly.

"Looking for you," she admitted. "Thought I might find you here. I just wanted to tell you how sorry I am…." Her voice broke as she thought of the calves.

Without speaking, he got up and walked a little distance away.

"So what does this mean?" Phoebe asked, her voice faint. "Bess thinks we'll get through it."

"Well, she's wrong."

"Wrong? I don't think so. Look at all—"

"We'll be bankrupt by summer," Mitch predicted, his voice devoid of emotion.

"No," Phoebe stated firmly. "Bankruptcy is not an option, remember?"

Mitch laughed but there was no humor in it. "It's our only option. With no calves, we've got a year to wait before we can get more milkers to just break even with what we were working at before."

"You'll have new calves soon."

"It'll be too late. We're out of time. By the time the new calves are old enough to give milk, this will be the bank's farm—" He glanced at her and then averted his face.

Her chest hurt at the sight of his red eyes. All she wanted to do was put her arms around him and tell him everything was going to be okay.

"Can you buy more cows to fill in the gap?"

"With *what?*" he snarled at her. "My father's good name that I've just made worthless?"

"No. Mitch." Phoebe moved very close to him, tugging lightly on his sleeve. "You haven't done any such thing. Remember, you told me there are always options. It's just money." She grabbed his forearm and felt the tension ripple through him at the contact. She held on even though he tried to pull away and continued speaking, her voice low and urgent. "Maybe you can find someone who will give you a break. The flood wasn't your fault. Even though you'd like to think you are, you're not God. You can't predict the weather."

Mitch was silent. And Phoebe stood there helplessly. Not knowing what else to say, she gave him a big bear hug, pressing her heart against his, even though he resisted, standing ramrod straight, his arms at his sides, hands tightly clenched. "It's going to be all right," she whispered. "I know it is. We'll think of something. We will."

Finally, his arms went around her, and he spoke, his voice low, haggard, his question breaking her heart. "What am I going to do, Phoebe?"

"Shave, first of all," Phoebe said practically, but when he didn't laugh, she said seriously, "You've got to get some sleep. Then, when you're rested, we can work on the next step."

"I've lost it all. Everything my father and

mother worked for. There's nothing left for Katie." He shook his head. "She won't be able to go to college."

Phoebe held him tightly and said in a forceful, positive voice, "Yes, she will. But guess what? Katie's not going to college for another two years and you've had no sleep in the past seventy-two hours." She stepped back and shivered. "And I'm freezing. So drive me home, Mitchell Hawkins, and put yourself to bed." Even as she spoke, her heart ached for him.

As they drove toward his trailer, Mitch couldn't even look at the empty corrals where the calves had been.

"You need sleep," she said as she got out of the truck. "Things will be better tomorrow. You'll see."

He didn't answer.

CHAPTER TWELVE

THEY SAT DOWN for yet another meal without Mitch, even though Bess had tried to bribe him by making his favorite—roast beef. Phoebe could tell Bess and Katie were concerned. They kept looking at Mitch's empty place.

"Mitch should eat," Phoebe observed.

"I don't think he can," Bess said quietly. Phoebe looked into her pale eyes, realizing that Bess saw and cared a lot more than she let on. "When we lost the other herd, we didn't see him for a week."

"It was worse than this," Katie agreed.

They fell into silence.

"But there's got to be a way to help," Phoebe reiterated just as much for herself as for Bess.

"There are always ways," Bess said. "But I'm not sure Mitch can see them now. He'll figure it out. He always has."

Phoebe wasn't sure if Bess truly knew how bad it was for Mitch. Katie believed that this wasn't nearly as bad as the last time, but for

Mitch it was worse. He was deeper in debt and he was tired. Phoebe guessed that without help, Mitch wouldn't find a way. Yet, there had to be an answer. Even though Mitch had said there were no solutions, Phoebe couldn't help but think there must be at least one.

After dinner, Phoebe went back to her room and paced. She flipped through her mail, noting a fat envelope from Diane. She put it down and stared out the picture window into the night. It bothered her that Mitch was shutting everyone out, just when he should be leaning on someone. *You don't know that,* she told herself. Yes, she did. She did know that. She knew he was spinning numbers, calculating, figuring, trying to find a solution.

"Is he okay?"

Phoebe jumped, startled out of her reverie and turned to find Katie hovering in the doorway, looking young and uncertain. "Katie, you scared me. Is who okay?"

"Mitch. Is he okay?"

Phoebe regarded the young woman, finally saying truthfully, "I think he's going to be okay. He's not okay right now, but he will be once he gets some sleep."

"Those calves meant everything to him."

"I know."

Katie started to leave, but then paused. "I wish—"

Phoebe couldn't help but think that in her high-neck nightgown Katie looked like a little girl. "What do you wish, Katie?"

"I wish there was a way to go—poof!—so we could get extra cows."

"What?"

"Extra cows. Stinky's family, the Whitfields, have so many cows. He said his dad was going to sell some because they have too many. Too bad—"

"I *knew* more cows would help," Phoebe said half to herself.

Katie gave her an exasperated look. "Of course they would. If we had more cows, then they'd give extra milk, extra milk means extra money and we could wait for the calves to come. And, if we had more cows, it'd mean we'd have that many more calves." She lost herself in the fantasy and then said sullenly, "But good cows cost a lot of money. It's hard to make money if you don't have any to begin with."

"How much do cows cost? How much is a lot?"

"More than we have." Katie rolled her eyes.

"Do you need to buy a whole herd? Or can you just buy one or two?"

"Well, I guess you can. I don't know what one or two will do. Ten or fifteen would help."

"Really?" Phoebe was thinking hard.

"Yes. Not that it matters." Katie walked to her door. "I'm tired. I just wanted to know if Mitch was okay."

"I think he's going to be just fine," Phoebe murmured, excitement building in her chest, as the younger woman shut her door. Just how much would new cows cost?

She looked at the envelope Diane had sent. With trembling fingers, she slit it open. It was fat with copies of papers she had already signed, but attached to the top of Diane's scrawl of congratulations was the check. It was a lot of money. Enough to pay her creditors. Or enough to buy a few cows, healthy milkers to give Mitch breathing space until he got his calves back.

He'd never take it. She shook her head and stared at the check. Then she threw it into a drawer. He had rejected her on more than one occasion, why should she bother? She lay on the bed. Because he deserved it, now more than ever.

Mitch needed something to hold on to, to break through his isolation and let him know he really wasn't alone. She grimaced. It seemed crude, to give him money. But she wasn't just giving him money, she was giving him a chance at freedom, at love.

She would benefit, too. Maybe she could stay. If she were his wife, they would share money as easily as hugs. If she were his wife, she would have no qualms about taking his hand, snuggling close to him, or buying more cows.

But you're not his wife—you're a tenant, someone who's leaving in two short weeks. He said he didn't love you. But Phoebe's heart knew he was lying. She knew he loved her desperately. *Now is the time to bother,* a voice told her. *Just this one more time, bother.* With a deep breath, Phoebe opened the drawer.

"You're it," she whispered and carefully folded up the check, putting it in her pocket and going to the kitchen, surprising Bess by volunteering in a loud voice to brave the bear and take Mitch a plate of food.

"I don't think that's a good idea," Bess warned. "I called about ten minutes ago and he said he'd pick something up later tonight."

"He needs it now," Phoebe said cheerfully. "I won't bother him. I'll just feed him."

She and Bess exchanged an understanding glance as Phoebe heaped a big helping of mashed potatoes and carrots, and several thick slices of roast beef on a plate. Bess put three rolls in a brown bag and tucked a liter of soda under Phoebe's arm.

Phoebe used the light in his trailer as her beacon across the dark yard. With a deep breath, she rapped firmly on the door, shifting the soda under her other arm and stepped down two steps to wait. After a full minute, the trailer moved and Mitch peered out the side window. His glasses were on so Phoebe knew he was deeply immersed in work, no doubt going through the data trying to find a solution.

"What do you want?" Mitch asked rudely. He looked annoyed, harried.

Phoebe wasn't going to let his tone bother her. "Hi," she said lightly, "I've brought sustenance. Open the door."

"I told my mother I wasn't hungry."

Phoebe gave him an impatient snort. "This isn't from your mother. It's from me. Now, open up."

The door cracked open, and Phoebe mounted the stairs, wriggling past Mitch.

"I don't remember inviting you in," he said, his voice weary. She studied his eyes, the heavy bags making him look terrible.

"I invited myself. Doesn't this look great?" she said with an overly cheerful tone.

"I'm not that hungry," he denied irritably.

"I beg to differ, sir," Phoebe said in her best Southern drawl, which wasn't very good. At least she drew a small smile from Mitch. She put the soda on the counter and walked into his small kitchen to pop the plate of food in the microwave.

"That'll take just a few minutes to heat up. Would you like ice with your soda?"

"No." Impatience edged Mitch's voice.

"No? You want to drink lukewarm soda?" She made a face. "Ick. But it's your soda." She reached for a glass and twisted open the plastic top.

"No. I don't want dinner. I don't want soda. I want you to leave."

"In a minute." Phoebe sat down on his couch and watched his face. "Did you get any sleep?"

"Some."

Phoebe nodded and said placidly, "Liar."

If she knew Mitch, he'd probably got none. He'd probably spent the whole afternoon, manipulating the books, looking at his loans. Searching for a solution. The width and depth of paper—ledgers and computer printouts—on his desk confirmed her hunch. "Have you found a solution?"

He laughed bitterly. "I found there is no solution."

"None?"

"None that have jumped out at me."

"One will," she said positively.

"I don't think you realize the loss—" He had hunched himself into the isolated dairy farmer pose that made Phoebe so mad she could spit.

"Oh, yes, Mitch," Phoebe said seriously. "I do realize the extent of the loss. I just can't but help think there has to be a way. You simply can't find it right now."

"Yes," he said deliberately. "There is a way. We sell the farm now before we go any deeper in debt, sell the cattle, the equipment, pay off all our outstanding loans and move to that piece of property my father saved for me. Then I'll get a job as a foreman on someone else's farm. It's easy."

"You'd hate it," Phoebe said shortly.

He turned away. Phoebe could tell from the set of his shoulders that he was tightly wired. Her hands itched to touch him, knead the tension out of his back and spine, just so he would know, truly know that he wasn't alone. She felt the corner of the check in her pocket poke at her.

The microwave dinged and Phoebe stood up, carefully brushing past him to get to the kitchen. Suddenly, the small trailer seemed even smaller—she could smell his shampoo, see the fine hairs on the nape of his neck. She took a hot pad and unwrapped the food. After clearing away his papers, she put the plate down, then got some ice and poured him a glass of soda.

"I'd get you a beer, but there is none," she said as she put the soda next to his plate. "Mitch, sit down at the table. Forget about all of that right now. There's nothing you can do tonight that you can't do tomorrow. Nothing. In fact, I'd say trying to tackle all of this tonight is going to put you in a worse frame of mind. After a good night's sleep you'll feel a lot better, less dense, and a solution will come. But for now, food will help. Come, sit." She tried to make her voice sweetly persuasive.

Mitch stared at her pensively as if he would really like to believe what she said. She patted the chair and gazed up at him, her eyes meeting his. They stared at each other for a full minute, Phoebe never breaking her gaze. Finally, with a deep sigh that came from the bottom of his lungs, he capitulated and sat. Phoebe nodded approvingly, much relieved. "I knew you couldn't hold out, especially with the smell of Bess's roast beef tempting you."

She sat across from him, wondering why she found this stubborn man so dear, even when he tried to push her away and isolate himself further. She knew the answer. It was because in the past few months she and Mitch had become inextricably entwined. Just as he could feel her panic at the thought of opening past due notices, she could feel the weight of this latest tragedy, the burden that lay squarely on top of his broad shoulders.

And she also knew that if anyone could get Mitch to ask for help and accept it graciously it would be her. She gave him a big smile. A difficult task, but she had gotten him to sit down. He was eating food. He was accepting, albeit not graciously, her company. It was a start.

MITCH ATE SILENTLY, surprised to find himself ravenous. Phoebe watched him silently, not one bit in a hurry or nervous. Even though he indicated to her on more than one occasion that she didn't have to stay and keep him company, she seemed to ignore him and settled herself more firmly in her seat, carefully piling up his folders and papers to the side. Now, she sat, her chin propped on her right hand, her right elbow irreverently balanced on the stack.

When he was finished, she automatically stood and whisked his plate away, negotiating his small kitchen with practiced ease. Tonight she was wearing a green flannel shirt over a pair of jeans. Even in dairy clothes, she looked as if she'd just stepped out of a salon. He was surprised that he noticed her clothes, surprised that he was eating. For some reason those two things were clear evidence that the world had not yet come crashing to an end. She glanced at him curiously and then smiled.

"So are you going to fess up that you were hungry?" she asked cheerfully. "Do you feel better?"

He had to admit he did. He supposed the world would come crashing to an end tomorrow, but right now he actually felt just a tiny bit of relief. He studied the piles of papers and then realized how her presence had broken up the frenzied atmosphere of this afternoon, when he'd desperately calculated how the loss of the calves would affect the farm. Figuring, projecting. They'd limp along for the next year, and then there'd be a problem. A big problem, just when Katie'd be trying to go to college. He shook his head. Phoebe was right. There was nothing more he could do tonight. Mitch looked at her and acknowledged gruffly, "Thank you."

"You're welcome," she said simply. "Sometimes we need people who aren't so close to keep things in perspective. I'm just returning the favor."

"Returning the favor?" Mitch looked at her puzzled, wondering why he'd never noticed that her eyes were pure emerald-green. He took his glasses off and rubbed his forehead and looked again. Yes, they were green, sleepy half moons, almost the exact color of her flannel shirt.

"Yes." She finished wiping the glass and returned it to its place on the shelf.

"What are you talking about?"

"I'm talking about your helping me through what I thought was the worst period of my life. I lost my job, I had a boxful of bills that I couldn't open, my mother pressuring me. I was pretty desperate," she said carefully. "But you looked after me, made sure that I had all I needed so I could do what I had to do. That's what I want to do for you now."

"What?" Mitch asked, his voice a little hoarse.

"I want to make sure you have all that you need so you can do what you have to. Food. Comfort." Her voice trailed off with a small smile.

"I don't think I helped all that much," he mumbled. "You can handle anything."

She wagged a slender finger at him. "I think

someone is telling a fib. You know how desperate I was." She sat down, obviously comfortable with his presence.

He laughed reluctantly, surprised at the peace that had suddenly washed through him. She was right. There wasn't anything he could do now. Nothing. Except enjoy her company. Take her comfort.

"I had an idea," he admitted. "But I also figured you'd probably find an answer. Which you did," he pointed out. "People like you always land on their feet."

"People like me?" She raised an eyebrow. "I hope you mean that in a flattering way."

Mitch smiled at her look of affront. "You're like a piece of fluff, moving with the wind, getting out of one scrape, moving headlong into another."

"Hmm. That doesn't sound any better," she observed, a smile still evident on her lips. "Try again."

"You are such a capable woman that wherever you go or whatever you do you're successful. The likelihood of your failing at anything is pretty remote. You proved that to me pretty early on."

"Much better," she nodded approvingly. "I did. But I was able to do it because you gave me time. You let me work for you instead of having to pay rent, and you sorted out all my debts, so I would know how much I owed. You've done a lot for me."

Mitch looked down, her gaze too intent for him. He shook his head. "It's nothing that anyone else wouldn't have done."

"I disagree," Phoebe said. "I think that very few would have done that. I just wanted you to know I appreciated it."

"Well, thank you for coming and feeding me."

Phoebe smiled. Then she nodded to his work. "Are you going to do more tonight?"

He started. If she hadn't come, he wouldn't have stopped until he'd dropped from exhaustion. His headache had subsided substantially, probably from the food, and with a flash of clarity, he realized that he was probably still in shock. It was what had happened when the botulism hit.

"Is this the same?" Phoebe asked softly.

"What?" he looked at her, startled.

"Is this the same?" Phoebe repeated. "I remember you telling me that you lost another herd."

"It feels the same," he said and was silent for a long time. "My dad had just died a few months earlier. Mom wasn't in the best of minds. Katie was just a little thing." He glanced at the paperwork, his stomach starting to churn. "But I think this is a much worse situation."

"Why?"

"Because we still have the loans out on the cattle. We're not nearly as solvent as we were before. We suffered from my father's death personally, but financially we were doing very well. In fact, my father and I had just finished the renovation of the milking barn so we could increase the herd. Then it was gone." He spoke honestly. "The banks had established a good relationship with my father, but he was considered the backbone of the farm. So when they lent us the money, they were also looking to see how I ran this farm." He couldn't help the bitterness and defeat that crept into his voice. "After two lost herds, they're not going to be willing to invest in a third."

"You can't know that," Phoebe said passionately, the translucence of her cheeks flushing with her urgency. "It's not a whole herd, just calves. I'm sure they know—"

"They know that I've lost more cows in the past two years than my father did in the past twenty."

"It wasn't your fault," Phoebe said stubbornly. "They will know that. You can't be sure what they're thinking. You can't. Even I was forgiven. And I did that all to myself."

He looked at her, not sure he wanted to believe what she was saying and then shrugged and smiled dimly. "You're right, I can't know what they're thinking."

Phoebe was curiously silent, just staring at him, studying his face. Mitch wanted so much to accept her comfort. As if reading his mind, she took his hand and led him to the couch. She laid her head on his chest, her face pressed against his thudding heart, her hand resting lightly on his arm. She fit as if she belonged there.

She shifted, snuggling to get, if possible, closer to him. He studied the small, fine sparkling gold streaks in her hair. Then the feelings he was normally able to keep at bay became overwhelming. The need to feel something other than desperation over the dairy and the numbers and the tragedy was urgent. She looked up at him, and he saw such love, such compassion in her eyes. He knew there was no turning back. This was the only thing in his life that felt right. He bent to kiss her.

But was it fair? Fair to Phoebe?

"Don't think, Mitch," she whispered. "Just feel. It's okay."

"No, it's not okay." Mitch pulled back, gently displaced her and stood up, suddenly wondering what they were doing.

Phoebe reached toward him. "Don't think, Mitch," she pleaded.

"I think we'd better think. Why is it that the only times we end up like this are when—"

"—we need each other the most," Phoebe finished. She looked at him levelly. "That's not a bad thing, Mitch. It's a good thing. When everything is okay, your concerns are about the dairy, Katie, Bess, your books and numbers. You're so busy you don't even let yourself need anyone. You won't even let me get close."

"That's not true," Mitch denied.

"That's very true," Phoebe said sadly. "Or you wouldn't be insisting that I take the job when all I want to do is stay with you on the dairy for better or for worse."

Mitch was silent, a cauldron of emotion bubbling inside of him.

Phoebe continued, her voice low and honest, "You know, Mitch. It's when the worst happens that we need to connect to all the things that are good. It's the worst that shows us we need to touch and be touched. When we're getting by, when life's treating us okay, it's easy to say that we don't need love. But everyone needs love, Mitch—all the time. You just don't know what it feels like because you've been living without it for so long. When things are bad, it's the love that gets you through, that tells you losing all your calves isn't the end of the world and that together we'll find a way."

Phoebe stood and drew his stiff arms around her waist, staring imploringly at him, her eyes bigger than he had ever seen them.

"You can't tell me you don't feel what I feel. I know that the words scare you, but they don't scare me. I love you, Mitchell Hawkins. I love you."

Mitch could feel her warmth pressed against his chest. She pulled herself as close to him as she could. If he returned her embrace, all would be lost—*he* would be lost. With a deep sigh, Mitch carefully, softly, regretfully put her aside and stepped back.

"You need to go," Mitch said, unable to look in her eyes as they radiated with her love for him.

"No."

"Then I'll go," he muttered gruffly as he turned toward the door.

CHAPTER THIRTEEN

PHOEBE COULDN'T BELIEVE what she was hearing and couldn't stop the tears that fell at Mitch's rejection.

"Mitch," she called loudly, afraid that he wouldn't stop, that she would have to chase him outside. But he did stop. He stopped as if he was suddenly bolted to the floor. She hastily swiped at her tears, her anger getting the best of her.

"I've got to get out of here," he insisted, still not looking at her.

Phoebe gave a toneless laugh. "You must think I'm some kind of idiot."

"No. I don't. I just—"

"I know. You can't. You can't love me." Phoebe took a series of deep cleansing breaths. "I don't know why I haven't gotten the message so far. I guess I keep forgetting."

"Forgetting what?" he asked quietly.

"That we're not what I keep thinking we are," she said frankly.

"If you think we can be something permanent—"

"Yes," she said fiercely. "For some silly reason, I keep thinking that we can. I know you love me—"

"Phoebe, you don't realize how bad things are," Mitch implored her to understand. "They're only going to get worse over the next few—"

"This isn't about the calves. Or how many gallons of milk the cows produce or whether or not the dairy is going to die a slow, torturous death. It's about you, Mitch. It's always been about you."

Mitch gave her a ghost of a smile. "Phoebe, all that *is* me. We're the same. This dairy and me. I can't work under fluorescent light for eight hours a day. I'm going to slog away at this job until I die. Just like my father did, just like my grandfather did."

"Yes, you are," she said abruptly, feeling in her pocket for the check. "But you don't have to do it alone. If you want one, I have a solution for you."

"Phoebe." Mitch's voice was full of regret.

She pulled out the check and thrust it at him.

"What's this?" He took it cautiously.

"The check from the sale of my condo. My

Realtor already paid off the bank. That's what's left."

"That's nice." Mitch looked up, a question in his eyes.

"It's a lot of money." Phoebe stated the obvious with a tentative smile. "It can get you started again."

"What?"

"Won't this buy more cows? To tide us over until new calves are born."

Mitch immediately shook his head and handed the check back. "We—I can't take this."

"Why not?" Phoebe had been prepared for his resistance. "If we buy more cows, you'll be all set."

"But what about you?" Mitch asked pointedly.

"What about me?"

"How are you going to pay your debts?"

"I'll wait for a job in town. I told you I've applied—"

"I can't support you, too, Phoebe," Mitch said heavily.

"You won't have to support me. If you take the money, you'll have more cows. If you have more cows, they'll make more milk—"

"It's not that easy."

"Really?" Phoebe looked at him skeptically.

"I think it is. Besides, if the dairy's going to be okay, then there's no reason for me to go."

"No," Mitch said, his voice sharper than Phoebe would have liked it to be. Then he sighed and gave her a pained look. "Use your money to pay off those credit cards. Start fresh with a new job rather than fantasize about being a dairy farmer's wife."

Phoebe felt her face grow hot with indignation, hurt. She opened her mouth to say something then closed it and took another deep breath. Finally, after carefully choosing her words she said in a low voice, "Is that what you think I've been doing, fantasizing?"

Mitch had the grace to look ashamed. "No, I don't think that. But it doesn't change anything. I won't take your money," he said firmly.

"Why not?" Phoebe persisted.

Mitch looked away, his patience fraying and then said quietly, "You don't want me to answer that honestly."

"How do you know that?" Phoebe crossed her arms over her chest, surprised by how much his words hurt. "Why? What is so important that you won't accept this gift?" She tried to hold back the tears, her voice shaking with the word gift.

Mitch was silent for a long time. He walked

across the room to put physical space between them and said in a strained voice, "Because I'll always wonder why you were trying to buy me."

Phoebe took a step back, blinking, trying to absorb what he was saying. She tried to control the tremble in her voice when she asked, "What do you mean—buy you?"

Mitch gave her a piercing stare. "Just like you did with Katie."

Phoebe felt as if she'd been punched in the stomach. Her world whirled as she tried not to panic. "Katie?"

"Those Christmas boots for Katie."

"I don't understand." Phoebe's voice was weak.

"I know you wanted her to have something that all her friends had, but it was too much. It seems—" Mitch paused again.

"Tell me," Phoebe insisted, feeling her heart shatter into little pieces.

"It seems that whatever you want, you try to buy." His voice was very quiet.

"Is that what you think? I was trying to buy Katie?" She laughed a little hysterically.

"Phoebe, you're up to your eyeballs in debt and without a second thought you go and buy Katie designer boots. You can't tell me you weren't trying to buy her. I can see that she decided to like you a lot more after Christmas—"

"Things aren't always what they look like," Phoebe said.

"Well, that's what it looked like." He stared at her painfully. He paused a moment as if debating whether or not to say anything. Finally he said heavily, "And Tucker."

"Tucker?" Phoebe felt herself panic. "What does my brother have to do with this?"

"You need absolution for something you believe you've done wrong. So you keep sending money to your mother for any scrap of information she deems to give you. None of it has done any good. If you really wanted to find Tucker, you'd have used the money to hire a private detective, not subsidize your mother's—"

"Mitch," Phoebe broke in, distress tearing at her. "You can't believe that's the same as— You can't."

"What can I believe, Phoebe?" Mitch asked. "Now that you've given me all the money you have, so that I can buy more cows and you don't have to leave."

"I can't believe—" Phoebe felt as if she'd choke on her tears.

"I don't mean it in a bad way, Phoebe,"

Mitch said helplessly. "But I'm not for sale. I guess you were right."

Phoebe didn't like the sound of that. "About what?"

"This isn't about the money. It's about me. If I wanted to marry you, I would. If I wanted you to stay, I'd ask you. I haven't asked you."

Phoebe gasped, her heart frozen from the chill in his tone.

"I know it sounds bad," Mitch said in a low voice, "but once you start working in that nice clean hospital, you won't even think twice about the dairy. This isn't your life. Your life is in the city, with a job in an office and a man who can—"

"Who can what?" Phoebe asked angrily. "Who can pick me out of the depths of financial depression and show me there's light? Who can make my heart pound just by entering the room? Who's shown me in a thousand little ways that he cares for me? Mitch, that's *you*."

Mitch shook his head, apparently at a loss for words, then said heavily, "I can't do this anymore." He turned to leave.

"No." It took everything for Phoebe to rise and walk past him. Devestation didn't begin to cover it. "I'll go."

She stopped at the door. After a long moment, she said quietly, "You know, someone very wise once told me during a horrible time that things are never as terrible as they appear. I didn't believe him." Her throat was closing so she could hardly talk. "But guess what? He was right."

MITCH WATCHED HER retreating back, emotions churning inside him. He lay against the couch, dismayed that the whole trailer smelled so much like Phoebe. But his rational mind soothed him. A little hurt today prevented the big hurt tomorrow. He rubbed his chest, surprised at how painful heartache was. It was for the best. Phoebe didn't belong on the dairy. The poverty, the worry, the day in day out work would drain the life out of her, just like it had to his mother, just like it was doing to him.

AFTER BREAKFAST THE NEXT morning, Phoebe approached Bess who was working quietly in the living room, a half-finished quilt spread out before her.

"Can we talk?" Phoebe asked.

Bess glanced up and smiled. "About what?" she inquired, her voice soft, the needle still moving.

"I talked with Mitch last night."

"Is he okay?" Bess looked at her with maternal concern, something flashing behind her eyes. Regret?

"No," Phoebe said, her voice blunt. "He's not okay. He's going to go down with the dairy."

"He's always worked it out before," Bess said, looking away, but Phoebe saw her fingers falter.

"But he can't do it alone anymore. He needs you."

"What can I do?" Bess asked, helplessly. "If I could have stopped the flood, I would have. But bad things happen to us all the time and there's nothing that we can do about it. We'll get through this just as we have everything else."

"But at what cost, Bess?" Phoebe said, her voice urgent, her tears almost overwhelming her. "You have a daughter who's so lonely she'll do anything just to feel connected to you and a son who can't accept love when it stares him straight in the face because he's so wrapped up in the problems with the dairy."

"The dairy is our life." Bess's tone was defensive.

"But his life could be more than just hard. His life could be fuller, happier."

Bess stared at her, assessing her words, then

said, "And I suppose you want to make his life—er, full?"

Phoebe looked away embarrassed. Finally she said quietly, "I love Mitch, but I know that he's not going to let me help him." She placed a gentle hand on Bess's forearm. "But he will let you."

"I don't know what I can do that Mitch can't do," Bess replied, her voice uncertain.

"I know exactly what you can do," Phoebe said firmly. She took out her check and put it on the quilt in front of Bess. "You can take this money and buy the dairy more cows."

The older woman was quiet for a long time. Then she finally observed, "It's not going to make him love you any more."

Phoebe swallowed hard and then smiled feebly. "I know that. In fact, if you take this check and buy more cows behind his back, he'll probably hate me. But maybe, eventually, he'll understand. He's already let me know he wants me gone. I've got a new job, so I'm leaving next Tuesday."

"So soon?" Bess looked shocked.

"Yes. So I need you to do this." Phoebe pushed the check toward Bess.

Bess picked up the check and studied it. "This *would* buy us some time, but we can't accept it."

"Yes, you can."

"Don't you need this money?"

Phoebe laughed and looked out the window, her eyes watching Mitch maneuvering the tractor. "You know, a few months ago I was desperate for that money. But now, I realize it's just money. I've got enough to get me started." Her voice trailed off as she tried to hold back her tears.

Bess stared at her for a long time. When she spoke again, her voice was gruff. "Do you really love him?"

Phoebe nodded, swallowing her tears. "With all my heart."

"I loved Mitch's father like that."

"I had a feeling that you did," Phoebe said.

"I think I loved him too much because when he died, I didn't know how to live without him." Bess looked down and confessed, the sorrow in her voice making Phoebe's chest tight, "I burned all the family albums."

Phoebe looked at her in surprise.

"I was so angry I burned everything." Bess's voice was filled with pain and regret at her actions. "Our wedding pictures. Mitch's and Katie's baby pictures. Everything. I don't think there's a photo left of my husband anywhere." She shook her head. "I haven't been able to love them the same. Mitch and Katie look so much like him. I couldn't look at them without seeing him." She gave Phoebe a tearful glance. "For some, I suppose your children are your comfort. For me, they were just painful reminders that I would never see my husband again. Now the photos are gone and I can't see him again."

Phoebe held her breath, debating whether she should say something. It was another confidence of Mitch's that she would break, but she realized she had very little to lose.

"Yes, you can," Phoebe whispered, her voice tight. "I've seen Mitch's father."

"What are you talking about?" Disbelief and confusion filled Bess's face.

"Mitch showed me. He didn't let them burn. He saved the albums and put them away."

"No," Bess denied, with a stunned shake of her head. "I saw the ashes."

"No, you saw a bunch of newspapers burning. He saved all the photos. He has them all."

Bess was silent for a long time and then she started to cry. Phoebe scooted closer to give her a hug and said in a voice choked with emotion. "You have a son and a daughter who love you very much. And me—" Phoebe gave Bess a weak smile. "I love you and Katie, too. You've been the mother that my mother could never be. Mitch and Katie are very lucky."

There was a long pause and then Bess shook herself, searching for a tissue. She looked out the window at Mitch. "He's a lot like his father. Very proud."

"Yes. He is that," Phoebe agreed.

"It's been hardest on him. He's had to do it all."

"But it doesn't have to stay hard," Phoebe said, then asked bluntly, "Will you buy more cows?"

Bess studied the check, then looked at Phoebe and said faintly, "I'll think about it."

"I'll tell you what," Phoebe said, taking the check and turning it over, fumbling for a pen in her back pocket. "I'll sign this over to you. You can do whatever you want with it."

Bess didn't move. She just stared out the window intently watching Mitch. Phoebe took a deep breath and headed toward her room. She opened her closet door and surveyed what was left of her wardrobe. Would she feel the same when she put on her suits? Or had the dairy altered her forever? Would she find herself allergic to fluorescent light?

"What are you doing?"

Phoebe jerked in surprise and then forced a smile at Katie who leaned petulantly against the door. "Just sorting things out," Phoebe said briefly.

"Why?"

Phoebe glanced at Katie in surprise. "Didn't Mitch tell you?"

"Tell me what?"

"You're going to get your room back. I found a job."

Katie looked shocked. "No. You can't leave." She sounded genuinely dismayed.

"I have to—"

"But you can't go," Katie insisted.

"Why not?"

"Because—because, I thought that you and Mitch—"

"Mitch and I were?"

"You know— Does he know?" Katie demanded.

"Yes." Phoebe took a deep breath. "Yes, Mitch knows."

"So you're running out on us when we need you the most." Katie's voice turned hard, her anger bubbling up.

"I am not running out on you," Phoebe corrected. "Mitch and I talked about it and decided it was best—"

"But I haven't paid you back yet—" Katie grasped at straws.

"That's okay. You don't have to pay me back."

"You don't like it here?"

"I love it here," Phoebe said with a catch in her throat.

"So why don't you stay?"

"I wish I could, but I can't. I have a job that I've already accepted." Phoebe wasn't feeling too good about this conversation.

"Would you stay if I was nicer to you?" Katie's voice was small.

Phoebe laughed, feeling a little bit of a sob coming up, catching her unaware. "Oh, Katie, you've been nice enough."

"No, I haven't. I was really rude at the beginning."

Phoebe gave Katie a big smile and admitted, "Yes, you were, but you know what? That's okay, too."

"Why is that okay?" Katie looked at her skeptically.

"Because it's not the easy friendships that last," Phoebe said, as she folded three suits and put them in a box. She stopped what she was doing and gave Katie a soft smile. "After all we've been through together, I'd like to think of you as a friend."

Katie's eyes brimmed with tears. "I never told Mitch or my mother about what I did to you," she said roughly, her arms crossed.

Phoebe regarded the teenager with compassionate eyes. "How does that feel?"

"Terrible. I've never kept a secret like this from them."

"You don't have to tell."

"Are you leaving because I didn't tell?"

Phoebe shook her head. "No. I'm leaving for lots of reasons, but they don't have to do with that."

"Is it because of Mitch?"

Phoebe swallowed hard and said noncommittally, "Why do you think it's because of Mitch?"

Katie shrugged. "I don't know. Maybe it's the way he looks at you and the way you look back. I thought you'd get married or something. Maybe I wanted you to."

Phoebe wanted to cry but forced a cheerful laugh. "The last thing your brother wants to do is get married. Especially to me." She pushed some clothes aside in the closet, turning her head away from Katie.

"Would it help if Mitch knew about what I did?"

Phoebe bit her lip and said, "You need to do what you can live with. If you want to tell Mitch, you should because it's the right thing to do. Not for any other reason."

Katie nodded and then abruptly turned away.

CHAPTER FOURTEEN

BESS APPROACHED MITCH as he assembled a mid-afternoon snack. He'd noticed Phoebe had made herself scarce, not even showing up for lunch. He didn't like the way the meal had felt. Everyone had been subdued, Katie giving him furtive glances and then looking away, pushing her salad around on her plate. Carlo watchful but as silent as ever. He'd gotten used to lively talk and laughter. Mitch summoned a smile for his mother as he unscrewed the lid to the mayonnaise. Bess cleared her throat.

"Phoebe offered me a check this morning."

"What?" Mitch was so startled he actually dropped the piece of bread on the floor. He picked it up, brushed it off, then blew on it.

"Phoebe signed her equity check over to me," Bess said, her voice stronger than he had heard in years.

Mitch looked at her, not understanding the sudden rush of anger that he felt. "Tell me you're kidding," he said, his sandwich forgotten.

"No." Bess fished it out of her shirt pocket and gave it to him. He turned it over hoping not to see Phoebe's signature.

"We can't take it," he said shortly.

"She also told me you saved the family albums," Bess continued, taking the check back from him.

Mitch felt Phoebe's betrayal slice through him. "She had no right—"

"Is it true?"

Mitch stared at the mayonnaise jar. Finally, he looked his mother in the eye. "Yes. It's true. I did it for Katie," he said a little defensively. "And for you. And me."

Bess just gazed at him, her lips tight. Mitch looked away again, not wanting to apologize for something he didn't feel sorry about.

"Thank you," Bess said finally, her voice cracking.

"What?" Mitch looked at his mother in surprise, finding her eyes welling with tears. He hadn't seen Bess cry since the funeral.

"Thank you, Mitch. You have no idea how much I've regretted doing that. Knowing they're safe is a great weight off my conscience." She gave him a big, strong hug. "You're a good son. You've done a wonderful job in terrible circumstances. I'm so proud of what you've done in spite of how I've been these last years." She quietly added, "Your dad would be, too."

Mitch felt his throat closing, his anger at Phoebe still simmering, but his mother's admissions lifting a great weight off *his* conscience.

Bess pulled away and said, "I also told Phoebe that we'd manage."

"And what did she say?" Mitch was perversely curious.

"That it could be better."

Mitch laughed, no humor in his tone. "She's right about that." He finished spreading the mayonnaise and assembled the sandwich quickly. "So will you give the check back to her, or shall I?"

Bess didn't look at him as she put the mayonnaise back in the refrigerator, but assured him, "I'll take care of it."

MITCH RETURNED TO HIS trailer, sandwich in hand, his mind still spinning from what Bess had confided in him, the strong hug she had given him. Phoebe just couldn't keep her mouth shut. What made that woman think she could go behind his back and— He opened the door of his trailer, surprised when Phoebe nervously jumped up from the couch.

"Phoebe," Mitch said, his voice clipped. "What can I do to help you?"

He wasn't pleased when she actually stepped back from him.

"Hi," she replied and wouldn't meet his eyes. "I'm sorry to bother you, but I need one last favor."

"You never bother me," Mitch said automatically, momentarily forgetting he was very angry at her, wishing with all his might that she wasn't such a busybody and that the circumstances were different. "What do you need?"

"A letter of reference."

"Reference?" He had to admit, he was surprised.

She nodded, not looking at him but staring out the window. "Uh, yes. I need to look for an apartment and if I have a letter of reference with me it might help me find something faster."

"Certainly." He sat down, pushing his sandwich aside, his appetite completely gone. "When do you need it by?"

"Friday would be good," she said and then added hastily, "if it's not too soon."

"No. It's not too soon."

"I thought I'd spend the weekend looking for an apartment."

Did her voice break or did he just imagine it?

"Left it kind of late, didn't you?" He didn't know why he said that, especially when her hazel eyes looked so sad.

But she recovered quickly and shrugged it off, remarking, "I'll find something. I met someone from the hospital who offered to put me up for the weekend and show me around the area."

"Someone?" Mitch raised an eyebrow.

"Coworker to be," Phoebe said briefly. "I'm sure he'll have suggestions."

"He?" Mitch didn't like the feeling of jealousy stabbing at him.

"And his wife," Phoebe supplied smoothly.

A silence fell between them.

Finally, Mitch heaved a big sigh. "It's for the best, you know."

Phoebe started toward the door. "I'm sure it is," she said clearly. "So will you give me a reference?"

Mitch regarded her for a long moment. "Of course."

With a brief nod of thanks, Phoebe turned and left.

Mitch watched her walk away, his stomach clenched with regret. *She loves you and all you have to do is say the word and she's yours.* But he had nothing to offer her. She was starting a new life and hadn't changed. He shook his head, trying to squelch his envy. He envied Phoebe's freedom, her mobility. Not that he wanted a different life than what he had. He couldn't imagine life without the dairy. But he didn't like the feeling of being left behind, that things would get better for her—without him.

There was a tentative knock on his door. His pulse rate accelerated. Phoebe. He smiled and lunged to open the door.

"Did you forget some— Katie," he said with surprise, trying to hide his disappointment.

"I've got to talk to you," she said baldly as she rushed in. She looked extremely uncomfortable, nervously crossing and uncrossing her arms.

In the most reassuring voice he could muster, Mitch said, "Sure, go ahead. You want a seat?"

"You're not going to like it," she predicted gloomily, as she plopped onto the couch. She studied the scuffed toes of her shoes, her arms still crossed defensively.

Mitch sat down and looked at the sandwich, his stomach churning. "Okay. Tell me something that I'm not going to like."

"You promise not to tell Mom?" She gave him a suspicious look.

Mitch sighed. He usually made a conscious effort to be patient with his younger sister, but Phoebe had just about exhausted all the patience he had left. However as he stared at Katie, he saw she looked terrible, guilt-ridden. "You know I can't promise anything like that," he said, trying to make his voice reasonable. "But, maybe I can help you."

Tears welled up in Katie's eyes. "I'm so ashamed. Phoebe's leaving because of me."

Mitch cleared his throat, avoided looking at her and asked quietly, "Why do you think that?"

Katie's words rushed from her. "She said she wouldn't tell. That I had to."

"Had to tell about what?" Mitch looked at Katie puzzled. "You're not making sense."

"I've done an awful thing."

"What have you done and what does this have to do with Phoebe?"

"H-her c-credit c-cards." Katie could barely talk. She wrapped her arms around her body and sobbed, her small shoulders heaving.

"Her what?"

"I t-took her credit cards the d-day the cow died last fall. I took all the jackets in and

found them when I put your cell phone back.
I—I took two. I knew you'd never notice."

Mitch felt the blood drain out of his face.
He could barely speak. "Go on."

Katie avoided looking at him. "I was going
shopping that Saturday with Denise and I
didn't want to look like I was poor. I wasn't
going to use the cards, but—it was easy.
They didn't even ask for I.D. I bought some
stuff—"

"Stuff?" Mitch couldn't control the sharp-
ness in his voice, even though Katie visibly
cringed.

"A j-jacket," she whispered. "The boots—"

"The boots that you got for Christmas."

"We took the jacket back. I've been paying
her back since then, out of my allowance, and
she agreed to give the boots to me for Christmas so you and Mom wouldn't find out. She
was really cool about it all."

Mitch just stared at her not believing what
he was hearing. His mind spun. Phoebe hadn't
tried to buy Katie, but why hadn't she told?

Katie looked away and continued, "Phoebe
said that if I wasn't going to tell, you and Mom
would never know."

"So why are you telling me now?" Mitch
wasn't sure why he was so angry. Was it because Phoebe, yet again, had gone behind his

back or because he was proven wrong about her or because this felt like just another ploy to manipulate him? Fury burned in his throat. "So did Phoebe persuade you to come talk to me?"

"No. No! I just found out that she's leaving and if I had only been nicer... Even when I was really mean to her, she never told on me, Mitch. Never. Will you talk to her? Will you make it so she doesn't have to go? Will you tell her I'm sorry?"

"You should be the one to tell her you're sorry," Mitch said, his fist clenching and unclenching. He could feel the muscles in the back of his neck tightening.

"I tried but she said it was all okay. But if it was all okay, she wouldn't be leaving."

"She has a job to go to," Mitch said shortly. "God, Katie, I can't believe—"

"I'm sorry. I just thought she had so much—"

"I think you should leave now," Mitch said suddenly, his mind imploding from the implications of everything Katie had told him. Did it change anything? He shook his head in answer to his own silent question and shot a hard look at his younger sister, who sat huddled, her body still shaking with her sobs. "Katie, please leave. I'm very angry now. We'll talk about it later."

His words made her sob harder. "Mitch, I'm so sorry. I didn't mean—"

Mitch took a deep breath, a wave of sympathy flooding over him, battling with his anger. As hard as Katie tried to be a grown-up, she was still a child.

"Please, Mitch," Katie begged. "Don't be mad at me." *Love me, still love me,* her blue eyes pleaded.

Mitch reached out and pulled Katie to her feet, giving her a strong hug. Katie cried harder, burying her face into his chest. He whispered in her hair, "I'm very mad at you. But that doesn't mean I don't love you. No matter what a squirt you are, you're my sister and I'll always love you. Always."

AFTER KATIE LEFT, Mitch paced the length of his trailer. He couldn't ever remember being as angry as he was. Right now, his life was just a blurry, explosive fiery ball of—oh, he didn't know what. But he knew Phoebe was responsible for all of it. He didn't appreciate her using his family to manipulate him. Using his mother to take the check, and now Katie. He laughed grimly because he'd actually felt sorry for her when she'd asked for her reference. What she hadn't said was *why* she had left it so late. Of course. She'd never intended to leave.

"If Phoebe Douglas wants a reference, she'll get one," he muttered, ignoring the rational part of him that warned him to wait until the intensity of his feelings had passed before he committed any words to paper. Letting his anger get the best of him, he wrote just what he thought of her. Irresponsible. Disruptive. Evasive. With grim satisfaction, he signed the letter with a flourish at the bottom and then purposely hand-delivered it. He found her in the barn, chatting with a newborn calf, just born that morning.

Her cautious hazel gaze, only deterred him slightly.

"Here's your letter," he said briefly.

"Thank you," she replied and put it in her back pocket. She turned her attention to the healthy calf. "She's a sight for sore eyes, isn't she? The last thing you need is another run of bulls."

No, Mitch thought. *That last thing I need is some city girl who thinks she can buy what she wants.* Rather than replying, he asked rather cryptically, "Are you going to read it?"

PHOEBE STARED AT MITCH. She didn't recognize him. His normally gentle brown eyes blazed with fury. She felt her heart sink. Had he found out about what she and Bess had talked about? She lifted her chin. What could he do, except rant and rave? She knew the money wasn't going to get him to love her any more, not to mention that her going to Bess would probably make him angry. But she wasn't offering them the money because she wanted to buy anyone. She was giving them the money because they needed it more than she did. She took a deep breath.

"I'll read it," she said cautiously.

"Please do." His voice was dangerously pleasant.

Phoebe studied Mitch warily. She didn't like the anger in his eyes, the aggressiveness of his stance. Silently, she pulled the letter out of her back pocket and opened it, trying to keep her fingers from trembling. It took her only a few seconds to read, and she felt as if she had been stepped on by one of the cows. If she had nurtured any remaining hope of staying on the farm, this letter effectively killed it.

"Well, thank you for telling me what you really think," she said quietly.

"Anything you want me to explain in further detail?"

"No, thank you. This about covers it." She averted her face so he wouldn't see the tears. "Don't worry, I'll be out of your hair soon." She turned her attention back to the calf.

MITCH FUMED AT HER dismissal. He didn't know what he wanted her to do, but this wasn't it. He stared at her as she bent toward the calf, wisps of light hair framing the nape of her neck, the rest of her hair tamed in her familiar French braid. He knew exactly what he wanted her to do.

He wanted her to take him on, pick a fight, so they could get everything out in the open, so he could yell at her about the money she'd tried to give Bess, so her eyes could blaze with exasperation, as her words slapped some sense into him. Most of all, he wanted her to explain to him one more time why he needed her because he couldn't explain it himself. But she didn't look as if she was in any shape to pick a fight. He felt no victory in knowing he had beaten her. Now that he had finally made himself clear, he wondered why he felt so empty.

Because he couldn't leave things alone, he said quietly, "You know, Phoebe, I expected you to be more honest."

"More honest?" She looked at him, tears

glittering in her hazel eyes, more gray than green today.

"Than using my mother and sister to further your cause."

"My cause?" she asked dully.

He could see confusion on her face and the hollow in his chest widened.

"I don't appreciate you going behind my back, trying to buy my mother's approval."

Phoebe gave him a piercing look, snapped out of her trance. "Guilty as charged."

"How convenient that Katie came, too, to tell me about her credit card theft."

The glance she gave him was truly surprised. "I didn't tell her to do that," she said shortly. She got up and started to lead the calf into a freshly cleaned pen.

"And telling my mother about the albums—"

"You know, Mitch. I don't think I want to talk about that. You've told me what you think about me, so let's just call a truce." She took a deep breath. "You win. I lose. Thank you for the reference."

This wasn't quite the fight he was looking for. But before he could reply, she finished the conversation by walking away. Woods and roses wafted past him and he wondered what it was that he'd just accomplished. He caught her arm, and her body stiffened with his touch.

"Let me go," she choked out.

"Phoebe…" But he didn't know what else to say.

"You know, Mitch, because of you, I've discovered all sorts of freedom that I never could have imagined." She gave him a sad smile. "You helped me conquer what kept me captive. Maybe you need to think about doing the same for yourself, because it's not the money or the farm or the cows that keep you chained." With those words, Phoebe jerked her arm out of his grasp and hurried away.

As PHOEBE WALKED ANGRILY to her room, her first impulse was to find Bess and try to take the check back, but then she stopped, struck by Mitch's observations. If she did that, she would indeed be trying to buy them. She sat on the bed and with shaking hands reread Mitch's reference letter. It was still awful. She stared at the juvenile initials carved into the headboard, wondering if the small boy had been as stubborn as the man. She took a deep breath. The Hawkinses were honorable people. If they decided to accept the money, they would find a way of paying her back.

However, she didn't have to wait for them

to reject that, too. She would just leave now, come back next week to pick up her things. She would use the time to acclimate herself to her new life. Maybe meet a few people at the hospital a day or two early, get her bearings. It had to help the pain in her chest. Anything would be easier than worrying about Mitch, about his stupid farm, his stupid pride, about what he really thought of her.

What hurt most was that she desperately cared what the farmer thought about her. Mitch had found his way into her very soul. She took out the letter one more time and reading it more carefully, seeing herself as Mitch did. Irresponsible. Disruptive. Evasive. She crumbled it up and threw it away. This was getting her nowhere. She pulled her duffel bag from out of the closet, tossed enough clothes in it for a week, and was out the door. She almost made it to the car.

"Going somewhere?"

She whirled, relief washing over her when she saw it was Carlo. She smiled weakly. "I've got to find a place to stay."

"Your place is here."

She shook her head. "Not anymore."

Carlo nodded. "Yes, it is. You'll see. Good luck with your trip." He gave her a toothy grin and waved her away.

IF MITCH THOUGHT he would feel better after confronting Phoebe, he was sorely mistaken. His stomach churned with mixed emotions, and Mitch felt awful because he didn't know what made him angriest—the fact that Phoebe looked so attacked or that both Bess and Katie were involved in his personal life or that he would have no personal life in a matter of days, or that even though he felt his world crashing around him, essentially nothing had changed.

After feeding the cows and revving the tractor back and forth rather unnecessarily, he had cooled down considerably. He would talk with Katie about what she had done later. He wouldn't have handled the situation the way Phoebe had, but he reluctantly admitted that she'd responded wisely and creatively. With so long to ruminate, Katie had had plenty of time to repent. He doubted that he could have handled his sister as well.

When he climbed off the tractor, he was surprised to find Phoebe's car missing from its place in back of the house. He clicked his tongue, annoyed that he was looking in the first place. However, the first thing he did back in his trailer was redraft her reference letter. He'd been out of line and had never intended it to be considered by a potential landlord. It was just a way for him to let her know how angry he was.

He spent the better part of two hours writing her a genuine letter, highlighting her dedication and determination, her steadiness in the face of crisis. As he wrote, it became uncomfortably clear to him how much he was going to miss her when she left. But it was for the best, he told himself. She would be much happier in the long run.

He stared pensively out at the land, his father's land. He could barely support his mother and Katie from one year to the next. Could he support a wife? *Even if she was willing to stay?* He shook his head, with profound regret. He wouldn't do that to Phoebe. Maybe in three or four years, with Katie safely away at college, when he was on his third or fourth generation of calves, maybe he could find Phoebe and ask to start over.

But three or four years was a long time. Phoebe was a generous, funny, giving woman. She would be snatched up by any man with eyes and a heart. Mitch closed his eyes. *It's not the money that keeps you chained,* her soft voice whispered in his ear. He looked out at the fields and wished his father were alive. He could use someone to help him make sense of this whole mess and then he laughed bitterly, his heart shattering when he realized that someone should have been Phoebe.

He reread the letter, made a few changes in wording and printed it, stuffing it into an envelope before putting it in his jacket pocket. He'd give it to her after dinner with an apology. That was the least he could do. The very least. Maybe after, she'd agree to go for a walk, despite everything he'd said. She would do it, too, because she was a kind, forgiving person. When he walked up the back steps, he tried to think optimistically. They still had a week to work this out. She had taken worse verbal blows from him. For better or worse, she had said.

For better or worse.

"Where's Phoebe?" Bess asked as they all settled down to dinner.

"I'll go check her room," Katie volunteered.

"She's gone," Carlo announced as he scooped some green beans onto his plate.

"Gone? When's she coming back?" Mitch helped himself to a biscuit and passed the basket on.

"She said next week," Carlo said.

Bess shot a concerned look toward Mitch.

"You mean she's leaving next week," Mitch corrected him, his brain not registering what his old friend was saying.

"No," Carlo said complacently. He buttered his biscuit. "Said she'd be back next Tuesday to pick up her things."

Dinner was very subdued. Katie couldn't meet his eyes, Bess became quiet and Mitch had a taste of true loneliness. *But everyone needs love, Mitch—all the time. You just don't know what it feels like because you've been living without it for so long.* Before Phoebe, he hadn't even known that he was lonely. Then she barged into his trailer, talked to him, loved him, made him feel as if he was the most successful man alive even in the face of his failures.

After dinner, he walked alone, checking the barn, making sure she wasn't there. Even though she was gone, there were signs of her everywhere. The milk buckets neatly stacked upside down to drain against the wall. He smiled faintly. Phoebe would bring those same organizational skills to her new job. She would meet new people, eventually meet a man who wasn't too proud to accept her gifts. And he would go back to his old life, juggling debt on a daily basis, running from one crisis to the next, inserting himself between Bess and Katie. Then at night, he'd be by himself in the trailer with no one to talk to.

THE SUBSEQUENT DAYS passed slowly, giving Mitch plenty of time to contemplate how Phoebe had made his days go by faster and his work lighter just by her presence alone. He no longer had a reason to keep an eye on her, and that meant he wouldn't see her smile at him from the barn or wave to him from her bedroom window. That knowledge, however, didn't keep him from looking for her light to switch on in the early mornings when he rumbled past her room on his tractor.

The rest of the family also seemed to notice the loss. Katie had tried to make herself extra helpful. But now that there were only a few calves to feed, the once burdensome chore became simply an afterthought.

"Need help?"

Mitch looked up from the hinge he was fixing. He shook his head. "Nope. I think I have it." He stood up and swung the gate back and forth. "Good as new."

"Finally fixed it, huh?"

"Yeah. Phoebe complained about it enough."

Silence fell between them. "I guess she's supposed to be back on Tuesday."

Mitch didn't say anything, just fiddled with the hinge.

"I guess she's just going to pick up her stuff and move," Katie said flatly.

Mitch looked up at his sister's tone. "You'll get your room back."

"I don't care about my room."

"Do you want something, Katie?" Mitch asked directly.

Katie shook her head, but didn't move.

"Are you sure?"

"Yeah."

Mitch stared at his sister, who gave him a quick glance and then looked away.

"So, Katie?" Mitch said casually.

"Yes?" She looked at him hopefully.

"Are we okay?"

"Okay?"

"You and me. Are we square?"

Katie bit her lip and looked down at her feet. She gave him a slow nod. "I'm really sorry."

"I know."

"I'll never do anything like that again," she said. "I love the boots, but I felt guilty when I wore them, and then once Phoebe found out, I felt even more guilty because I thought she would tell. But she didn't, even though that messed things up between you two."

"Between us?"

Katie rolled her eyes. "I know you guys love each other."

"How do you know that?"

"The way you look at her. The way she looks back."

"Well, she's gone."

"She's not moving to Alaska. And it's not like your truck is broken. You can go visit," she said with adolescent simplicity.

Mitch stared at his sister, seeing a calm settle around her that hadn't been there six months earlier. He cleared his throat, knowing exactly how Phoebe had felt the day she decided to cover for Katie. He said gruffly, "I don't think there's any reason to tell Mom."

Katie gave him a look of relief. "Thank you."

"But that doesn't mean you're off the hook."

"I'm still going to pay Phoebe back," Katie said hastily.

"Good."

"Good." Katie gave him a big smile, her eyes mysterious. "Things are going to get better."

He looked at her curiously. "Yes. I suppose they will," he replied with false optimism.

"No, really, Mitch," Katie insisted, with a quick giggle. "Things are going to get better. Like today."

He looked at her sharply. "Why do you say that?"

She shook her head and laughed, then started to run toward the house, calling back, "I just know. Oh, yeah. Mom wanted me to tell you that lunch is going to be at one."

One o'clock? Lunch had been at noon forever. Things were changing.

At noon, he found out why lunch was late. The rumble of trucks and the mad barking of the dogs made him look down the road. Three trucks hauling very full cattle trailers pulled onto the property. Puzzled, he went to meet them. The dogs gathered around the back of the trailer, their tails wagging with excitement. Bess came out of the main house, wiping her hands.

"Hawkins, come give us a hand," Gil Whitfield said as he swung out of the nicest and newest truck. His son, Stinky, stuck his head out of the passenger side with a big grin plastered on his face.

"What's this, Mr. Whitfield?" Mitch asked.

"Your cows," Stinky hollered with a whoop.

"My cows? There must be some mistake."

"There's no mistake," the elder Whitfield said matter-of-factly. "Where do you want them?"

Mitch blinked, temporarily distracted by a young man, hair cropped close, getting out of another truck with Jay.

When Mitch didn't answer right away, Bess said, "Over there, Gil. Thanks."

"Sure thing, Bessie. Stink, tell your girlfriend to shake her butt and come help," Gil teased his son.

Stinky turned bright red up to his ears when Katie appeared in the doorway, but waved her over. Katie ran to them, almost bouncing with excitement. Mitch watched dazed as Gil Whitfield preceded to unload some of his best Holsteins, healthy, fat with milk, and at the same time, wondered who the young man with Jay was.

"We'll talk about this later," Mitch whispered to Bess, jerking his gaze toward his mother.

"Hello," Mitch called to the young man who approached them cautiously. "How can we help you?"

"Hi, there," the young man responded politely, a military issue duffel bag slung over his shoulder. "I was looking for Phoebe Douglas. These guys gave me a ride. Told me that she'd be here."

"She's not here now," Mitch said sharply. "She won't be back until Tuesday."

The young man looked deflated and started to turn around with a nod, "Okay. Thank you, sir."

"What do you want with Phoebe?" Mitch asked curiously, his eyes studying the stranger.

The young man hesitated and then said, "She's my sister."

CHAPTER FIFTEEN

KATIE TURNED immediately. "You're Tucker?"

"Yes, ma'am. Tucker Douglas." He put out his hand to shake Mitch's. "I just got stationed here in California. I'm on a week's furlough to find my sister."

Mitch stared at the young man, seeing the resemblance to Phoebe now that he knew to look for it. He glanced from Katie to Bess, who stepped forward and gave Tucker a big hug. The young man seemed disconcerted by the embrace.

"We've been expecting you," Bess said simply. "Are you hungry, Tucker? You're just in time for lunch. As soon as the trucks are unloaded, everyone's invited."

"Thank you, ma'am," Tucker flushed. He looked speculatively at Mitch and then offered, "I can help with the cattle. I did some time on a ranch in Montana."

"We could use it." Katie said with great enthusiasm, and Stinky gave Tucker a competitive glare. Tucker dropped his duffel bag on the porch and quickly strode to them.

Mitch pulled his mother to the side and demanded, one eye on the cows being unloaded, the other on Tucker. "What have you done? Why are we expecting Phoebe's brother? You took her money!" Mitch couldn't sort through all the stimuli bombarding him.

"I took her money. I bought cows. And after all that Phoebe has done for us—for me—I decided to finally end her misery." Bess looked a little abashed. "When I talked with Gil about the cows, I asked him how I could find a missing person on the internet. I used some of her money to find Tucker." Bess actually beamed with pride at her investigative work. "It took just two days to find out Tucker had joined the Marines. Then, only a couple of phone calls to find out where he was stationed. I emailed him."

"You said you were going to give Phoebe's money back," Mitch accused.

"No," Bess corrected. "I said I would take care of it. It was a generous offer and I thought we should take it. Your father's friends were more than happy to help out. We have sixty cows coming over the next three days. Gil is giving us fifteen more and it took less than an hour for him to find three other dairies willing to give us cows at a discount."

"No." Mitch looked at the cows that Katie, Carlo and Tucker and the Whitfields were unloading, mentally tallying what sixty cows meant. He shook his head in disbelief. "How can you do this? We can't take her money."

Bess stared directly into her son's eyes, her eyes burning bright blue, her cheeks flushed, some of her old spark in her tone. "We've already taken it. I've deposited her check and I've paid for the cows."

"How could you do that without consulting—"

"Because there are a few things you're not the best judge of."

Mitch opened his mouth to protest and then closed it as he watched Jay pull the second trailer up.

"This has nothing to do with the way you've run the dairy," Bess said her voice even. "Mitch, you've done a fine job. In fact, you've carried this farm these past two years with almost no support from me."

"That's not true," Mitch muttered.

Bess continued, "If Phoebe's money is going to make it easier on you, then I'm more than willing to take it."

"Does she know?"

Bess shook her head and said carefully, "I'm not sure. She knows she gave me the money. She doesn't know whether or not I've done anything with it."

The last of the cows came off the trucks.

"I thought it best that the cows be delivered this week, so she can see solid evidence of her investment before she leaves," Bess added, a self-satisfied note in her voice. "I think she'll be happy for us. How nice that her brother was able to make it as well."

WHEN MITCH WAS ALONE in his trailer, he wondered at just what point he'd lost control over his life. Bess had invited the Whitfields to stay for lunch, something else that hadn't happened since his father died. Gil Whitfield accepted with easy grace. Jay unmercifully teased Stinky about the way Katie was hanging on Tucker's every word. Stinky glowered, obviously unhappy that Tucker sat on the other side of Katie. Bess fussed over them all. When Tucker got ready to leave to find a room in town, Bess insisted he stay, bunking on Mitch's couch, until Phoebe returned.

Before they'd left, Mr. Whitfield had clapped Mitch on the back, saying in a low voice, "I've just been waiting for your mother to say the word. Your daddy would've been proud of you." Mitch closed his eyes, his throat tight. Would his father have been proud of him? Would his father have been proud of the way he'd run Phoebe out?

The question plagued Mitch through the weekend. Tucker turned out to be quite knowledgeable about cattle and helped him tag and inventory.

"How long has it been since you've seen Phoebe?" Mitch asked.

"Twelve years," Tucker answered as he studied the belly of the cow he was tagging. "I think this one's carrying."

Mitch joined him to inspect the Holstein. He had been pleasantly surprised to find nearly half of the new cows pregnant. Gil Whitfield had been very generous. Phoebe would be delighted.

"You know she gave us the money for these cows," Mitch said, not really knowing why he was telling Tucker, surprised that his soul didn't burn with shame at the admission.

Tucker nodded and pushed back his cap. "I heard you had a run of bad luck."

"Do you have a problem with that?" Mitch asked, still probing.

"Why should I?" Tucker responded briefly and then looked at Mitch in a way that was much older than his twenty years. "Look.

We're family, but you know her better than I do. I don't know if she even wants to see me."

"She wants to see you," Mitch said.

"Maybe. But when I got the email from your mother, I knew I had to try. Phoebe practically raised me."

The two men lapsed into silence for several minutes, until Mitch ventured, "She doesn't talk much about her family."

"It's not much of a family to talk about," Tucker replied. "She was the only family I knew."

I love you, Mitchell Hawkins. You're my family.

By Sunday night, he finally, truly understood what Phoebe meant, what she had been trying so hard to get through his thick head. *It's not the money that keeps you chained.* Mitch closed his eyes as a huge burden lifted from off his shoulders. If he wanted to, he could be free.

PHOEBE TOOK A DEEP BREATH as she turned up the dirt road to the farm.

Her time in Santa Rosa had been miserable. But she found that if she flung herself into the experience of being somewhere new, the sharp, stabbing pain in her heart subsided to a persistent radiating ache. Working would help, too. The hospital looked like a great place and her coworkers-to-be had proved to be instrumental in securing an apartment even without a reference.

Now, it was simply a matter of closing this very painful chapter of her life. The dairy looked deserted, which was just as well, because she had formulated her plan all the way down to the smallest detail. Glue smile on face. Pack. Get in and get out. No long goodbyes. No humiliating tears. Get in and get out. If she was lucky, Mitch would be busy in the trailer or better yet, in town, and she wouldn't even have to see him.

She parked in front of the house, angry at the tears that welled up unexpectedly. She squeezed her eyes tight, fighting for control. Get in and get out. She took a deep breath and opened the door to the house. Just pack and leave. Just pack and leave. Her heart sank when she heard a full-blown, animated conversation taking place in the living room. She swallowed when she heard Mitch's deep laugh. She hesitated by the door.

"Phoebe, is that you?" Bess called.

"Yes, Bess." She forced herself to sound cheerful. "I'm just going to pack and then I'll be out of your hair."

"Why don't you come to the living room first and meet our visitor?"

Phoebe sighed and pasted on her most polite smile as she rounded the corner. "Sure. Hi—" She froze, her voice caught in her throat as a young man rose awkwardly, wiping his hands on his pants, grinning a familiar grin.

"Don't recognize me, do you, Pheebs?"

Phoebe didn't recognize the voice. It was a man's voice. She shot a look at Bess and then noticed Mitch, standing back in the corner, watching her, his eyes compassionate. She blinked, trying to comprehend who this was.

"It can't be," Phoebe said, her voice returning with a croak. She walked toward the young man. He was so tall, as tall as Mitch. His shoulders broad, posture military straight. "You grew," she breathed.

Tucker wrapped her in a big hug. Phoebe felt herself being squeezed, his love passing to her. "You shrank," he replied.

And then she hugged him back, as tears coursed down her face. "How— Why are you here?"

"Mrs. Hawkins emailed me."

"Emailed you? Where were you?" Phoebe touched his face, patted his arms and hugged him again.

"Stationed back East. Between tours."

"Stationed? You're in the military?"

"Marines. I'm training to be a pilot when I get my degree."

"Your degree?"

"I'm going to college in the evenings."

"College. Oh my God. You're in college? How did you do it?"

"I took a page from your book. I left."

"Oh, Tucker." Phoebe sat down, accepting the tissue that Bess pressed into her hands. She dabbed at her eyes, not caring that Bess and Mitch were listening to every word. "I didn't want to leave you—"

"I know," he said gently as he sat next to her. His eyes were rimmed with red. He swallowed. "I hated you, at first. But as I got older, I knew why you had to leave. If I'd stayed, I'd be like Todd. And I wanted to be like you. I saved every postcard you sent. I wanted to go to the university just like you did—"

"Tuck." Phoebe started to shake, her emotions so frazzled. She took a deep breath and blew her nose. Mitch handed her the box. She looked up at him helplessly. He smiled back.

"I didn't know if you wanted to see me—"

"I've asked and asked about you. But Momma—"

"Let's not talk about Momma," Tucker said, his voice darkening, then it softened. He hugged her again. "I just wanted you to know that I turned out fine."

"Tucker is staying until Thursday," Bess put in.

Phoebe looked at her brother for confirmation and he nodded.

"Maybe you can wait and leave tomorrow, Phoebe," Bess suggested, with a quick look at Mitch. "I'd like to fix us a nice family dinner tonight."

Phoebe stared at Bess dazed and then nodded, her voice unsteady. "I guess I can leave tomorrow. I don't start work until Thursday."

"Good. It's settled then." Bess shot another glance at her son. "We'll leave you two alone so you can catch up."

When Mitch passed by, Phoebe carefully averted her eyes, not wanting to meet his gaze.

MITCH WORKED OUTSIDE, strategically positioned where he could see any movement from the house. He expected that Phoebe and Tucker would have a lot to talk about, but he hoped that sometime over the next thirty-six hours, he would get the chance to talk to her alone. He had many things to share with her, things he'd learned since she'd been gone. He squinted in the direction of the back door and adjusted his cap. Katie had gotten home from school nearly an hour ago, but nobody had come out at all.

Finally, just as he finished feeding the cows, he saw Phoebe wander out to the big corral. She kept her distance from him, but was obviously interested in seeing the new cows. When he waved to her from the feed wagon, she hesitated and then turned to walk back to the house.

"Phoebe!" Mitch called hastily, clambering down, work boots hitting the dirt, his heart beating fast as he walked purposefully toward her. "Wait. Please."

She stopped and turned slowly back.

"I just came to see the new cows," she said quickly, looking back at the house.

"Let me show them to you," he replied, taking her elbow to lead her toward the newest arrivals. Her arm stiffened under his touch. He held on gently. "See? They're beautiful. The Whitfields and my father had registered herds from the same lines. These are very much like the ones my father had."

She studied them carefully and then gave him an uncertain look.

"Come on." He walked over to another set, hoping she would follow. He exhaled in relief when she did. She climbed up on the fence, craning her neck, counting the cows.

"About half are pregnant," Mitch told her, talking quickly. "We'll have a busy crop of calves soon enough. Katie's refused to take care of them." He gave her a sidelong look. "I guess I'll have to find someone who will."

"So you're not going to go bankrupt," she observed, ignoring his innuendo.

Mitch was not able to look at her except in quick glances. "No," he finally said. "We're not going to go bankrupt."

"I'm happy for you." Her voice was flat.

They both lapsed into silence. After a few moments, Phoebe started to climb down from the fence.

"Phoebe," Mitch said quietly, gently assisting her. "We need to talk. I wasn't kidding about getting someone to take on the calves. I thought you'd be perfect."

What little color she had in her face drained away at his words. She shook her head, her voice tight as she replied, "I'm not perfect and I really can't talk today, Mitch."

IT WAS TERRIBLY HARD being back, Phoebe realized, as she looked into his dear familiar face. During her reunion with Tucker, she'd fervently wished he wouldn't look at her so intently, with such love in his eyes. It made leaving that much harder.

"Come for a ride with me," Mitch blurted and then added as an afterthought, "Please."

Phoebe looked at him, tears burning in her throat. She shook her head, the feelings she had spent the last week trying to subdue flooding to the surface.

"It's almost dinnertime," she said abstractly. "Bess is cooking something special for Tucker. I don't want to be late."

Mitch looked up at the sun. "We have about two hours before dinner. I think that's time enough to get us started."

"I don't want to, Mitch," she said as carefully as she could, not looking at him because she knew she would cry. "I don't want to go for a ride with you. I just want to spend time with my brother and then leave."

"Please, Phoebe. Just one last ride." The urgency in his voice made her look into his eyes. And her tears spilled over. He was begging her to stay. How could he ask this of her? She looked away, dashing away the tears with the back of her hand. She had seen his soul several times and every single time she responded that hard head of his took over.

Please, it begged.

She shook her head.

"Please, Phoebe." Mitch's voice was low, pleading.

Finally she asked, not being able to mask the pain in her voice, "Why?"

Mitch stared at her a long time. "Because I've learned a few things that I need to tell you."

"Tell me here." She crossed her arms over her chest, thinking that if she created enough pressure it would stop her heart from breaking.

"No," he said gently. "Come for a ride. I'll bring you back here and no one will be the wiser."

Mitch stared at her, willing her to trust him one last time. Phoebe shifted her feet, her red eyes studying the dirt. Finally, after a long time and a deep breath, she nodded.

"Thank you," he breathed in relief. "Stay right here. I'll go get the truck." He walked quickly toward his truck, hoping he would be able to conjure the words he needed. He drove up next to her and jumped out of the cab to open the door for her, but she was climbing in by the time he got there. He shut the door and ran back to the driver's side.

She had already fastened her safety belt and slid as far away from him as she could.

"Good thing you've got a door there, or you'd fall out," he observed.

She didn't even smile.

Mitch drove her to their grove of eucalyptus trees. The ground was damp, but Phoebe walked across it and found a place to perch herself. Silently, she stared out into the direction of his property.

"I've sold it," Mitch said quietly.

Phoebe looked up at him in surprise. "You what?"

"I sold the property. Or I've got a buyer for the property."

"But that's where you were going to move Bess and Katie when you went bankrupt next year." She didn't try to disguise the bitterness in her voice.

"That's one of the things I learned."

"What?"

"That I need to let go of some things. That piece of property was dead weight to my thinking." He cleared his throat and sat next to her, close enough to feel her tremble.

"I don't understand."

"I always looked at that property as my last resort. But last week, I realized that if I sold it, I could invest the money back into the dairy. Make it easier on all of us."

Phoebe didn't say anything.

"Your cows helped a lot," he added. "Thank you."

She glanced at him and said defensively, "I wasn't trying to buy you."

"I know you weren't." His voice didn't sound like his own.

The look she gave him almost killed him. She tilted her chin up at him and said, "How do you know that?"

He took a deep breath. "Because I know you. I was wrong. You weren't trying to buy us, you were trying to heal us."

PHOEBE STARED AT MITCH, not believing what she was hearing.

"Another thing that I learned," he continued, "was that I could only have one of two things." He ran a gentle finger down her cheek, then he pushed a silky strand of hair behind her ear.

"What?" she asked.

"My pride or you."

Phoebe hardly dared to breathe.

Mitch gently placed his lips on her temple and said softly, "I chose you."

Phoebe closed her eyes. "I-I'm not sure what you're talking about."

"Once I chose you, I understood everything that I have to thank you for."

"Th-thank me?" She started to shake, and immediately, Mitch moved closer, pulling her against his heart. She could hear it thud heavily.

Mitch continued to speak, his voice a bare whisper. "I want to thank you for giving us cows. I want to thank you for giving Katie and me back our mother. I want to thank you for loving me, and talking to me, and caring for me, for *us* even though you didn't have to."

Phoebe closed her eyes again, blinking back the tears, the knot inside her heart slowly unraveling. "I wanted to," Phoebe said shyly.

"So…" He shifted away from her, taking both of her hands to warm them in his and knelt before her. "Can I ask one last favor from you?"

"What?" She looked at him uncertainly, her heart pounding in her ears.

"Will you do me the honor of becoming my wife?"

MITCH HELD HIS BREATH. Phoebe's silence seemed to last an eternity, her eyes changing from gray to a vivid green as she digested his question.

Finally, she pulled her hands away and said sharply, "No!"

Mitch laughed, more from nervous energy than humor. He had expected she might say that. He recaptured her hands, which trembled violently, and tugged them close to his heart, so she could feel how fast it was beating. "Will you at least think about it?"

"I can't believe—" She pushed him away and jumped up, walking back to his truck. "It's getting dark. I want to go back," she said, her voice angry.

"Phoebe—" Mitch followed her.

"I can't believe your gall, Mitchell Hawkins." She whirled so suddenly that he almost knocked her over. He put his hands on her arms to steady her. "You put me through every bit of hell that you could and then think because you learn something, thank me and apologize, that I want to marry you, you stupid, stubborn man?"

"Well, I'd hoped so, yes." Mitch laughed again, genuine relief flooding through him. If Phoebe was angry, she was thinking about it. If she was thinking about it, she would eventually talk about it. If she was talking, she was loving him. He knew her like he knew no other woman.

"I don't want to marry you. You probably just need me to take care of the calves."

"Yes, you do want to marry me," Mitch said positively, but added, "and yes, I do need you to take care of the calves—and me."

She glared at him in exasperation. "I've put a deposit on an apartment."

"We'll get it back."

"I've got a ton of debt."

"Me, too."

"You don't trust me. You think I'm irresponsible, disruptive and evasive."

"You *are* disruptive," Mitch interjected. "You've disrupted my life since the day you moved in."

"*Ooooh!* You have a lot of nerve."

"A lot of nerve. I need it to compensate for all my stupidity at not seeing what was right in front of me."

"You are stupid," she agreed, her anger leaving her.

"If insults help," Mitch said seriously, "you can insult me for the next ninety years."

"I don't want to insult you," she said quietly. "All I wanted to do was love you."

"And I want you to love me, because Phoebe, I love you."

Phoebe stared at him hard and then gave him a watery smile. "This doesn't mean I want to marry you."

"Yes, it does."

"You should suffer the way I've been suffering."

"What makes you think I haven't?" Mitch

wasn't joking. He spoke painfully, "I've been suffering from the moment I found out that you'd gone, remembering that you'd left with the letter I wrote about you."

"That letter was terrible—"

"I was very angry, confused. Katie had just told me about what you did for her and I thought—"

"That I put her up to it." A silence fell between them. Then, Phoebe confessed. "I didn't put her up to it. I didn't ask her to go to you, but I wanted her to tell you what she had done. As much for me as for her." She looked at him uncertainly. "Every time I think we're getting closer, you pull away. How do I know this isn't just the same thing?" Her voice broke. "I can't take another rejection, Mitch. If you're not serious, let me go now so I can start my job."

"I'm very serious. But I have proof if you want."

PHOEBE LOOKED AT MITCH not believing what he was telling her. Her chest was tight because she so much wanted this to be true.

"What proof?" she asked warily, tamping down her hope.

"Come on, I'll show you." He opened the truck door for her and helped her in. She could feel his fingers lingering on her elbow. As he drove, he said casually, "You'll find something that might interest you in the glove compartment."

Phoebe with a trembling hand, opened it up. There was a thick envelope with her name on it.

"What's this?"

"Look."

Phoebe took a deep breath and opened the letter, her eyes not really able to focus. "What is it?" she asked again.

"What's it look like?"

"I don't know."

With a grin, Mitch flipped on the overhead light.

"What's it look like now?"

Phoebe still shook her head. "I don't know."

"It's a contract."

"A contract?"

"Yes. A contract making you part owner of the dairy." Mitch's voice deepened with his emotions as he concentrated on driving straight and not running them into a ditch. "You just have to sign. If you sign that makes our life yours. You'd become one of the family. With the extra cows that your money bought, along with the sale of the property, we'll have enough to pay off both the cow loan and your credit card debts almost completely by the end of summer. Fall's a nice time for a wedding," he added meaningfully.

Phoebe stared at the documents in her hand-for a long time. Finally, she said, "I don't know what to say."

"Say you'll marry me." Mitch's voice was sober.

"Why?" she asked, annoyed that her voice was a squeak.

Mitch stopped the truck in the middle of the road. It was now dark. The main house glowed just yards away.

Phoebe searched his honest brown eyes.

He touched her face, and then very gently kissed her, his hand behind her neck. "For better or worse, Phoebe we're family. That's what it's about. For better or worse. That's why."

Phoebe remembered to breathe. "Yes," she whispered. "I will marry you. For better or worse."

* * * * *

REQUEST YOUR FREE BOOKS!

2 FREE INSPIRATIONAL NOVELS
PLUS 2
FREE
MYSTERY GIFTS

LIREG11B

REQUEST YOUR FREE BOOKS!

2 FREE RIVETING INSPIRATIONAL NOVELS
PLUS 2 FREE MYSTERY GIFTS

Love Inspired.
SUSPENSE

YES! Please send me 2 FREE Love Inspired® Suspense novels and my 2 FREE mystery gifts (gifts are worth about $10). After receiving them, if I don't wish to receive any more books, I can return the shipping statement marked "cancel". If I don't cancel, I will receive 4 brand-new novels every month and be billed just $4.49 per book in the U.S. or $4.99 per book in Canada. That's a saving of at least 22% off the cover price. It's quite a bargain! Shipping and handling is just 50¢ per book in the U.S. and 75¢ per book in Canada.* I understand that accepting the 2 free books and gifts places me under no obligation to buy anything. I can always return a shipment and cancel at any time. Even if I never buy another book, the two free books and gifts are mine to keep forever.

123/323 IDN FEHR

Name _____ (PLEASE PRINT)

Address _____ Apt. #

City _____ State/Prov. _____ Zip/Postal Code

Signature (if under 18, a parent or guardian must sign)

Mail to the **Reader Service:**
IN U.S.A.: P.O. Box 1867, Buffalo, NY 14240-1867
IN CANADA: P.O. Box 609, Fort Erie, Ontario L2A 5X3

Not valid for current subscribers to Love Inspired Suspense books.

**Are you a subscriber to Love Inspired Suspense
and want to receive the larger-print edition?
Call 1-800-873-8635 or visit www.ReaderService.com.**

* Terms and prices subject to change without notice. Prices do not include applicable taxes. Sales tax applicable in N.Y. Canadian residents will be charged applicable taxes. Offer not valid in Quebec. This offer is limited to one order per household. All orders subject to credit approval. Credit or debit balances in a customer's account(s) may be offset by any other outstanding balance owed by or to the customer. Please allow 4 to 6 weeks for delivery. Offer available while quantities last.

Your Privacy—The Reader Service is committed to protecting your privacy. Our Privacy Policy is available online at www.ReaderService.com or upon request from the Reader Service.

We make a portion of our mailing list available to reputable third parties that offer products we believe may interest you. If you prefer that we not exchange your name with third parties, or if you wish to clarify or modify your communication preferences, please visit us at www.ReaderService.com/consumerschoice or write to us at Reader Service Preference Service, P.O. Box 9062, Buffalo, NY 14269. Include your complete name and address.

REQUEST YOUR FREE BOOKS!

2 FREE INSPIRATIONAL NOVELS
PLUS 2
FREE
MYSTERY GIFTS

Love Inspired

HISTORICAL
INSPIRATIONAL HISTORICAL ROMANCE

YES! Please send me 2 FREE Love Inspired® Historical novels and my 2 FREE mystery gifts (gifts are worth about $10). After receiving them, if I don't wish to receive any more books, I can return the shipping statement marked "cancel". If I don't cancel, I will receive 4 brand-new novels every month and be billed just $4.49 per book in the U.S. or $4.99 per book in Canada. That's a saving of at least 22% off the cover price. It's quite a bargain! Shipping and handling is just 50¢ per book in the U.S. and 75¢ per book in Canada.* I understand that accepting the 2 free books and gifts places me under no obligation to buy anything. I can always return a shipment and cancel at any time. Even if I never buy another book, the two free books and gifts are mine to keep forever.

102/302 IDN FEHF

Name	(PLEASE PRINT)	
Address		Apt. #
City	State/Prov.	Zip/Postal Code

Signature (if under 18, a parent or guardian must sign)

Mail to the **Reader Service:**
IN U.S.A.: P.O. Box 1867, Buffalo, NY 14240-1867
IN CANADA: P.O. Box 609, Fort Erie, Ontario L2A 5X3

Not valid for current subscribers to Love Inspired Historical books.

Want to try two free books from another series?
Call 1-800-873-8635 or visit www.ReaderService.com.

* Terms and prices subject to change without notice. Prices do not include applicable taxes. Sales tax applicable in N.Y. Canadian residents will be charged applicable taxes. Offer not valid in Quebec. This offer is limited to one order per household. All orders subject to credit approval. Credit or debit balances in a customer's account(s) may be offset by any other outstanding balance owed by or to the customer. Please allow 4 to 6 weeks for delivery. Offer available while quantities last.

LIHI1B